A CAREFUL HEART

What Reviewers Say About
Ralph Josiah Bardsley's Work

Brothers

"A stunning success...This is a novel you don't want to see end."
—*American Library Association*

"In the realm of understated family drama, this book rushes to the front of the pack"—*Convergence Book Reviews*

"Bardsley's writing style is flawless and elegant."—*Inked Rainbow Reviews*

The Photographer's Truth

"...love, with all of the beauty, and seriousness, and disruption it can sometimes bring...another absolute winner from Bardsley!"—*South Dublin Libraries*

"The photographer carefully constructs the photograph...in much the same way that the fiction writer constructs a scene...both use lies to tell a deeper truth."—*Lambda Literary Review*

"It's a happy ending, though not, in any way, a fairytale-like one..."
—*Just Love Romance Reviews*

By the Author

Brothers

The Photographer's Truth

A Careful Heart

A Careful Heart

by

Ralph Josiah Bardsley

2017

A CAREFUL HEART

ISBN 13: 978-1-62639-887-0

This Trade Paperback Original Is Published By
Bold Strokes Books, Inc.
P.O. Box 249
Valley Falls, NY 12185

First Edition: March 2017

CREDITS
EDITOR: JERRY L. WHEELER
PRODUCTION DESIGN: SUSAN RAMUNDO
COVER DESIGN BY DANA SHORT
COVER PHOTOGRAPH BY SHUTTERSTOCK, INC—OLLYY

Acknowledgments

Thank you Dana for your constant love and support in this process and for always believing in me. Thank you Ma and Dad for everything. Thank you Club Café for the years of inspiration. Thank you Erin Bush for taking the first read of this. Thank you Melinda Cordner, Tanya Ricci, Mary Squires, Janet Short, Eleanora Paciulan, and Kate Bardsley for your help in the editing process. Thanks to Dana Short for the cover.

Thank you Radclyffe, Sandy, Ruth, Cindy, Jerry, and the whole crew at Bold Strokes Books for being amazing to work with.

Dedication

For the silent

PRELUDE

Gabe walked slowly over to the edge of the water and looked down. The ripples of current caught the moonlight in their creases and pockets, shining back up at him like shards of glass in the black of night. He took a sharp breath, unable to fill his chest. The air was thick, and his lungs felt tight all of a sudden, as if the salt of the sea were rising up and clinging to him, pulling him down under the surface of the water and out of the harbor with the tide, to the open ocean. He let out the breath. It was done. There was nothing more to think about, and he could never, ever, tell another soul.

2001

NEW HAMPSHIRE:
TWO BOYS GROWING UP TOGETHER

I don't think I can go in there, Travis," Stephen said to his best friend as they stepped off the bus in front of Northwest New Hampshire Regional High School. The squat modern red brick structure was nestled in against the base of a trio of heavily forested mountains, twenty miles from his home. The early September air was still heavy with the heat of summer, but Stephen shivered as he looked out across the parking lot at the building that would be the center of his world for the next four years.

Travis stood next to him, a backpack slung over his left shoulder, nodding his head slowly. If he was scared, he didn't show it. "Come on," he said. "It'll be an adventure."

"Sure, right." Stephen gulped, slipping his own backpack off and holding it loosely at his side. "Adventure."

"The world's big, Stevie." Travis elbowed his friend gently in the shoulder. "This is just the beginning. You're going to love this, I promise."

"Right." Stephen watched the rush of other students flowing around them, as they stood like two rocks in a river.

The boys had different homerooms, so they started the day at opposite ends of the school. Stephen tried to ignore the butterflies filling his stomach as he left Travis and walked alone to his own classroom. But it wasn't long before he saw Travis again; many of their classes were freshman requirements, so they had four out of six periods together.

At noon, the two of them filed out of Algebra One into the cafeteria. To Stephen, lunch was a free-for-all, a giant room full of panic and disorganization topped off with food. To Travis, it was a moment of amazement. The noise of all those people energized him—so many different conversations going on at once. He listened intently, picking up bits and pieces of what people said, straining to hear as many of the voices as he could. He marveled at the sheer number of people in a single place. He had always known that the world was bigger than his tiny single-street hometown of Forestville, but this was the first time he was actually getting to see that, feel it.

"Did you bring your lunch?" Stephen asked Travis.

Travis nodded his head, unable to take his eyes off the crowd.

"Where do you want to sit?"

"Over there." Travis pointed to a crowded table with two empty seats toward the middle of the cafeteria.

Stephen's stomach tightened. He had spent most of the morning with strangers. At least in class, he didn't have to make unstructured conversation. Here, he would have to worry about making the right impression, being judged by everyone at the table, saying the right thing. "Okay," he finally managed as he followed Travis over to the table.

The magic of Travis and Stephen's friendship was that even though Travis loved crowds of people and rooms full of activity, he never left his friend behind. He somehow managed to drag Stephen with him, into conversations in crowded cafeterias, onto the high school basketball team, into school dances. Everywhere Travis went, he was popular. People liked him; they liked to talk to him. And Stephen went with him, standing reluctantly beside him, watching and sometimes participating in the conversations and games that seemed to erupt around the energy of his best friend.

Stephen had substance; beneath his silence there was a quiet determination about everything he did. Stephen almost never said a word during basketball practice. The first time he led a game in free throws and three pointers the crowd went wild while he calmly, almost sheepishly, stayed focused on the ball.

"Stevie," one of the point guards said after the game was over and they were all sitting around at Morey's Diner for hamburgers and fries. "Where did that come from?"

Stephen just shrugged his shoulders. "Dunno. I just had some open shots, so I took 'em."

Travis was sitting across the table from him. "You never know exactly what he's thinking, but he's always thinking," he said, reaching over the table and messing up Stephen's hair.

"It's like it came out of nowhere," the point guard continued. "Like you were just kind of invisible until you decided to show yourself and score twenty-one points in a single game."

Stephen winced at the term invisible. He never knew why people felt that they had to be loud to be seen.

"It's like he's a ghost," said another player who was sitting beside Travis.

"Stevie the Ghost," said the point guard.

Stephen looked over at Travis, and Travis smiled.

Freshman year passed into sophomore year, and the two boys had settled into the routine of high school. They had fewer classes together in their second year, and gradually each was beginning to be a little bit more his own person. Stephen was still shy and a little quiet, and Travis still thrilled at the opportunity to be in front of any crowd, no matter how big or small. But both had grown to realize Northwestern was not really such a big place.

One day early in February, after a particularly grueling basketball practice, Travis left the locker room early, without a word to Stephen. Stephen didn't think anything of it at the time, figuring they would catch up outside in the gym. Some of the team hung around after practice, even playing a quick game of Horse before they finally headed home. Stephen finished showering and got dressed, gathering his workout gear and shoving it into his duffle bag. He spent a few minutes on the locker room benches after everyone was dressed, listening to the rest of his teammates recount the practice and discussing what their strategy would be for the game later that week. He had even offered a few of his own thoughts about the other team, a private high school from a town sixty miles south, which they had played before only once during Stephen's freshman year.

After he'd heard enough of the recount, Stephen made his way out of the locker room to find Travis.

Sometimes, after practice, a few of his teammates would hang around accompanied by a couple of the cheerleaders who routinely spent time on the bleachers during practice. But a quick glance out at the basketball court told him that the place was deserted. The court was still. The janitor had already shut down the main lights, and the bleak shadows of basketball nets and steel rafters stretched across the wooden floor in the dull sulfur-yellow glare of the auxiliary lights.

Stephen took a right and bypassed the court, instead heading to the gym lobby. The wide linoleum floors of the lobby were silent. Glass cases around the sides of the room housed trophies of the school's old basketball, baseball and football wins. Photographs of teams and occasionally pictures of single star players dotted the spaces between trophies.

Stephen crossed the lobby and stuck his head out of the front door, being careful not to close it. He knew it was already locked. "Travis?" Stephen called out, his voice echoed in the frigid New Hampshire night. The two of them had agreed to drive home together, and Travis didn't usually break plans. Stephen ducked back inside and looked around the lobby again. He decided to double back into the gym and check the court again. Maybe he had missed Travis on the bleachers. It was unlikely, though. Travis was never quiet enough to miss. But as he turned around and retraced his steps, he heard the soft thud of something dropping to the wooden floor of the gym. It wasn't quite like the sound of a basketball, more like someone had dropped a heavy backpack or gym bag. The sound had come from the corner of the gym, in the little cubby that formed when the bleachers were retracted half way up to the closed position against the wall. Stephen walked the twenty or so steps it took for him to get to the half line of the court, when he heard more sounds coming from the same spot. This time it sounded like the rustle of clothing, then the squeak of sneakers against the wooden floor.

"Travis?" Stephen said his friend's name again under his breath, stopping for a few seconds at the half line and continuing toward the noise in the back of the gym. When he got closer, he could hear whispers coming from the closed off area behind the bleachers. He could identify one of the voices as Travis's, but he couldn't recognize the other. He moved closer until finally he could see beyond the corner. What he saw stopped him dead in his tracks. Without thinking, he dropped his gym bag. Travis was kissing another boy in a red sweatshirt and a pair of blue jeans, his arms wrapped around the boy's waist. It was Danny Plymouth, one of the point guards on the Northwestern basketball team. Danny was a stocky kid, short and thickly muscled with the olive skin and deep brown eyes that hinted at some type of Eastern European heritage.

Danny was from another small town about ten miles East of Forestville, so Travis and Stephen rarely saw him outside of school. But he had started sitting with them occasionally at lunch. Travis had been hot and cold toward Danny. Sometimes he welcomed him into their conversations, shot the breeze or talked about upcoming games or maneuvers from the previous day's practice. But other times, he was cold and quiet when Danny sat down.

Because of Travis's popularity and their being on the basketball team, different people always joined them for lunch or sat with them before school or in between classes. So it wasn't really odd that Danny ate with them. Travis was friendly to whomever sat down next to him. But he was unpredictable around Danny. Sometimes he was glad to see Danny, making room for him to squeeze in next to him at the table, but other times Travis looked down at his lunch when Danny approached and didn't even make eye contact with him. The mixed up reactions to Danny had struck Stephen as odd, but he hadn't ever mentioned it.

Now, standing in the darkened gym, watching his best friend grabbing clumsily at Danny, Stephen realized there was much more to the relationship than he had known.

"Umm." Danny put his hands on Travis's chest and pushed him slightly away.

Stephen could hear Travis's muffled voice as he tried to stop Danny from pushing him away. "It's all right."

"Umm." a tone of panic started to build up in Danny's voice. He was looking over Travis's shoulder, directly at Stephen's silhouette. His olive skin had turned bright red, and he was trying desperately to push Travis away.

"What?" Travis said, backing up and looking directly at Danny's face.

Stephen meant to turn around at that point and walk away. He thought maybe he should leave and give his friend the privacy this moment deserved. But he was so shocked, he found himself frozen. His feet just wouldn't move. So, when Travis finally did register from the shocked and panicked look on Danny's face that something was wrong, he turned around to see his best friend standing stock still, staring at him. Stephen's hands hung loosely at his side and his gym bag sat beside him on the floor.

"Stevie." Travis said. His face went blank.

Danny scrambled out from behind Travis, grabbing his own gym bag and heading out for the lobby. His walk transitioned into a jog as he got farther away from them, speeding up to a full-on run by the time he reached the door.

"Danny," Travis called after him. "Wait." But it was too late. Danny had already burst out of the gym doors, and he was probably halfway through the parking lot by that time. "You forgot your jacket."

"Oh well," Stephen said, searching for the right thing to say. "I guess you can give it to him tomorrow." Travis's eyes were glassy. Stephen added quietly, "I'm sure you'll see him."

Travis nodded slowly. The two boys stood staring at each other for a few minutes. Stephen could see, even from a few feet away that Travis's lips were chapped and his face was red and blotchy, especially on his chin and around his mouth.

"Stevie, I..." Travis paused.

Stephen said nothing.

"I don't...this isn't...I didn't..." Travis was stuttering. Stephen couldn't process this. Travis was usually so polished, so absolutely on top of his game. He was always the one talking, telling the story, so well composed. Stephen was usually the one uncomfortable in his own skin, unable to relate to the people around him, nervous and just a little sweaty. But as he looked at his friend tonight, Stephen could see no trace of Travis's cool collectedness.

"I..." He struggled to continue but he couldn't manage to get a word out.

Stephen shrugged. "Don't worry about it," he finally said. "It's not a big deal. And besides, I won't tell anyone."

"I…" Travis looked down at the floor. He took a few steps and closed the space between them. Stephen could see the tears welling up in his friend's eyes. Travis clamped his eyes shut for a few seconds and opened them again, looking left to right, but still looking down at the floor.

"Come on." Stephen put his arm around Travis's shoulder, corralling him toward the lobby. "Still want to drive home?"

Travis nodded, and the two of them started to walk toward the exit. But Stephen stopped after a few seconds, realizing they had forgotten Danny's coat. He released his friend and jogged back to grab it off the floor. "Can't forget this, can you?" he said.

The winter air was cold against his skin as Stephen held Travis's shoulder in the crook of his arm. But the night was clear and the stars were brilliant, filling the sky with a dazzling display of bright yellow pinheads against the blue black of the galaxy. Travis shuddered against the cold as they crossed the parking lot, and he unlocked his dad's Subaru station wagon.

"I don't want to go home," Travis said as he opened the door and pressed the unlock key to let Stephen in on the passenger side.

"Okay." Stephen ducked into the car and closed the door behind him. Travis stood outside for a few more minutes and reluctantly climbed in, but did not immediately put the key into the ignition.

"Can we go for a drive?" Travis said. "I really just…I really just need some time to think."

"Do you want to be alone?"

Travis shook his head and slid the key into the ignition switch. The Subaru sputtered to life in the cold New Hampshire night, and Travis put the car into gear and pulled out of the high school parking lot without another word.

They drove up past Forestville, over the bridge and out into the Vermont countryside. The hum and sputter of the little car marked the passing time. Travis popped a tape into the cassette deck, and Bruce Springsteen came on the tinny factory speakers.

"So." Stephen was the first to speak. "Are you and Danny boyfriends?"

"What? No!" Travis looked at Stephen, but only for a couple of seconds, until Stephen looked directly back at him. Then he couldn't meet his friend's eyes any longer and looked straight out the windshield to focus on the road. "It's not like that," he said after a few minutes.

"Well it should be," Stephen said sharply.

"What?"

"You were making out. You shouldn't be making out unless he's going to be your boyfriend."

"I was just experimenting. It's not who I am." Travis's voice was different now; the familiar energy of his 'on voice' was back. Stephen recognized it and rolled his eyes.

"Travis." Stephen put his hand on his friends shoulder. "Don't"

"Don't what?"

"Don't do your crowd voice on me."

"What?"

"Travis, you're my best friend. We've known each other since we were born. I know your fake voice. Whatever happens, you can't use that voice with me—first, because you won't get away with bullshitting me and second, because I'll be really, really pissed off at you for even trying."

Travis kept his eyes on the road ahead. Stephen could see his face in the instrument lights, and he watched as a single tear formed on the outside corner of his right eye and slid silently down his cheek.

"It's okay, Travis."

"Boyfriend." Travis repeated the word from a few minutes earlier in a whisper and shook his head.

"Do you like him?"

Travis pursed his lips together as if to speak, but he didn't say anything for a few minutes.

Stephen grinned. "Well, do you?"

"He's kind of hot," Travis finally said, and both boys erupted into laughter. "But he's a little clingy."

Stephen nodded. "Is that why you sometimes ignore him when he comes to sit with us at lunch?"

"Yeah, I guess. I don't know."

That night they drove around for hours. Stephen called their parents so they wouldn't wonder where they were. Then he was silent and let Travis do the talking. He didn't interrupt him once. He let him speak about the things happening in his head and his heart.

❖

The next morning, Stephen found Danny in between classes. He was at his locker putting some books away when Stephen walked up and handed him the jacket he had left on the gymnasium floor. "You left this after practice last night."

Danny turned scarlet as he took the coat from Stephen's hand. "It's not what it looked like," Danny said.

Stephen smiled softly. "Yeah it was, Danny." He patted Danny on the back. "It's cool. Believe me, I'm not going to say anything. Travis is my best friend. I don't care who he likes."

Danny let out a sigh of relief. "Thanks."

Stephen smiled, and then he punched Danny gently on the shoulder and turned to make his way down the hall.

As Stephen walked away from Danny that day, something pulled at his chest from the inside. He had listened to Travis's confession the night before. At first, when he'd discovered Travis and Danny together, he had felt as if he had interrupted something very personal, something he shouldn't have seen. But he wasn't really sure if he was surprised. He hadn't ever thought about whether Travis was gay or not. There'd been nothing to indicate a preference one way or another. He and Travis had talked about movie stars they thought were 'hot' or 'fine' but for Stephen, those conversations had always felt slightly aloof—regurgitated from the dialogue they had heard in movies or from older kids in the cafeteria.

But then, as they had driven around the back roads of eastern Vermont, and the initial surprise had worn off, he realized with deep sadness that Travis had felt he'd had to keep it a secret. Something just didn't fit with that.

Stephen decided to push the thoughts of Travis and Danny to the back of his mind. He couldn't help thinking they were like clouds on a beautiful day, a mild threat of derailing an otherwise pleasant experience. Stephen shook his head and tried to shrug off that feeling. A second later, the class bell rang, and he broke into a slow jog. He still needed to get to his locker before he went to class. He would definitely be late.

❖

Travis and Stephen decided to go to different colleges. Stephen packed his bags and went to Bellard College, a small liberal arts school in North Carolina, almost as an act of rebellion against his college professor parents. They had let it be known in subtle ways that they'd wanted their son to follow in their footsteps. His high school years were filled with science camp, writing camp, and trips to museums all around Boston and New York. When they looked at college campuses during Stephen's junior year in high school, his parents had suggested Yale, Stanford, Brown and other schools they thought Stephen should attend.

But Stephen had other plans. He wanted someplace small, where he wouldn't be overwhelmed with either the sheer volume of people or the academic pressures. He chose Bellard because he liked it. His parents tried to hide their disapproval, but it still shone through in small ways. They would forget the name of his school in mid-sentence or his father would come home and talk about some of his friends' children who were attending Harvard or Columbia. He would never fail to mention how Stephen was smarter then they were, but choices were choices.

Travis's parents were surprised he wanted to go to school at all. Travis had started working at his father's hardware store during high school and though nobody said anything explicitly, they assumed he would take on a full-time position at the store after high school. When he brought home a printed out application form for Emerson College in Boston, they pretended not to notice for a few days. But after he had spent several nights at the kitchen table staring at the application with a dull pencil in his hand, his mother finally helped him outline his essay and fill in the rest of the application, including the financial aid form. His father watched out of the corner of his eye from the living room while he pretended to pay attention to a Patriots game on television.

The summer before they left for college seemed to stretch on forever. The elation of graduating from high school, combined with the warm days and cool mountain nights gave those weeks a mythical quality. The two boys were inseparable during that summer. Their other high school friends had gone their own ways shortly after the week of graduation celebrations. All of them, that is, except Danny. He still came around from time to time. Stephen had actually grown to like him quite a lot.

But Stephen couldn't help getting a feeling of futility when it came to whatever relationship Danny and Travis still had. Travis was less and less interested. Perhaps he'd outgrown Danny after two years of being together, or perhaps it was Travis's impending departure for college. Danny was taking a different route—he had enlisted in the navy and would be heading to boot camp in August.

Stephen and Travis had never talked about Danny; he had just slowly become an adjunct to their friendship. He would pop up on weekends or if the boys went somewhere after school. Most of the time, he just slid in beside Travis, but some days he would show up, and Travis would be gone. He'd cross the fence from Travis's house to Stephen's. Stephen would be lazing about reading or maybe doing some yard work. On one day in particular, Danny showed up as Stephen was chopping wood in back of his house.

"Hey, Stevie." Danny had adopted Travis's nickname for Stephen somewhere along the way.

"Hi. Danny." Stephen tapped a steel wedge gently into a large chunk of oak with a sledgehammer until the wedge stood up on its own. Then he backed away and swung the sledgehammer down onto the wedge. The clang of the steel came first, followed up by a crack as the wood split into three pieces.

"Guess you won't be here to burn that wood this year." Danny watched as Stephen laid down the sledgehammer and picked up the pieces of wood, carrying them over and tossing them neatly on top of the stack of wood running along the fence.

Stephen laughed. "No, not for most of it. I'll be back for Christmas, though." He walked back toward the sledgehammer and rolled another stump over to his chopping area. "What about you?

How long will you be gone at boot camp? I don't expect they'll let you come home for long after you're done, will they?"

"Nah." Danny shook his head. "I'll get a little time off after boot camp, but then I'll probably put out to sea."

"So," Stephen paused for a moment from positioning the wedge on the next stump. "What's the deal with you and Travis, then? Are you guys going to try and do the long distance thing?"

Stephen watched as Danny shifted his weight back and forth from one foot to the other and dug his hands deep into his pockets. He'd never asked Danny directly about their relationship; he'd never even asked Travis about it. But something that afternoon made him wonder what was really going on.

"You know," Danny finally said. "Well, um, actually, how much do you know about, um, Travis and me?"

Stephen wiped his brow and shrugged. "Not much, I guess. I just, you know, figured that you guys were, whatever…together, I guess. Boyfriends."

Danny winced at the last word. "Yeah, well, I don't know about that."

Stephen was quiet.

"It's not really that kind of a thing." Danny tried to sound casual, but his voice sort of drifted off and he looked away from Stephen.

"But you wanted it to be, didn't you?"

"I don't know, Stevie." Danny shrugged. "It's easier not calling it something. Means I don't have to put a label on myself."

"That sounds more like Travis than you." Stephen picked up the sledgehammer again and gently tapped the wedge into place on the new stump, the clink, clink, clink of the metal on metal breaking through the quiet heat of the summer day. "Were you guys ever boyfriends?"

"I kind of thought we were. But Travis said he didn't want that." Danny looked away again. "I feel bad talking about it without him here."

Stephen lifted the sledgehammer above his head and brought it down in a loud crash, driving the wedge halfway into the stump, but not splitting it fully. "It's okay, Danny. I won't mention it to him if you don't want me to."

"For a while," Danny said, "I thought that you guys were, you know."

Stephen put the sledgehammer down and looked directly at the other boy. "What?"

"Well, you know, you're always hanging around each other. You're best friends and all. And, well, I see the way he looks at you all the time."

Stephen shook his head. "Nah. I love Travis, but he's like a brother to me. We grew up together, in these houses our whole lives." Stephen gestured to the two houses behind him.

Danny nodded silently for a minute, as if digesting things. "He never stops talking about you. Not when we're alone. It's always 'Stevie and I did this' or 'Stevie and I are going fishing next week.'" He stopped briefly. "At first, I was a little jealous, because I wanted him to want to be that close to me. It's not easy, you know, when you want to be close to someone, and you don't know how to say it. And then you see that person is really, really close to someone else."

Stephen could see the distant look in Danny's eyes shift from lost to just a little sad. "I'm sorry, Danny. I always thought he should pay more attention to you."

Danny waved his hand as if shooing away a mosquito. Stephen thought his eyes betrayed a little bit more pain than he wanted to show. "It's no big deal. Eventually I stopped being jealous about it and just took it for what it was—this awesome relationship that you two had. Have. You know what the funny thing was?"

Stephen shook his head.

"The funny thing was seeing how much Travis loved you, how much he was always looking forward to being with you or talking about you, made me love him even more because I could see how good a person he is. It just killed me a little he didn't feel the same way about me that I did about him."

"Danny." Stephen brushed the palm of his hand across his forehead, wiping away a thin layer of new sweat, and then he walked over and leaned against the woodpile where he had left a bottle of water. Danny followed suit, leaning back beside him and watching him take a swig. "What are you going to do about the Navy?"

"What do you mean?"

"I mean you're gay. Why are you going into the Navy when you know you can't be yourself?"

"I'm not sure I'm gay."

"Oh," Stephen nodded his head slowly. "This whole thing with Travis? The last few years? You don't think that's a pretty strong indicator?"

"It doesn't matter," he sighed, reaching over to pull a large splinter of wood off of one of the stacked logs. "They have the 'don't ask, don't tell' policy now, so I can go in with a clean slate. I just have to, you know, play by the rules."

Stephen nodded quietly. He didn't know what else to say.

The days of summer stretched on and on in a warm collage of chores and hikes and swims that year. June and July were eternities to themselves, but eventually August rolled around, and it seemed as if summer would actually come to a close after all.

In the final days leading up to Travis and Stephen's departure for school, the two families held a cookout to celebrate. The two young men sat next to each other in a pair of old wooden Adirondack chairs, surplus products from Travis's dad's hardware store. Amid the hamburger and charcoal smoke of the afternoon, they talked through the highlights of their four years in high school, a small crowd of family and friends listening and sometimes adding color to a particular story. The evening seemed to Stephen to possess a sense of fulfillment, of the end of one major set of accomplishments and the dawn of his "real life." It was unclear to him, though, if his friend shared the same sense of accomplishment. Travis, usually at his best and most showy in front of a crowd, had been strangely quiet all afternoon.

Stephen's mom eventually commented on the lack of Danny's presence. It was toward the end of the afternoon, when the shadows were growing long, and the air was just starting to cool off with the mountain chill that blankets the summer evenings of the New Hampshire mountains. Most of the other guests had peeled off, one by one, to their own homes, and it was just Travis and Stephen and their parents. "Funny Danny didn't show up today," she remarked as she picked up a few stray paper plates. "He hasn't headed off to boot camp yet, has he?"

Stephen watched as Travis's face darkened for just an instant before he recovered. "No, Mrs. D." Travis had referred to Stephen's parents as Mr. and Mrs. D. since he had been in fifth grade, the two-syllable Davis being too long for such a cool pre-teen to say. But the nickname had stuck. "He hasn't left yet. He was just busy today."

"Oh, well that's too bad. I'm going to miss seeing him around." She paused for a moment before heading into the house with the stack of used paper plates full of leftover hamburgers and potato salad. "I'm going to miss all of you guys. I can't believe it." She took a breath. The boys were silent, and she shook her head slightly and headed into the house.

Stephen waited for a few minutes after his mom had left before he said anything. The boys were alone now, and the only sounds were the river rushing through at the foot of the yard and the clank of dishes through the open kitchen window of the Davis's house.

"You never told your parents about Danny, did you?"

Travis exhaled a long, loud sigh and shook his head no.

"Right." Stephen shook his head in synch with his friend. "How could you tell them that without telling them the other thing."

"Stevie, not now."

"Look, dude, if you want to go off to college without ever telling them about who you really are, that's your deal. It's not my life, but..."

"That's right," Travis cut him off a little too quickly. "It's not your life. So stop trying to tell me how to talk to my parents, okay? I'm not ready to tell them that stuff yet."

Stephen shrugged and was silent. He had known Travis long enough to know there was no malice behind the tense words. The boys sat in silence for a few minutes.

"Are you nervous about school?" Stephen asked after a few minutes.

Travis shook his head slowly. "Nervous? Nah, not really." He let out a slow sigh. "I'm excited. I can't wait to get down to Boston, see a whole new city. How about you? You got a longer way to go. You nervous?"

Stephen nodded. "Yeah, a little, I guess." He stared out toward the river. "I'll miss this place. I'll miss you."

Travis winced and shook his head. "I'll miss you too," he finally said. "I wasn't going to think about it, though. I figure we'll see each other on Thanksgiving and Christmas and then again all next summer."

"Yeah," Stephen kept his eyes on the river. "I guess you're right."

The Boy From Watertown

There was just enough lawn to fool you into thinking it was a yard, but not enough to actually do anything fun like playing baseball or hide and seek. The house itself was a respectable two-story bungalow with a thick glossy coat of white paint that gave it a shine in the mid-morning sun and something of a glow in the rain. Green shutters framed out the windows, and well-manicured hedges added to the respectability and neatness of the place.

Gabriel Brennan had lived in this house for all of his sixteen years. For as long as he could remember, he'd had a bedroom to himself, but that hadn't always been the case. When he was just a baby, he had shared a bedroom up in the eaves of the house with two of his brothers. He was lucky, so his brothers told him. As the youngest, he'd gotten an entire bookshelf and a bureau to himself. His two older brothers had to share a bureau and neither one of them had a bookshelf. Of the four bedrooms in the house, his two sisters had shared the bedroom beside his, and his two oldest brothers split a bunk bed across the hall. His parents' room was the only bedroom downstairs on the main level.

Gabriel was the youngest, eighteen years younger than his oldest brother and ten years younger than his youngest older brother. His two sisters were in the middle—the order had gone James, John, Michael, Mary, Siobhan and Connor. Then Gabriel had rounded out the Brennan family long after anyone expected an addition.

Gabriel's brothers and sisters had all moved out of the house by the time he was sixteen and a junior in high school and the once loud and rambunctious home had become a slow motion version of its old self. Where there had once been the chaos of barely enforced routine, now there was simply the languid pace of morning after morning of getting up and greeting the day.

Gabriel, or Gabe, as his father and his friends called him, was quiet. It was as if the exhaustion of the house had somehow manifested itself in his personality. He was slow to speak and kept mostly quiet during meals. His parents had done their best to make sure he was involved in as many activities as possible, thinking that might make him more social. But he was as quiet at school as he was at home. However, thanks to his parents' efforts to bring him out of his shell, he played a number of sports at Saint Luke's, the Catholic High School he attended. He was good enough to get by in basketball and baseball. He had absolutely no talent in football, and only played for one season— and at that he never saw a game. He proved quite skilled at lacrosse, but he never really enjoyed it. His passion was for running, even if he wasn't the fastest runner on the cross-country and track teams.

Kids are often cruel to those who are quiet, but Gabe seemed to escape this fate. Playing sports kept him above reproach for the most part. Because he never said anything more than absolutely necessary, his fellow students never knew if he was smart or stupid; if he was quick-tongued or slow; or if he was good with the girls or not. He had the reddish-blond looks people talked about; all he had to do was flash his bright blue eyes, and he melted hearts. He was friendly enough with everyone but not close to anyone. He made it a point never to give anyone enough to judge him deeply.

The two exceptions to Gabe's stone-like silence were his two cross country and track teammates, Thom Green and Jack McClean. The three of them had run on the Saint Luke's cross-country and track teams together since their freshman year and had forged a deep bond through miles and miles of practice runs, races and cool downs. They had suffered through shin splints and ankle sprains and Charley horses together, and had become inseparable.

Both Jack and Thom lived in the same neighborhood in the nearby suburb of Waltham, about a ten-minute drive from Gabe's house in Watertown. But the boys had been like brothers since their freshman year.

Gabe was more talkative with Jack and Thom. Maybe the miles they'd run together and the races they loved gave him something to talk about with them. Maybe they'd experienced the euphoria of winning and the exhaustion of losing together. In some of his deeper moments of teenage self-reflection, Gabe had tried to pinpoint exactly what made him feel like talking when he was around Jack and Thom, but he could never quite figure it out.

If he had figured out how to warm up to the broader population of his school, or if he'd had the ambition to use his looks to his advantage, Gabriel Brennan would have been a very different kid. But he wasn't the least ambitious in that way. He didn't want the things that other teenagers seemed to want. He couldn't care less about popularity or girlfriends or cars or even grades. He sailed through classes, putting whatever effort was necessary in to his schoolwork. He studied when he needed to study and not when there was little or no use in it.

"Gabriel," his mother asked one Saturday morning when they were both sitting at the kitchen table. Gabe had his nose in a history book, studying for an upcoming test. He nodded and looked up briefly at her. "Have you given any thought to what you want to do for college yet?" She took a sip of her tea and turned the page of a Reader's Digest magazine she was re-reading for the tenth time.

"Not exactly," Gabe lied. He had started to think about schools, but he knew what he wanted to do didn't require a college degree. His parents' patience had worn thin after the last discussion they'd had about his future.

"You really should, you know." She played with the tea bag, dunking it swiftly a few times.

"I know," he said. "Can I borrow Dad's Jeep tonight?" He tried to change the subject.

She frowned. "Gabriel, I'm talking to you about college."

He slipped a napkin into the page he was reading and closed the history book. "I know," he said. "I'm looking at them, I just haven't really made up my mind yet."

"You know you're coming to the end of your junior year. I don't want to stress you out or anything, but you've got to get things in line for that. Senior year will be here before you know it."

"Ma, you know what I want to do, right?"

She nodded and took another sip of her tea, glancing down at her magazine. "You've said it a few times."

"I feel like you and dad aren't even listening."

"We're listening, Gabriel, we really are, but you know what your father thinks."

"Jesus, Ma."

"Watch the mouth." She looked up.

He shook his head slowly. He didn't want to get into it with her again. They had the same argument over and over these days. When he was younger and somebody asked you what you wanted to be when you grew up, it was perfectly fine to say you wanted to be a policeman. At sixteen, with the decision about what college he should go to in front of him, that answer just wasn't right for his parents any longer.

"I don't know why you won't listen to me," Gabe said. "I want to go into law enforcement. I don't need to go to college for that."

She looked at him in silence and took a heavy breath. "Gabriel, I think wanting to work in that field is noble. But—"

"—but you and dad don't think it's good enough."

"I think it's a very big decision not to go to school. You might find later in life that you wish you had."

Gabe looked at her but said nothing.

THE RACE

The Watertown public track was an old quarter mile loop of crushed rubber and asphalt nestled in among the rolling hills of thickly settled neighborhoods. It was about a ten-minute walk from the Brennan house, and Gabe ran on it during the summer and when he wanted to practice on his own. Almost all the cross country and track events Gabe ran were in meters, but he liked that this track was a quarter mile—what the old guys called a four-forty track. It was nostalgic and cool, a hold out against the progressing tide of the more modern four hundred meters.

"Four hundred and forty yards," he said out loud to himself as he closed in on the first quarter mile and looked down at his watch. A minute and twenty eight seconds. He focused on the asphalt. He was right where he should be to come in a hair under a six-minute mile. It wasn't the fastest quarter mile he could put in, but he wanted to pace himself. He hadn't been able to break six minutes this whole year, and the cross-country season would start in another month.

The early August morning air was still crisp and cool as he filled his lungs. Gabe had woken up ahead of his alarm clock and ambled down to the track while it was mostly still empty. This was his favorite time of the day to run, before the rest of the world woke up. The few clumps of walkers stayed mostly to the inside of the track. Gabe passed a group of them as he rounded out the second quarter mile. He looked back down at his watch. Two minutes and fifty-nine seconds. He had picked up an extra second in the second quarter mile. He drew in a deep breath through his nose and pushed it out through his mouth.

The running helped him clear his mind. He had lain awake most of the night after a particularly tough evening with Thom and Jack, his teammates from cross-country. The three of them had gotten together at Jack's house to watch a couple of old races—some their own, some college or IAAF races.

It was rough not because he had stayed up late, or worse, that he had been drinking, something he never did. Gabe wasn't particularly interested in being a goody two shoes, but he was afraid of what he might let himself do or say if he got drunk. No, the evening was rough because all night he'd been unable to stop staring at Thom.

He didn't know what had happened to him over the last year, but lately he'd been finding himself lost in thought about his fellow runners, or worse, staring at random guys he happened to see walking down the street. He'd notice the musculature of some guy's shoulders or his calves or glutes. He'd try to rationalize that he was only admiring them for the work they required, for the exercise and commitment to sport. But more and more often, he knew that wasn't why he was looking. What had made matters worse last night was that Thom was staring back at him. A lot. The three of them had been lying on the floor in front of the television, and Thom had adjusted his legs so that his calf was touching Gabe's calf, and he'd left it there. It drove Gabe insane, but he refused to acknowledge it, silently soaking up the heat of skin on skin.

He focused on the asphalt track in front of him. The sun was just starting to burn through the early morning haze, and he could feel the beginning of what would be a hot day. He cleared his third quarter mile and looked down at his watch to realize he was at four minutes and thirty-four seconds.

"Shit," he said out loud, feeling the burn in his lungs from just speaking that single word. He doubled his focus, did a mental inventory of his body—arches, fine, there was never an issue with them; shins, slight twinge of pain with each strike, the beginning of another bout of shin splints if he wasn't careful, he would have to ice them; knees, fine, a dull throbbing pain in each that was always there; glutes, ah, there was the problem. He wasn't engaging his glutes enough. He leaned slightly forward and purposely lined his legs up, lengthening his stride and intentionally pushing from his rear muscles. Each stride became more of a leap than a step.

He quickened his pace and raced against the thoughts in his head. He briefly pictured a team racing with him, edging toward the finish line. He imagined Jack and Thom next to him, running hell bent for leather, legs stretched out in front of them, spikes thumping in rapid succession as they hit the track. He looked down at his own legs, and the image in his mind blended with what he saw. It started to work. He felt the seconds ticking away, but he was going to come in just under what he wanted to for the first mile. He rounded the bend and crossed the finish line at five minutes and fifty-nine seconds. He kept going, to see if he could maintain the pace for two consecutive miles.

He let off the gas just a little bit, trying to find his momentum in the new pace. His mind wandered back to the imaginary team he had running against him. He saw the sweat dripping down Jack and Thom's faces. He imagined what Thom's singlet would look like, drenched from the center of his back down. He shook his head and tried to think of his breathing instead. The competition in his head was turning slowly into something else altogether, and if he let it go as he had before, it would end in something he was having trouble coping with.

Gabe continued around for another three laps, losing a couple of seconds on each split. He looked down at his watch as he rounded the first corner of the track on his final lap. He was set to make a second mile at just over six minutes and ten seconds. He pushed as hard as he could, his legs aching, a hollow feeling in his stomach as he tried to manage just how much he could sprint going into the last two hundred yards. He pushed harder, and the images of the other two boys crept back into his mind, only this time they were on the sidelines at the finish, shouting at him to run faster. In his mind, Thom's lips were dry and chapped, as they had been when he'd seen him the night before. He crossed the finish line, and the images vanished from his mind. He bent over, heaving and feeling slightly nauseous.

"Walk it out," a voice came from the side of the track. He looked over to see his father leaning on the waist-high fence that circled the track. "Don't stand still. You know better than that. Get moving into your cool down lap, go on."

Gabe nodded at his father and started off into a slow shuffling jog. He wondered when his dad had shown up to watch him, and he felt the heat of shame underneath the sweat from his work out, thinking of the things he'd been imagining in his father's presence. He shook it off. It wasn't like his dad could see into his head.

As he finished up his cool down lap, his father met him on the track. "Walk a couple more laps with me?" he said to Gabe.

Gabe nodded. He was slowly getting his breath back. "What'd you come down for Dad? You're usually at work now."

His father nodded. "I figured you'd be down here, and it seemed like a good chance to get my walk in."

Gabe nodded at him. "You want to talk about the college thing," Gabe said.

His father smiled. "Actually, yeah, Gabe. That's part of it."

"Only part of it, Da?" Gabe looked up and smiled at his dad. "Am I in trouble for something?"

Gabe noticed his father smiled at the antique word, "da." Nobody used that term. Even the Irish families had dropped it generations ago. But as children, the Brennan siblings had all called their father that. Gabe wasn't sure exactly why, but he had some vague memory of his mother laughing and telling him it had started because his oldest brother couldn't pronounce "dad" fully. Instead he'd called their father "da," and it had stuck through all the kids, though they had all shifted to "dad" as they grew older.

His father reached over and ran a hand through Gabe's wet hair. "When have you ever been in trouble?"

Gabe knew that his father was different with him than he'd been with Gabe's brothers and sisters. He was softer, more affectionate. Where the older Brennan siblings had faced a particularly strict and sometimes tough father, Gabriel had gotten the mild end of his father's parenting run. But Gabe never really did anything wrong.

His dad's life was also different now than it was earlier in his career. He had more job security, he worked fewer hours, and he had more energy to put into his family. He spent as much time as he could with Gabe. He attended all of his games, spent time teaching him how to work on cars—all the things he had missed with his other kids. When all of the Brennan siblings got together and their parents were not around, they would tell stories of the short-tempered, sometimes explosive man their father had been for them, and they would all kid Gabe about ending up with the softer, gentler set of parents.

The two of them walked along for half of the loop without saying a word. Gabe regained his breath and walked with his hands on his hips, swinging his arms occasionally and stretching them across his chest in a cycle of activities.

"Gabe," his father finally said as they closed the first four hundred and forty yards of walking together. "I've been thinking about a few things."

Oh no. Here it comes. Whatever it is, it won't be good.

His father must have seen the look on his face, because he smiled at Gabe and said, "Relax, it's nothing bad. I've been thinking about how you want to go into the police force."

Gabe nodded. He hated talking about this subject with his father, but this time his tone at least sounded better than it had in the past.

"Well, I know I've been a little stubborn with you on the topic."

"Dad," Gabe interjected.

"No, just hold on." His father put a hand on his shoulder as they walked. "Just let me talk for a minute."

Gabe let out a long huff.

"I know it's what you want to do, and if it is, then I'm behind you. But I want to have a serious conversation with you about it, and then we don't have to talk about it ever again if you don't want to."

They walked for a couple of strides in silence. Finally Gabe looked up. "Well, go on Dad. I'm listening."

His father took a deep breath. "Gabe, you know I love you, we love you, your Ma and I. A lot."

Gabe nodded but was silent.

"And, well..." His father trailed off and shook his head before he continued. "What I'm trying to say is that it takes all kinds of people to make the world go around, and I've been watching you for all your life, and well, Gabe, I think you're going to find as you grow up that you're a little different than other boys. Other men."

The hair on the back of Gabe's neck began to stand up, and he felt a chill across his shoulder blades. "What are you talking about, Da?"

His father stopped walking and faced him. They were in the outermost ring of the track, far away from either of the two groups of walkers. "I want you to know that different is a good thing. You should be proud if you're different. Your Ma and I love you for who you are, every fiber of who you are."

Gabe stood like a stone.

"I watch you Gabe, and I see you dealing with this. And I want you to know that it's okay. Whatever you're feeling and whatever you are, it's who you are and that's amazing."

"What does this have to do with being a cop?" Gabe's voice had a snap to it that even he didn't expect.

"If you want to be a cop because you feel like you need to prove something to yourself or that you need to somehow change who you are to fit into some kind of…I don't know, some kind of expectation, well, I want you to know that you don't have to do that."

Gabe looked away from his father and around the track. "Can we go now?" He asked.

His father sighed and followed his son's gaze out across the giant black oval. "Do you hear what I'm trying to say to you, Gabriel?"

Gabe wanted to be mad, but he couldn't. Maybe it was because he was tired from the run, maybe it was because the heat of the day was starting to come up and he could feel the salty crust of drying sweat across his forehead, or maybe it was because he was overwhelmed because his father had identified something he hadn't even been able to acknowledge. Not only had he identified it, but he'd also tried to let Gabe know that it was okay. But that just somehow seemed to make everything worse. He wanted to be angry. He wanted to yell and scream and take off running down the street as hard as he could. But the stillness between him and his father was like a spell, and he found it was impossible to be mad.

Instead, he felt a wave of exhaustion and frustration but on the edges of that combination of feelings was a thin, emerging glint of relief. "Da," he finally said after a moment of thought. "I don't want to be a cop because I feel like I need to prove something. I want to be a cop because they help people."

His father nodded.

"You know when Thom got in trouble last year?"

His father shook his head, a puzzled look crossing his face.

"Well, he did," Gabe said. "He was stupid and, well, it's not important, but he got caught in a lot of fights, some of them real bad, and he was about to get in a lot of trouble. This cop ended up having to take him in because he beat the crap out of some kid. But the cop wasn't a jerk about it. He took Thom outside the police station, bought him a can of tonic, and they sat down on a bench. And the cop, he just talked to him, let him know what was ahead for him if he didn't sort things out. Told him that everybody gets mad sometimes, but that he can't go around blowing a fuse at random people. And something clicked for Thom. Something the cop said. I don't know exactly what it was. He told me about it once, that's how I know all about it, but he didn't tell me everything the cop said. He just said that he was fighting with a lot of shit—sorry, Dad—I mean stuff. He was fighting with a lot of stuff in his own head. The cop was the first person to ask him about it, to try and hear him out for his side of the story. Up until that point people had either just let Thom do his own thing, or they'd been afraid of him, afraid of getting in a fight with him because he was a little crazy, really. But no one listened to him."

"What about you and Jack?" his father said. "You guys are his friends. Did he ever talk to you about any of the stuff he was going through?"

"No." Gabe shook his head. "Not until after it all happened with the cop. We knew something was wrong. He showed up to practice banged up and bloody a few times. We tried to say something to him once or twice, but he never wanted to talk about it with us."

"Do you know what it was that was bothering him? I know he didn't tell you, but did you have a guess?"

Gabe looked up, and he thought he registered something in his father's eyes but he quickly looked away. "No," Gabe said. "No, I didn't know what it was."

"Uh-huh." His father looked at him suspiciously for a moment, but whatever it was in his eyes vanished.

"Anyway, I want to be like that. I want to help people out and make the world a safer, better place. I can't do that as an engineer or an executive."

His father raised his eyebrows as if he were going to speak but thought better of it.

"I think I can make a difference as a cop."

"Okay," his father said. "Then here is the deal."

Gabe rolled his eyes. "I knew it, I knew there had to be a catch."

"There's no catch. You can't be a cop in any town that really matters until you're at least twenty-one."

"Yeah." Gabe nodded.

"So, I want you to go to college in between the time you graduate high school and the time you go to the academy. I don't care what you major in. If you want to be in law enforcement, study criminal justice. It will be a great fit for you, you can use it in your career as an officer, and you'll keep yourself out of trouble."

"Trouble?" Gabe squinted his eyes at his father.

"And," his father raised a finger. "I'll pay for it, so you won't have to get a job. You can focus on your studies. What do you say?"

Gabe shrugged, and they began to walk off the track in the direction of the Brennan house. "Okay," he finally said. "I guess I can probably go with that. But I'm not changing my mind about being a cop."

His dad smiled at him, and they walked the few blocks home.

2005

COLLEGE

Stephen walked into the dorm room and dropped his bag on the bed closest to the window. The white cinderblock walls had been painted in a thick glossy coat of paint, giving them the look of a dimpled white board. The linoleum floor had been waxed to within an inch of its life, and he could almost see his reflection in it. He took a deep breath and looked around the room a few more times, taking in the blank surfaces, the wooden built-in desks and bureaus, and the shelves. It was the first time he had stopped for even a second in his voyage down to school. He'd said good-bye to his parents in New Hampshire, and now he felt a profound sense of isolation.

But before he could stop too long to think about it, he heard a voice shouting from somewhere out in the hall. It took Stephen by surprise at first, but it wasn't an alarm or an angry shout. He poked his head out the door of his room to see a group of three kids his own age making their way down the hall, looking for their room numbers when they saw Stephen.

"Hi, are you on this hall, too?" one of the kids said.

"Yeah," Stephen said, cautiously extending his hand. "I'm Stephen."

"Stephen," the other kid said. "Good to meet you. Looks like we're all gonna be hallmates!"

Six hundred miles north, in a cramped hallway on the twentieth floor of a converted apartment building, Travis searched a confusing layout of pods trying to find his own room. He'd already been waylaid on his quest a couple of times. First, by a group of students watching

Project Runway in a dorm room with the door opened, second by a clutch of freshmen standing in one of the many common areas looking at a map of the campus, and the third time by a new RA who was apparently as lost as Travis was. All in all, it was a great start to his college career. He already had a date and about a dozen friends.

The traits that had defined Stephen and Travis as children never faded, but instead matured into characteristics that defined them as men. Stephen remained quiet and focused but he grew increasingly social at college. The casual dorm parties, the forced conversations in class, and the loud dining hall meals forced him out of his comfort zone until he became a chattier version of the high school boy he had been.

In his sophomore year Stephen met a girl he really liked. She was in his English Lit class. It was the first class he'd gotten a B in. She sat three seats in front of him, and he couldn't stop looking at the back of her head during class. He missed an entire lecture on Chaucer looking at her profile from a slight angle. Her name was Melanie, and she was from upstate New Jersey. She played women's lacrosse and had blonde hair she wore up in a ponytail most days to class. Stephen might have made it through the entire semester without saying a word to her except he saw her out one night at O'Dell's, the bar across the street from campus.

Stephen had gone out with a group of buddies from his hall on a Friday night that October. O'Dell's was a campus institution. It was located just across the street from the college's athletic center, a three-minute walk from the dorms. You could slip out for a beer and then head back to finish whatever project or term paper was due the next day. That had been exactly the type of logic Stephen's dorm mates had used to drag him out that night.

Stephen's crowd had been seated for only a few minutes, cans of Natty Lite in front of each of them, when Melanie walked in with a group of her lacrosse teammates. They sat at the table directly next to the group of boys. As Bellard was a small college, everyone seemed to know everyone else, and the two tables were essentially one big party of chatter before long. Stephen ended up standing next to Melanie's chair and, when the time seemed right, he leaned in and tried to start a casual conversation.

"So are you ready for that test tomorrow in English Lit?"

She shrugged. "I'm as ready as I'm going to be. It's not my favorite class."

"Mine neither," Stephen said. "I find it a little hard to focus in there." He didn't say it was because he was constantly watching her. He thought that might sound a little creepy.

"Me too." She gave him a mildly surprised smile. "Can I tell you something?"

He nodded.

"The reason I sit up front is to try and not fall asleep during class."

"What?" Stephen looked at her incredulously. "That makes no sense."

"Sure it does." She took a sip of her Natty Lite. "It's a little trick my dad told me about. The closer you sit to the front of the class, the more attention you end up paying to whatever is being said, and that makes it harder to fall asleep."

Stephen scrunched up his face. "And how is that working?"

She shook her head. "Honestly, not so great."

He laughed. "I know. I saw you dozing off the other day."

She hit him playfully on the arm. "You did not!"

"Sure did. I looked over at you during the lecture on Lord Byron—the part about the inspiration for his poem *Don Juan*. There you were, snoring zzz's."

"I don't remember a lecture on Byron." She started to get a worried look on her face.

"Exactly." He smiled at her. "That's because you were sleeping."

She stared at him for a second, and then she let out a laugh. "You're making that up."

He gave her his best serious face for as long as he could before cracking up in laughter. "I am making it up."

They both laughed and looked at each other for a moment. He caught her eye, and they seemed to connect for just a second before they were absorbed back into the larger group conversation about school and holidays and sports teams.

Melanie surprised the heck out of Stephen a week later when she agreed to go out on a date with him. Two weeks after that, they were inseparable. They spent the days together studying and hanging out. Though Stephen never said it explicitly, he was pretty sure Melanie guessed their first kiss together was actually his first kiss, period.

❖

"That's great," Travis said with a forced enthusiasm Stephen couldn't quite figure out. The two of them were home for Christmas break and sitting at the kitchen counter in Travis's house in front of two bottles of Rolling Rock beer.

Stephen had delayed his return to the last possible chance, staying until the dorms had finally shut down for the season. He'd wanted to spend the last few days with Melanie before going home. The two of them had said a long good-bye, spending their last night together in her room after Stephen had snuck in through a downstairs window of the women's dorm where she lived.

Stephen forced a smile. "I can't believe she actually likes me." He took a swig of the lukewarm beer. "I mean, she's amazing and, well, you know, a little bit out of my league."

"See, that's the problem with you, Stevie." Travis took a sip of his own beer and placed the bottle back on the counter with a loud snap. "You always feel like you're not good enough for other people. You've always been that way and it pisses me off."

Stephen was quiet. Travis's tone was almost nasty.

Travis went on. "I'm glad to hear that you met someone you like and I think it's great that she is amazing and beautiful and all that. But seriously, dude. You got to up your game a little, have some confidence. You're a good-looking guy, you're smart. Don't feel like you have to wait around for people to approve of you. Go out there and have some balls about it."

Stephen swallowed and nodded. "How about you? How are things at Emerson?" He tried to change the subject.

Travis nodded and shrugged. "Okay." He pivoted around on his stool and stood up, stepping over to the cabinet to grab a bag of chips. He brought the bag back and set it on the counter in front of them. "Pretty much the same. I think I did okay in all my classes. I'm moving out of the dorms next year. I hate my roommate. Oh, yeah, and I think I might have gotten a job."

"Oh yeah, a job?" Stephen was surprised. They'd both worked at small jobs during the summer but never anything during the school year.

"Yeah, coat check at a bar. Just to earn some extra spending money."

Stephen nodded, unsure what to say. He had just told Travis the most exciting thing that had happened to him since college began, and not only had Travis brushed it off, the only thing he had to add was that he was working as a coat check attendant.

The back door opened, and Travis's mom came in, letting in a gust of cold December air with her. She set two bags of groceries down on the counter in a huff, the cold emanating off her as she took off her gloves.

"Are there any more bags in the car?" Travis said.

His mom shook her head. "No, this is it. Just a few last minute things for dinner tomorrow night."

The two families had made it a tradition of having Christmas Eve dinner together since as far back as either one of the boys could remember. The two boys were silent as they watched Travis's mom move about the kitchen stuffing things into an already overstuffed refrigerator and into the cabinets and cubbies around the room. She made small talk as she moved, asking about studies and grades and even cafeteria food, to which Travis simply nodded or grunted or both.

As Stephen sat by and watched, it dawned on him for the first time since he'd been away at college that a gap was forming between Travis and his family. Stephen realized he'd been so caught up in his own journey at school and with Melanie, that he'd lost track of where and what had been happening at home. Travis looked increasingly bored as his mom continued to rush around the kitchen, pulling out a couple of bowls and setting them aside, talking about how she would use them later for making a dessert. Travis nodded but kept quiet. His mom finally looked over at him, but his head was down. She nodded quietly and left the room, planting a kiss on Travis's scalp and placing a hand gently on Stephen's shoulder as she walked out.

As soon as she was gone, Stephen looked over at Travis. "When are you going to tell her?"

"I can't." He shook his head. "Not yet."

"She's not going to care, Travis. Neither one of them are going to care. Can't you see what you're doing by locking them out? They think something's wrong."

"Nothing's wrong."

"I know that." Stephen inhaled deeply. "You know that. Why can't you just tell them?"

"So," Travis said with a smile. "Tell me more about this Melanie."

"Wow." Stephen shook his head.

"Wow what? I want to know about her."

"Two minutes ago, you couldn't care less about her. Now you want to know about her? Nice and subtle way to change the subject."

Travis laughed gently. "Okay, so maybe I am trying to change the subject a little bit. But I do want to know about her. Go slowly, though. I'll let you know if I'm uncomfortable with any of it."

"What?" Stephen leaned back on his stool. "Uncomfortable?"

"You know, with your alternative lifestyle and all."

"Whatever, dude. You're just weird."

❖

Stephen tried not to talk about Melanie too much over the break. Travis was obviously bored with hearing about Stephen's new love life. But try as he might, Stephen couldn't help bringing her up from time to time.

A week before Christmas, Travis and Stephen decided to make the trek down to Nashua, ostensibly to do some last minute Christmas shopping. But the two of them had grown used to the pace of college life and the quiet days of northern New Hampshire had proven to be very slow. They both liked the idea of a day of city life.

"Maybe I should call Melanie and see what she's doing," Stephen said. He was sitting in the passenger seat of the Gaines's Subaru station wagon, staring at his cell phone.

Travis smirked and shook his head silently.

"Why aren't you happy for me? I found someone I really like, and I thought you'd be happy for me." Stephen looked off to the left, out the car window at the snow-covered cornfields that seemed to speed past them.

"I am happy for you, Stephen. What do you want me to do—jump up and down to prove it?"

"What kind of question is that?" Stephen squinted his eyes. "You don't have to get hostile."

"I'm not hostile," Travis said quietly.

"Well, you're something. I don't know exactly what it is, but it's not you." Stephen sighed heavily and looked down at his hands.

Finally, after a few moments of silence, Travis spoke. "Do you want a bullshit answer, or do you want to know what I'm really thinking?" He stared straight ahead as he drove.

"What does that even mean?" Stephen said, glancing up from his hands and turning to look at his friend. "Of course I want to know what you really think. I wouldn't have asked otherwise."

"See, the thing is Stevie, I don't know what to think."

Travis looked briefly at Stephen, but then continued to stare out the windshield at the road ahead.

"Huh?" Stephen snorted. "What do you mean?"

"What are you, Stevie? No, don't roll your eyes and look away."

Travis took a deep breath. "I just think it's a little weird that you're into her."

"By into her, do you mean Melanie specifically?" Stephen said slowly. "Or do you mean into women in general?"

In the silence between the two of them, Travis angled his head to one side and rubbed his right hand on his temple as he drove.

"I've got news for you, Travis. Not everyone is gay."

"That's not fair, Stevie." Travis turned a shade of red.

"That's what you're implying isn't it?" He heard the thin hint of disgust in his own voice.

"No, I'm not implying that everyone is gay," Travis's voice grew slightly more irritated.

"Not everyone, then? Just me?" Stephen shook his head. "Jesus, Travis. I know you're having trouble with the whole coming out thing, but dragging me into this is not going to make it any easier. I'm not gay."

"Is that such a strange thing to ask you?" Travis had regained his assertive tone.

"Yes. It's a strange thing to ask me."

"No, it really isn't, Stevie. You've never once been interested in a single girl since the time we were in fifth grade. You never even talked about women, never looked at them, never got busted for trying to sneak a dirty magazine."

"So that makes me gay?" Stephen glared at Travis.

"It doesn't make you anything, Stevie. But it's a fair question to raise. I'm sorry if I pissed you off. But you said you wanted to know what I was thinking."

Stephen sat silently in the passenger's seat of the car, a strange mix of bewilderment and irritation consuming him. But the sharp spike of anger he'd felt a few minutes earlier had faded.

"I know it's stupid," Travis said, "but if you want to know why it's taking me so long to come out to my parents, I always thought we would do it together. We've done everything else together."

Stephen scrunched up his face in a bewildered expression. "You want me to be gay so it will be easier for you to come out? Fuck you, Travis." He sat silently for a few minutes, staring out the window. "That's such a screwed up thing to say to me."

"No, Stevie, that's not what I'm saying." Travis's voice was gentle now, almost apologetic. "I'm saying that I always thought that you were..."

Stephen let out a long breath. "Jesus, I hate this conversation." He felt no anger, no anxiousness any longer. It was as if all emotion had drained from him, and all that was left were a string of empty words filling the space between the friends.

"I'm sorry, but I thought that you were probably also gay, and it was just taking you a little longer to figure it out."

Stephen croaked, a dull sound just barely audible above the sound of the tires on the highway. "What?"

"And so, when you started talking about this girl, I just...Well, it just took me a little bit to re-adjust what I thought of, well, everything."

"Of everything..." Stephen echoed his friend's words, his voice soft and disconnected. "Well, I guess you would have to rethink everything."

They rode along in silence for the next ten minutes or so. Travis kept his eyes straight ahead of him on the road, and Stephen stared out the window at the winter landscape.

Travis was the first to speak again. "I'm happy for you that you found someone, Stephen. I really am. I owe you an apology, but I wasn't trying to be weird about things. I just…"

"It's okay, Travis." Stephen reached over and put his hand on his friend's shoulder, a gesture he had made a thousand times since they were kids. "I asked you to be honest."

"Are we good?"

"Yeah, we're good." Stephen briefly met Travis's glance, then looked straight ahead. Then after a few moments, he asked, "Do I look gay?"

Travis let out a gust of laughter. "What?"

"Don't laugh. You just told me you've thought I was gay for the last twenty years. It's not an irrelevant question. Do I seem gay? Do I look gay?"

"Stephen, I don't even know what that means."

"Yes, you do."

"No, I don't, and that's an offensive question. Gay people don't look a certain way. Do I look gay to you?" Travis had inadvertently sped up the car as he spoke.

Stephen smirked. "Sort of. The way you dribble the basketball is a little gay."

"You're a dick, and you're just bitter because I'm a better basketball player than you."

"Okay, okay, I know you're right. I'm generalizing."

"You're being a homophobe, is what you're being." Travis reached over and playfully punched Stephen in the arm.

"I'm not a homophobe. Some of my best friends are gay."

"I cannot believe you just said that." Travis's jaw dropped in mock horror. "I honestly can't believe I'm hearing this."

"Kidding, kidding." Stephen held his hands up. "I only have one best friend…"

"Unbelievable."

❖

The conversation in the car with Travis stuck with Stephen for months after he returned to college. He tried to forget it, but there was something about Travis's words that Stephen couldn't let go of. Travis had been his best friend—his brother almost—so who else had seen so deeply into his soul? At first Stephen tried to dismiss the conversation, Travis being Travis. He was wishy-washy at times and despite how kind he could be, he was also narcissistic by nature. Why wouldn't he think the whole world was just like him? Except, it wasn't. Stephen wasn't. Stephen told himself he was his own person despite what anyone else told him, even Travis, they could not control who he was or what he was.

"Folding laundry on a Saturday afternoon?" Melanie appeared at his door of his dorm room. He'd left it open, of course. It was always open. He smiled to see her, her long hair falling gently over her shoulders, a blue parka unzipped but clutched together between two bare hands. He knew she'd lost her gloves one night when they had all gone out for beers. Her face was red from the cold, and her eyes stood out even brighter than usual.

"Couldn't study," he said, looking back down at the basket of clothes he had been working on for the past forty-five minutes. A football game was on the television in the corner of the room, and he had gone back and forth between watching it and folding. He had a bad habit of waiting weeks to do laundry, until he had gone through everything twice and had nothing to wear that didn't smell like a dorm room sheet.

"What have you been up to this morning?" he said.

"This afternoon, you mean. Did you sleep late? I didn't see you at the cafeteria this morning." She pulled her coat off and dropped it on the armchair. Stephen had his own room that semester. A shortage of students meant that most of his dormitory hall were single rooms, so he had removed the second bed and set it up with a couple of chairs and a small coffee table he had inherited from an upper classman who had left school half-way through the fall term.

"Yeah." He watched her slide into the chair and pull out her mobile phone. "Woke up at noon today." They had been out together for most of the night at an off campus party. But she had left early, complaining of an upset stomach, leaving Stephen on his own. "I stayed a lot later than I expected to last night," he said.

"I heard." She was busy tapping something on her phone.

"It was nothing crazy, I didn't actually drink that much," Stephen said absently. Tom Brady had just thrown a touchdown pass, and he was looking at the television screen.

"I know. I got the full download of the party this morning in the cafeteria," she said. Stephen could imagine the same breakfast conversation as every weekend morning, a detailed recount of the two or three parties everyone had been to the previous night. Who was there, who got too wasted and had to go to the hospital, who had hooked up with whom. "They said you talked to everyone, but drank nothing. I found it a little hard to believe."

He laughed vacantly, still staring at the television. He didn't think it was necessary to mention that he had spent a particularly long time talking to a beautiful freshman, and that she had tried to kiss him. He had dodged the kiss, letting her land a peck on the cheek, and then he had politely left her to talk to someone else. He hadn't committed any transgression, but still, he thought it better not to mention. "Which part?"

Out of the corner of his eye, he saw her look up from her phone and smile. "The talking part, silly."

Her smile distracted him from the game. He picked up the remote and turned the TV off. "I don't know, I just got to talking about stuff—God, politics, sex."

"Really? All that deep stuff? Who did you find to talk about all that with?"

"Are you jealous?" He was teasing, of course, but he was also changing the subject. She was never jealous, never petty, never possessive. She had a wonderfully warm way of being his friend and his girlfriend and never worrying about anything else. When she had left the party the night before, she had simply leaned down and kissed him and told him to enjoy the rest of the night and not to have too much of a hangover the next day.

Her smile broadened. "Not jealous. Just kind of amazed you found someone to have that deep of a conversation with at a Bellard party."

"What have you been up to today?" he said.

"Nothing."

"Me too. Totally bored."

She got up off the chair and walked over and kissed him on the lips, closing the door on her way. "I know something else we could do…" She smiled, and then she kissed him again.

Stephen smiled back and put his arm around her waist. Travis could go take a flying leap, Stephen thought. He didn't know the first thing about his heart.

But not long after that weekend, Melanie began to grow cold and distant. She stopped going over to Stephen's room and was noticeably absent from meals and classes that he was in with her.

On weekdays, the two of them usually saw each other first at breakfast, then lunch, then from about three in the afternoon after their last classes until well into the evening. That Tuesday, Melanie didn't show up at either breakfast or lunch. When Stephen texted her after his last class to say he was heading over to her room to study, she texted back that she was busy and needed to study alone.

When the same series of events happened the next day, he could feel the beginnings of a pit forming in his stomach. His mind crawled back over the incident with the freshman girl at the party, but he dismissed it. He hadn't done anything.

"Is everything okay?" He texted her on his walk back to his dorm room.

"Why? Is there something you want to tell me?" She texted back.

"No?" He gulped as he pressed send. The pit in his belly was growing deeper by the moment, but Stephen figured things might solve themselves if he left them alone.

"I'm fine." Came her final text of the day.

On the third day of Melanie's hiding, Stephen decided to go to her room anyway.

"What's going on with us?" Stephen said, standing in the doorway of her room.

"What do you mean?" She was looking down at a notebook, doing the best she could not to make eye contact with him.

"I mean things haven't been the same since that party last weekend, did something happen?" She shrugged, and he marveled at all of the different things that simple gesture could mean.

"Are you mad at me for something?" He leaned on the doorjamb. "Because whatever it is, I didn't mean it."

"No, I'm not mad." She kept her eyes on her notebook.

"Because I'm pretty confused right now."

"I just don't know you like I thought I did."

"What? What is that supposed to mean?"

"It means I need a little space from you right now."

"Well, do you want to talk—"

"No." She suddenly threw down a pen that she had tapping on her notebook with. "I don't want to talk about it, Stephen. I'm just…" She looked up at the ceiling as if searching for the right word. "…I'm just in a mood. Leave it alone."

"A mood?" He thought about telling her about the party, trying to explain that he hadn't done anything. But he couldn't bring himself to do it.

"Yes, a mood." She glared up at him, but only for a second. "Just leave it at that, okay."

He sighed heavily. "I guess I should go then?" It was more of a question than a statement, for Stephen really had no idea what was happening to their relationship.

"Well, I doubt we're going to have much fun here," she said.

"Okay then." He stepped into the room and leaned down to kiss her, but she kept her eyes down on the desk in front of her and he could only put his lips to her forehead. "Good night."

"Good night, Stephen." She was silent as he backed out of the room and turned to go.

As Stephen walked away that evening, back out across campus to his own dorm, he had a sinking feeling. Something had changed; some switch had been turned off and he had been locked out of something that had once, just a few short days ago, seemed so warm and promising.

Someone must have told her about that freshman at the party. He tried to subtly fish around among the people he knew had been at the party to find out. But nobody said anything to him. Melanie didn't confront him about it, so he never mentioned it, afraid to bring it up. But his silence only seemed to make things worse.

He tried to give her some space. At some level, he hoped leaving her alone would give her time to forgive him. But instead she only wanted to see him less. Their final conversation came a few weeks later when they ran into each other on front campus. She was on her way to class and he was on his way to the cafeteria—something he had grown used to doing alone again. It was late February and the mild Carolina winter had gotten as deep as it was going to get. The temperature was somewhere in the low forties and the grey, lifeless branches of the oaks above the brick path gave the whole setting a tired and soppy feeling.

Melanie had stopped walking the second she saw Stephen. She looked up at him, then looked away, as if deciding whether or not to turn around. But she didn't. She stayed and stood still, hugging a stack of books to her chest.

"Hi," he said gently as he approached her.

But she didn't say anything in return.

"I've been thinking about you," he continued. "There is something I want to say…"

"Stephen, don't," she said. Her voice was flat, and she sounded like she was starting to get a cold.

"Melanie, I think I might know what this is about?"

She shook her head. "I don't want to talk about it. I know about you and that freshman, but I don't want to talk about it. I don't—"

"No, It wasn't what you think. If it was that stupid freshman girl, nothing happened. It wasn't anything."

She held up her hand, shifting the stack of books down to her side. "Look, Stephen, please. I said I don't want to talk about it."

"Melanie, I honestly mean it. Nothing happened."

"But you wouldn't tell me about it, would you? I had to hear rumors about you and some little slut, and you didn't even have the guts to bring it up and tell me about it."

He could see the trail of her breath in the cool morning air. She shook her head slowly and finally reached out and put her hand on his shoulder. The warmth of her touch was reassuring, but at the same time, Stephen could feel it was at odds with the watery gloss of her eyes.

"Stephen, I don't want to see you anymore." She looked at him straight in the eyes, and he could see a pained resolve in her expression.

"What?" There was that pit in the center of his stomach again. Only this time it felt more like a swirly black hole, sucking in everything around him. "You're breaking up with me? Over something that didn't even happen?"

She shook her head sadly and withdrew her hand from his shoulder. His skin, underneath his coat felt cold and blank where her fingers had been. She looked away from him and continued on her way to class, leaving him staring after her.

Stephen's studies suffered, and the books took second priority in his life after the romance that had bloomed in the fall finally dissolved that winter. Stephen, so smitten with her, tried everything he could to heat things up with her, but it never worked. The last time she talked to him was to briefly tell him she would be transferring next year and would not return to Ballard. At least, Stephen thought, he would not have to see her around campus the next fall.

"That's too bad," Travis said in the car ride from Boston's Logan Airport after Stephen had told him the entire story. He'd driven down to pick up Stephen at the airport. "Did you think about transferring too?"

Stephen shook his head. "I was obsessed, but not quite that obsessed."

The two of them were quiet for several minutes as Travis maneuvered the tunnels leading away from Logan and the car emerged on route 93 heading up toward New Hampshire. Stephen hadn't been back since Christmas and the bleak grey and brown of the winter had given way to light greens and pinks and yellows of spring. He took a deep breath, glad to be heading home.

"I have some news," Travis said after a few miles on the Expressway.

"Boyfriend?"

"No," Travis shook his head. "Well, actually, yes, a few. But that's not the news." He was silent for several seconds.

"Well, are you going to tell me?"

"I told my parents."

"Told them what?" Stephen thought for a split second. "Oh, told them-told them?" His voice raised in a sharp staccato tenor. "Really?"

"Really." Then, after a second. "Well, sort of."

"What do you mean sort of?"

"Well, my Dad kind of knew already. He actually came down to see me during the spring semester, and we went out to eat."

"And?"

"And I don't know what happened. I was sitting there across from him at P.F. Chang's, you know the one down by Boston Common?"

Stephen didn't know where that was, but he nodded anyway, not wanting to stall the story.

"Well, we're sitting there and he's talking about everything at the hardware store—how sales are looking good this spring since it got warm earlier than usual, and how garden hoses are selling out like crazy. And I don't know what happened, I just blurted it out."

"Blurted what out? I mean, what exactly did you say."

"I said, Dad, I think that's great about the garden hoses. It's probably because everyone held off buying them last year. And I'm gay."

"You said that?" Stephen's jaw dropped.

"Yep." Travis smiled and struggled to keep his eyes on the road. "Just like that."

"And what did your dad say?"

"Well, that's the crazy thing. He just sat there across from me with his fork half-way to his mouth for about a minute. Then he put his fork down and he said, 'Well, it's about time you said something about it.'"

"That's it?" Stephen said. "That's all he had to say?"

"Well, no. But that's what he said right off the bat. Then, of course, we talked about all sorts of stuff. He said he and mom had known for a really long time, but they wanted to let me come out with it on my own terms."

"Just like that?" Stephen was in awe.

"Yeah, just like that. It was kind of weird, actually." The car veered slightly toward the edge of the lane before Travis focused on the road again, correcting the drift. "I kind of always thought they knew."

Stephen rolled his eyes. "Of course they knew. They're your parents. And besides, you weren't exactly subtle about it."

Travis gave him an irritated glance, looking away from the road again for a split second. "What's that supposed to mean?"

"Nothing bad," Stephen said.

"Are you saying I'm obvious? A flamer or something?"

Stephen couldn't suppress a giggle. "No Travis, not at all. Relax, you're totally back woods New Hampshire, all the way, dude. But, come on? All that time you spent with Danny? They had to have suspected."

"Oh, yeah, there's one other thing, and it's kind of awkward. They thought you were gay too."

"Oh." Stephen absorbed the news slowly, gradually shifting in his seat. He leaned his head back against the headrest. "Really?"

Travis smiled. "Does that make you uncomfortable?"

Stephen paused for a moment before he spoke. "No, I guess not." He looked back at Travis. "I guess it's not really a big deal to me."

"Uh-huh...Right. You're freaking out." Travis laughed. "I can tell you're totally freaking out inside, even if you're being quiet and all stoic."

"I'm not freaking out. I don't think I care," Stephen said. He raised his hands in front of him, palms up, as he spoke. "It's just not really a big deal if they thought that or not. It's not like it's an insult or anything."

"Let me guess." Travis flashed him a broad, bright grin, "Some of your best friends are gay?"

"Whatever." Stephen rolled his eyes and looked back out the window. "You make a joke out of everything." They rode in silence for a few miles, watching the suburban setting slowly transform from housing to more patches of green trees and fields. "They really thought I was gay?" he asked after a while.

"Relax." Travis reached over and gently punched Stephen's shoulder. "They just wondered if maybe there was something between you and me. I told them there wasn't."

Stephen turned to look at him. "They thought what?"

"Don't give me that face," Travis said. "What were they supposed to think? Danny was only ever around sometimes. You and I hung around every minute of every day."

SENIOR PANIC

S tephen hung up the scarf behind the door of his bedroom. He shed his coat and laid it on the bed and then sat himself down in the chair in front of his desk with a thunk. The winter in North Carolina was nowhere near as cold as it had been in New Hampshire, but Stephen had become acclimatized. Thirty-eight degrees now seemed like a frigid arctic wasteland.

He looked down at the blank laptop screen on his desk and took a deep breath. Spring mid-terms were a week away, and he had spent the last four days studying. It was unlike him to study this far in advance of a set of tests. And the truth of the matter was he wasn't even really all that worried about the exams. He was in the spring semester of his senior year, and he was finishing up on a set of elective courses. He didn't even need half the credits to graduate.

The intense early studying had been part of Stephen's way of taking his mind off the future. Every day that passed was a day closer to graduation, an event that both excited and terrified him. It was like some great big beginning that he had no choice but to wait for. In every single thing he did, day in and day out, he sensed things were coming to a close, and that scared him more than a little.

He flipped the lid of the laptop closed and stood up again, pacing to the corner of the room and then back. He looked around the desk at the notebook full of scribbles and lecture notes he had obsessed over for the past couple of months. He had nothing left to do. He could not cram another minute of studying into his head. He suddenly leaned over the desk and swept it all to one side. The notebook, papers and pen went flying. He grabbed the laptop, and a swell of tension ran up from his stomach to his throat. He paused and took a deep breath, putting the computer down, refusing to completely give in to his general feelings of frustration. He backed up and sat on the bed, grabbing his cell phone out of his pocket and dialing the familiar number he'd known by heart ever since he could remember.

"Hello." Travis picked up on the first ring. "What's up Stevie?"

"I'm so fucked," Stephen said. He could hear music in the background, something like a guitar and a strained female voice.

"Fucked as in a good way or a bad way?" Travis laughed.

"Travis, what the hell am I going to do after I graduate?"

"Oh, that?"

"Yeah, that." Stephen rolled over on his stomach so he was practically bowed over the bed sideways, his feet touching the ground on one side, his head about six inches off the ground on the other side.

"Stevie." Stephen could hear Travis walking. A door creaked and the music ceased. "It's going to be okay. You're going to move up here to Boston and get a job in an advertising firm. We're going to share an apartment, and we'll be okay."

"We will?" Stephen hadn't thought about any of this. They had talked about it only briefly during the holiday break that year. Stephen had mentioned a contact at an advertising firm in Boston that the college's alumni association had put him in touch with. He'd thought Travis had barely been listening to the conversation, but here he was, describing things as if they'd been working it out for months and were just settling the details. Stephen hadn't even reached out to the alumni contact in Boston.

"Of course we will. What did you think was going to happen when we graduated?"

"Well…" Stephen took a deep breath. He felt his ribcage expand against the mattress. He instantly felt relieved. "Well, I hadn't really thought about it." He paused for a second. "I've been freaking out here."

"I know," Travis said. "Me too, a little bit. It's all going to be over, all of it. We worked so hard for the last four years, not to mention the four years before that when we worked our asses off to get into college—well, sort of. Anyway, now it's all done, all that structure."

"It's just starting to sink in for me." Stephen was exasperated. Travis had said exactly what he'd been feeling. "I'm scared of not knowing what I'm supposed to do next. There's always been a catalog and a set of credits and requirements. Always an instruction set for life. Not anymore, not after May."

Travis laughed, and the phone buzzed with static as he spoke. "We get to make our own instruction set after May. It's kind of exciting, isn't it?"

"I guess." Stephen's lower back started to ache. He rolled over on the bed and propped himself up on his elbows. "So, where are we going to live in Boston?"

"I've been looking at a few places. Do you really care or do you just want me to try and pick a place?"

"How are we going to afford it? It's not like I have a job."

"Well, you have to call that guy the college put you in touch with, the one at the advertising company. Then you come up to Boston for spring break and do interviews."

"Spring break is a week and a half away," Stephen said.

"Well, get your train tickets or plane tickets or whatever."

"Have you interviewed anywhere?"

"Well…" Travis hesitated.

"Travis?" Stephen prompted him.

"I had a few interviews," Travis said. "I think I'll get one offer from a financial services company in downtown Boston."

"That's great," Stephen said. "Isn't it?"

"Yeah, I guess. It wasn't my first choice, but it's a good firm."

"What was your first choice?"

"Another firm," Travis said. "It was in New York."

"New York?"

"Yeah…"

"So, wait…" Stephen sat up on the bed and ran his hand through his hair. He wondered why he suddenly felt a pang of hurt. After all, it wasn't like Travis had an obligation to take care of him. Still, it had been nice to think he'd had a plan in place where Stephen himself had only been wallowing in a mixed state of panic and denial. "So all that talk about moving in together in Boston, that was just because you didn't get the job you wanted? I was your back up plan?"

"No," Travis said quickly. "Boston may be my back up plan, but you aren't. If things had turned out differently, we'd be moving to New York, but we'd still be moving in together."

"Oh." Stephen relaxed his scrunched up forehead, relieved that he, himself hadn't been an afterthought.

"Look," Travis said. "I know you're panicking right now, but don't. Get your ass up here next week. You can stay with me in my dorm room. Bring a sleeping bag."

"Okay," Stephen said. "I'll ask my dad to get me a plane ticket."

"Sounds good." Something crashed in the background. "I've got to go now. Text me your flight details."

"Okay, bye." Stephen clicked the end button on his phone and set it down on his chest. He lay there for the next several moments, staring up at the ceiling and trying to think of nothing at all.

2009

MOVING INTO BOSTON

Travis and Stephen moved in together on the fourth floor of a walk up apartment building in Boston's Fenway, a part of town just beside the much more posh Back Bay. They picked it because it was within walking distance of the places where they worked, and it was in stumbling distance to most of the bars and clubs in Boston. At twenty-two years old, they had a lot going for them. They were freshly out of college, each with a Bachelor's Degree. Both of them had been picked up by prominent firms—Travis in a financial services company and Stephen in an advertising agency. They worked crazy hours, but the weekends were their own.

The building was a yellow brick monster, built some time in the late 1800s or early 1900s. Their apartment had been partitioned several times from its original configuration. The molding indicated it must have at one time been an elegant single bedroom apartment with a couple of alcoves and maybe a dining area and a living room. In his more nostalgic moments, Stephen imagined some studious banker wearing a smoking jacket with a tobacco pipe, reading from broad leaf editions of the *Boston Herald*. The rooms had since been chopped up to accommodate the city's growing population of students and twenty-something junior executives. Whatever elegant layout had originally been there was now a two bedroom with a small kitchen area and a bathroom.

The boys moved in on the thirty first of August, and their parents had surprised them by pitching in and taking care of the first two months of rent, a generous gift that left Travis and Stephen speechless.

The move-in day went quickly and slowly at the same time—parking in the crowded streets where almost every other apartment was switching hands, lugging tons and tons of materials up the steps over and over again. But then it was finished. The six of them sat on what little furniture there was in the common area of the apartment, a couple of old dining room chairs, a small couch, and a beanbag chair Travis had brought from his dorm room. They drank beers and shared a pizza and talked about the neighborhood, where they would shop, how long their walks to work would be. Underneath it all was a split in the room. While the parents sat still, each with an expression of varying degrees of anxiety or melancholy; Stephen and Travis had a sense of something just starting. Their short bursts of conversation about innocuous things like the shopping and commuting only served to highlight how they avoided the deeper conversations about leaving home and not settling down in New Hampshire.

"You know they're never going to stop talking about how amazing New Hampshire is and how dangerous Boston is, right?" Travis said as they sat in the common area of the apartment after their parents had finally left that evening.

Stephen smiled and picked up a beer he'd been nursing since they had left. "I think they expected us to take a little more time after school before we left home again."

Travis shook his head. "No jobs up there, no life."

Travis arrived home at almost eight o'clock in the evening on his first day of work looking almost like he'd been run over by a Mack truck. His tie was askew, and his face had a sheen on it like he'd been sweating for hours. Stephen looked up from the still new-smelling Ikea sofa on the other side of their sparsely furnished living area.

"Rough first day?" Stephen said.

"I should have looked for the place before I started." Travis sounded out of breath. "Everything went wrong today. First, I couldn't find the office." He walked across the room to the tiny galley kitchen, opening the fridge and pulling out a can of Pabst Blue Ribbon beer his father had left in their refrigerator. "Want one?" He looked at Stephen.

Stephen nodded. "Sure, what the heck."

Travis opened the cans and joined his friend on the couch, handing him one of the beers as he landed.

"I thought you knew that area of town," Stephen said.

"I thought I did, too, but it turns out there are a lot of little hidden streets and alleyways around there." He took a gulp of his beer. "I wandered around until about nine fifteen trying to find the place. When I finally did, I was late and all sweaty and gross. Not the best way to make a first impression on your new boss."

Stephen laughed. "How was the rest of your day after that?"

"Not stellar." He sighed. "I managed to break the copier machine, hang up on one of the vice presidents, and almost flood the kitchen by screwing up the single-serve coffee machine."

"Excellent." Stephen took a sip of his own beer and toasted his friend.

"But," Travis said as he clinked his can to Stephen's and smirked. "The day wasn't without its bright spots."

"Yeah?"

"Yeah. It turns out there are quite a few hotties at the office."

"God, Travis, do you ever stop thinking about sex?"

"Nope." He shook his head. "Not since junior high school. Anyway, I'm not sure what the G-factor is in the office. Everyone seems pretty buttoned up. So I'm not about to go hitting on anyone."

"G-factor?"

"Gay factor—duh."

"Right. Sorry, I can't believe I missed that one."

Travis shook his head again. "Sometimes I wonder about you, Stevie. How was your first day at the advertising agency?"

Stephen shrugged. "It's okay. It looks like I'll be doing a lot of research."

"On what?"

"Just stuff. Audience demographics, message resonance, that sort of thing."

"Any cute girls there?"

Stephen smiled.

"Come on, don't get all shy on me. I know you noticed."

"I wasn't scoping out the women on my first day at work."

"Bullshit, Stevie. I know you. You won't admit it, but you were looking. Jesus man, you don't have to be such a saint all the time."

"Okay, okay there may have been a few good looking women there."

"A few?" Travis practically jumped off the sofa, almost spilling his beer. "It's an advertising agency, Stevie. That's supposed to be the number one type of company for hot women in Boston."

"I'm guessing finance must be the number one type of company for hot guys?"

"Why else do you think I'd work at one?" Travis smiled and Stephen just shook his head.

A Day at the Office

Stephen's cube was just outside a small conference room the executives used for their more sensitive meetings because it was somewhat out of the way of major office traffic. Three of them had been in there for the last two hours. During that time he had tried to focus on his work—developing a research report on the demographics of consumer banking customers in the Northeast, but the loud, angry voices coming from behind the wall made it hard to focus.

The research work was easy, and he plowed ahead with it. It was exactly what he knew it would be when he joined Boston's only real advertising agency as a research assistant for the media buying department. Graduating with a bachelor's degree in English Literature hadn't left him a ton of career options. You can only do so many things with an in-depth knowledge of the novels, poems and plays of the nineteenth and early twentieth century. He hadn't actually aimed for a job in advertising, but that's where he'd ended up through the miracle of alumni connections. And luckily, it suited him. It wasn't the kind of flashy creative stuff Travis and most people assumed it was. They had that department at the place he worked, but Stephen's job was in the department that figured out where to buy advertising space to put all the flashy creative stuff. They looked at audience demographics and statistics and something called "reach." When Stephen had to explain what he did, he often ended up saying it was like constantly working on a term paper. Most people frowned when they heard that description, but the truth was, it was perfect for him, and he was happier than he'd expected to be after school.

He also had some money for the first time in his entire life. It wasn't much but it was still something. Growing up in New Hampshire, he'd seldom had much reason to think about money. His parents had had enough, but there had never been anything for him to be in charge of. No allowance to manage. Although rent and groceries took a chunk out of his paycheck, he still had a considerable amount of money at his disposal and the freedom to spend it how he decided. However, he found the freedom to be flat broke by the tenth of each month was also his. He got caught in that situation once or twice, and it was painful enough that he didn't ever want to repeat it.

As he sat that afternoon scanning through numbers and making notes on a pad of paper, he couldn't help overhear the conversations in the small conference room next to him. He couldn't hear the full dialogue. Some voices were more resonant than others, and he strained to hear when things got quiet.

"What's going on in there?" He looked up to see the blonde bob and pale white skin of his manager, Melissa. She liked to call herself his boss or his mentor, but Stephen could hardly bring himself to call her that when she was only eight months older than he was, and she'd only been working there for six of those months. She was technically at the same level he was, but because she had seniority, she was responsible for parsing out the work and reporting up to their real boss, Susan Calvin. In contrast to Melissa, Susan had been doing her job for close to two decades with more than half of that time at the firm.

Susan happened to be one of the three people in that small conference room next to Stephen's office. He shrugged at Melissa, who was still standing in front of him. Her cube was across the office on the other side of the building, which he was happy about. She had a tendency toward finding teaching moments for him. She reminded him of what over-anxious mothers-to-be must be like when they babysit other people's children. At least with her across the office, he had time to work on his tasks, uninterrupted by her mentorship.

"Can you hear any of it?" she whispered.

"Not really," he said in his normal voice, not too loud, nor too soft. She flinched and put a finger to her lips. "What?" he asked in a slightly lower tone.

"They can hear you through the walls," she mouthed in big letters, pointing to the wall behind his cube.

"Ah." He nodded his head slowly and tried to keep from smiling. Her penchant for drama was off the charts, but she wasn't the only one in the office like that.

"Nothing?" she asked again, nodding her head slightly at the wall.

"No," he whispered to her this time. "Sorry. Haven't been paying attention."

"Ugh," she said, shaking her head. "Stephen, you've got to think team."

"Sorry?"

"I said you've got to think team. There are a whole bunch of us in this office. Even if you're not interested in hearing what our executive team is talking about, you've got to at least make an effort. Several of us would like to know what's going on in there. Don't be so selfish."

Stephen tensed up for a minute until she smiled, letting him know she was only kidding. He smiled back at her, and she came over to his desk and leaned on it, facing him. "You thought I was serious, didn't you?"

"Well." He shrugged. "You were pretty convincing."

"I know. It's a gift." She continued to gaze at him for a few seconds longer. "Hey, Stevie…"

He hated when she called him that. It seemed so contrived.

"Mmmmm?" He was looking back at his computer now, which was slightly awkward with her standing there leaning against his desk.

"A few of us are going out for drinks tonight after work." She said the words with a forced casualness.

"Mmm?" Stephen all but ignored her words, focusing instead on the research numbers now up on his screen.

"You should come. It's a lot of fun." She paused. "I mean, most of the time it's fun. Sometimes things get a little out of hand when someone has a little too much to drink." She let a little-girl-chuckle slip at that point. Stephen looked up at her, and she covered her lips with her hand. "Not that I would ever talk out of school. And not that I would ever be the one that has a little too much."

He nodded slowly, wondering what was going on with her and why she was still at his desk. She couldn't possibly be trying to overhear the execs on the other side of the wall; she was talking too much. "Uh, thanks for the invite. Not sure what I'm up to yet," he said in the most dismissive but polite tone he could muster.

"Well," she took one final look around, before slowly standing up straight. "I suppose I should get back to work."

"Okay," Stephen nodded, still staring at his computer screen.

"Let me know if you have any trouble with that report, I'm happy to go through it with you and help explain things again."

He glanced up at her. The report was really one of the most straightforward parts of his job. He'd been doing it for over three months now, and he couldn't imagine what he would possibly need explained at this point. "Okay," he said, forcing a smile. "Thanks."

"No problem," she said, slowly meandering away from his desk. "Happy to help when I can. I know how daunting it is when you start this job."

Stephen had to concentrate on not rolling his eyes. Instead, he simply nodded at her until she'd left. When she had, he looked at the clock on the bottom of his computer screen. It was almost 12:30. He looked around him to make sure that Melissa had really cleared the area, and then he grabbed his coat. He was supposed to meet Travis for lunch that day and if he didn't hurry he would be late.

A few blocks away in the second highest floor in a skyscraper on State Street, Travis filled four cups of coffee, adding just the right amounts of sugar or milk to each one. He carefully slid all four of them onto a hardcover notebook and ever-so-carefully made his way into the large conference room at the end of the hall. The inside wall of the conference room was all glass, and he could see the entire city of Boston and beyond, to the hills of southern New Hampshire.

"Thank you Travis," came the gravelly voice of one of the execs in the room.

"No problem," Travis said, carefully setting the mugs out in front of the three execs, and then taking his own and opening his notebook. This was a weekly meeting for these three middle managers to discuss the different funds they were responsible for and what they expected to happen over the next week. It was Travis's job to take notes, type them up, and send them out to each one of these men. He was not expected to contribute to the conversation. In fact, the brief interchange about the coffee was more than he normally felt permitted to utter in this meeting.

The first time he'd been dragged into the meeting and told what his role was, he didn't believe it. These three men couldn't take their own notes? For a meeting that was only between the three of them? Travis wanted to roll his eyes every time he thought about it, but instead he just gritted his teeth and took the notes. At least he had a cup of coffee as a distraction this week. He'd forgotten it last week, and he hadn't realized what a valuable asset a cup of coffee was during a meeting this boring, how even the act of picking up the coffee and taking a sip could be a relief from such extreme boredom. The feel of the warmth in his hands, the texture of the rim against his lips, the brief relief for his cramping hand. *God, this is pathetic*, he thought.

The meeting usually ran long, starting around nine in the morning and going until just about noon, when the three of them would break and each take a short walk for an expensive lunch that would probably cost half of Travis's wages for the week. But he pushed that thought away as he settled in and glanced up at the clock in the room. He had exactly two hours and forty-five minutes of mind-numbing note taking to go this morning.

When the meeting finally ended, Travis massaged his mangled, cramped mess of a hand. The three execs cleared out of the room, leaving their empty coffee cups and an odor of staleness behind them. It was just twelve thirty, and Travis knew he would be late to meet Stephen for lunch. He dug his phone out and texted him. *Leaving now. Five minutes late.*

They met up in front of the brick arcade in Faneuil Hall. It was a giant colonial era warehouse that had served as a stopping point for tea and other goods coming into and going out of Boston Harbor. It had been ground zero for the American Revolution in Boston and had somehow survived the urban planning of the 1950s and the interstate highway movement that had torn up and gutted much of the surrounding neighborhoods in the twentieth century. Today, cobblestones and bricks still paved the ground around the place, but instead of sacks of flour and crates of tea, the buildings held food stalls, restaurants, and stores like Abercrombie and Urban Outfitters.

Stephen arrived first and stood outside the building with his back to the brisk autumn wind. Boston was cool that fall, and the day was crisp bordering on cold. Stephen had only worn a light jacket, and the wind from the harbor was coming up sharp against his skin. He could smell the salt from the water just a block away. He was still getting used to the smell even though he'd been in the city for a few months.

"Hey Stevie. Sorry I'm late."

Stephen saw Travis coming across the cobblestones toward him. He smiled. "No worries," he yelled back as Travis jogged the last few yards. "I was just taking in the afternoon."

They stood in line at one of the sandwich counters, squished in among the pretzel vendors, cookie stores, and coffee shops. This seemingly endless hall of fast-serve food was one of the wonders of Boston. It was quick, but not the best quality, though neither one of the guys had ever left a meal unfinished.

"We should really start packing lunches," Stephen said.

Travis nodded as they advanced a few steps in the sandwich line. "We'd never get up in time to make them in the morning."

"That's true."

They got their lunch and found a seat in the round atrium at the center of the building. It was loud and a little cold, but it was a spot to sit indoors, and they didn't complain.

"So, any progress with the boss?" Travis said.

Stephen raised his eyebrows. "Melissa? She's not my boss."

"Whatever. She's the one you want to bag."

Stephen shook his head. "I don't want to bag her. I can hardly stand her."

"Uh-huh. Sure. That's pretty much just subliminal flirting."

"What are you talking about, Travis?"

"Trust me, I know this kind of stuff. It's subliminal flirting. Your brain secretly wants her, but you just don't know it yet. So you flirt with her, but not in a way you recognize. Instead of being all nicey nice and complimenting her and laughing at her jokes, the attraction manifests itself as irritation."

"Oh, geez, thanks oh wise one." Stephen took a defiant bite of his ham and cheese sandwich.

"You should just find a closet, make out with her one day, and get it over with."

"What are you? Twelve years old? We're not in middle school, and I'm not about to go play seven minutes in heaven with some girl at work I can't stand to be around. Do you ever think of anything but sex?"

Travis looked up toward the ceiling, pretending to think seriously about the question. "Nope. Sex is pretty much it. Oh, and food. Yeah, I think about food a lot, too."

"How are things going at your office?"

"Oh," Travis sighed. "You mean land of the lame? Fine, I guess. My lifelong goal was always to get coffee for old white guys and take notes while they talk for hours about stupid shit, repeating themselves over and over again."

"Oh, that sounds fun."

"Trust me, it's not. I totally picked the wrong job. There is not a single gay person there besides me."

"You can't know that."

"Oh, yes I can." Travis put down his sandwich emphatically as if to punctuate his point. "I thought, financial services. Okay, I can do that. Lots of young guys, sharp looking, well dressed. It must be crawling with the gays. Nope, nada, zilch."

"Well, it's probably best not to fish off the company pier anyway," Stephen said.

"That's bullshit. Fish where there are fish, that's what I say."

Stephen laughed at his friend. "You haven't seemed to have a lot of trouble fishing since we've moved to Boston." He looked Travis square in the eyes, and Travis smiled and looked away.

"Well, it has been a kind of busy few months," Travis said, the smile clinging to his lips.

"How many...er, dates, are we talking so far?"

"A few," Travis said, "but they're not really even dates. They're just hook ups, and it's not the same. I would like to have some gay colleagues at work, just because it would be nice not to feel so alone there. It's not really like I am looking to fish off the company pier."

"Uh-huh," Stephen said, his voice low and doubtful. "Travis, who was the last gay guy you knew that you didn't sleep with?"

"What?" Travis looked shocked and a little wounded.

"Seriously," Stephen said. "I'm not trying to be mean here, but really, when did you have just a 'gay friend?'"

"Well, there was Danny."

"No, there wasn't Danny. You were sleeping with him from the middle of high school on."

"Well, not anymore, and we're still friends."

Stephen frowned.

"Well, it's true."

"Okay, you get that one on a technicality. Any others?" Stephen finished the last bite of his sandwich without taking his eyes off Travis.

Travis tilted his head and looked away for a few seconds before looking back at Stephen and chuckling. "No, I guess not."

"So what's the big deal? It's probably better that you don't work with many gay guys. You'd just get yourself in trouble."

"Well, there is this one guy. His name is Benson," Travis said. "But he's one of the bosses. So, even if he is gay, which I'm sure he's not...but he does kind of trip off my gaydar..." Travis took a final bite of his sandwich, chewing while he spoke. "But anyway, even if he were gay, it's not like he would even talk to me."

"Why not?"

"The execs do not talk to us peasants." Travis wiped his mouth with his napkin. "It just doesn't happen, so it's no use even thinking about it. But he is kind of hot."

A Year and Christmas in Boston

The days passed one into the next until they had lived in Boston for a year. The winter had seemed to take up most of that first year, and it felt like they were perpetually fending off damp feet and cold hands. Stephen laughed to remember how he had thought the mild Carolina winters were cold when he was at school. The Boston winter was dark and snowy and much longer. But when spring came to the city, it did so in a rush.

The cherry trees along the Charles River were out in a white and pink bloom that lit up the entire town. The Boston Commons and the Boston Gardens, the two parks that formed the heart of the city, were planted with roses and daffodils and crocuses, bringing the whole town to life with color. The trees along Newbury Street and throughout the Back Bay willed themselves into timid, light green tips at first, progressing until they were a lush canopy.

Even the Fenway, the brackish marshes that flowed into the Charles from up behind Back Bay, woke up from its brown grey winter slumber and burst to life in a sea of green reeds. The transformation was miraculous. Stephen and Travis, who had been shut up in their apartment or confined to offices and bars since the fall, made it a point to be outside as much as possible, walking all over the city and spending their spare hours in the street cafes and slowly-awakening parks.

Summer extended the greenery of spring into a damp heat that came and went as the winds from the Atlantic either rose up to cool things off or laid low and let the population simmer in its cement and brick casing. Tee shirts and shorts grew shorter and the crowds of twenty-somethings that wore them parading down Newbury Street grew skinnier. Every night, Stephen and Travis made their way down to Emack's on Newbury for an ice cream, followed by a beer on the patio at Daisy Buchannan's just a few doors down.

As summer slipped into their second fall in the apartment, Stephen's wide-eyed wonder at the noise and the crowds that surrounded his every move eventually gave way to a casual sense of ease, as Boston became his city. Some of his rural habits remained, though. He still stopped and waited at crosswalks while the Boston masses plowed across, oblivious to oncoming traffic; he still said please and thank you to waitresses and bartenders; and he still opened doors for people when he went into buildings. Others found these traits both parochial and charming, and without his even knowing or realizing it, these little tells went a long way toward helping him build friendships.

In their early days of living together, Travis's status as the veteran city dweller proved to be conditional at best. While he had told Stephen that spending four years at a college in the city made him an expert, Travis soon realized how sheltered his life had been at school. He got lost all the time. The financial district gave him the most trouble. Boston was a maze of twisting streets and towering glass and steel structures peppered with tiny brick shops left over from the colonial days.

Before long, it was Christmas. The brisk chill of the Boston fall turned salty cold, and the wind stung where it touched their bare hands and noses. The two young men worked through the challenges of shopping on a limited budget and still meeting the social obligations of seasonal celebrations with friends and workmates. Stephen's firm had their party first, in early December, and Travis's fell just before Christmas. They planned to go home to New Hampshire on the twenty-third of December, a day after Travis's holiday party.

"Why am I going to your holiday party with you?" Stephen said as he fumbled with his tie. He stood in front of the bathroom mirror, which was just a little too low to see himself in without crouching down, which made it difficult to get his half-Windsor knot just right.

"You're going because I need to bring a plus one, and I don't have a plus one except for you." Travis was in the tiny kitchen polishing the pair of wingtips his father had given to him earlier that fall.

"Isn't a plus one supposed to be a date?"

"No," Travis said. "It's just someone from outside the office so we don't all have to talk about work all night long."

"Do you think that will actually happen?"

"Huh?"

"Do you think you'll actually talk about anything else besides work? If it's anything like my work party, you'll just all stand around, talking about office gossip or whatever you forgot to get done that day. Then you'll drink some—maybe too much. Then you'll go out to a bar with the coworkers you like and ditch the ones you don't, and half the people will be hooking up with each other."

"Well, there is one guy who's going to be there that I wouldn't mind hooking up with." Travis finished buffing his shoes and put the rags and the tin of black polish back into a plastic bag sitting out on the floor beside him.

"Great," Stephen said. "Do I get to play wing man tonight?"

"Not a chance." Travis laughed. "His name is Benson, and he's about ten years older than me. And he's out of my league."

"What?" Stephen finished his tie and walked out into the common room. "That's a first. Someone out of your league?"

"Even I have my limits," he said with a smile. He slipped on the wingtips he'd been polishing, and then he washed his hands in the sink. "Come on, we've got to catch the T or we'll be late."

Benson Harvey was the closest thing to a modern Boston Brahmin Travis had ever known. And to say Travis knew him was stretching it. He had seen Benson in a couple of all-company meetings and once in a while he would see him in the hall. If he had some reason to walk over by executive row, the set of offices that housed the firm's president and CFO, he would try as casually as possible to steal a glance through Benson's door.

Benson was old by Travis's standards. He was thirty-five, which gave him more than a decade on Travis. But he worked out every day. Travis made it a point to be somewhere in the vicinity of reception at one thirty every day, the time when Benson usually headed out on his lunch hour, carrying a gym bag. Travis would watch out of the corner of his eye as he pretended to be flipping through the newspaper searching for an article or looking for something on the receptionist's desk. He'd even volunteered to answer phones at the front desk during the receptionist's lunch hour. Travis thought the work outs must be pretty aggressive; Benson had broad shoulders and well defined arms, at least as far as he could tell through the long-sleeved Brooks Brothers dress shirts Benson wore every day. He was fairly tall, standing just about six feet two inches, and his jet black hair was trimmed short except for the front, which was just long enough to brush up and over to the side.

Everything Travis knew about Benson he gleaned from his covert stares and through the internet. In between actual work, Travis spent a great deal of his day searching for details on the life and past career of Benson Harvey. From his online stalking, he had learned that while only thirty-five years old, Benson had worked at three management consulting firms on large projects. He was from Boston. The only addresses Travis could find going back two decades were in the Back Bay. He'd attended Boston Latin high school and, later, Harvard. Travis had searched in vain for more information, but the only other thing he could come up with were occasional stories in the *Boston Business Journal* that either listed Benson as an employee or announced that he had been hired somewhere. Travis had stifled the urge to actually follow him out on one of his lunch breaks to find out where he worked out and what his routine at the gym was. While young and infatuated, he told himself he wouldn't cross the line to stalker, yet.

The holiday party that night was at Locke-Ober's, a Boston institution that went all the way back to colonial times. It was located in the center of Boston's financial district, a dark and somber place with burled walnut paneling, ancient oil paintings, and a serious amount of brass. Dinner would have cost a week's salary for either Travis or Stephen, so it was unlikely either would see the inside of the place again for years to come.

The pair stood at the bar in the private dining room reserved for the party, each with a Heineken in one hand and the other hand in his pocket.

"So how many of these people do you actually work with?" Stephen said, watching as the eddies and swells of people clustered and chatted around them without stopping to say hello or even look at them. There must have been over a hundred people in the room and it was still early. Not a single one seemed to notice them. This was not the Travis he had known at high school. Not Mr. Popularity.

"Oh." Travis coughed slightly and cleared his throat. "You know, it's a big office. How many people do you know at your work?"

"Everyone. But, it's a different place." He felt bad. "We're a lot smaller than this. There are only about one hundred people working there total."

"Travis, right?" Benson's voice came from behind them, seemingly out of nowhere, as if on cue. Travis turned first. Stephen followed suit just a few seconds later, but the guys had different expressions on their faces. Travis nearly dropped his beer, but Stephen had a slightly amused look. He had guessed, given his friend's expression, who the owner of the voice was.

"Yes." Travis swallowed hard, looking at the tall, dark-haired man standing in front of them. He wore a navy blue suit with a white button-down shirt and no tie. The suit was slim cut with narrow lapels and obviously hand tailored to emphasize the broadness of his chest and the narrowness of his waist. "Hi," Travis eked out.

"Benson." The man stuck his hand out, and Travis slowly reached out and shook it. "Benny, actually. You're sort of new, right? I think I've seen you out on the floor."

"Yes sir," Travis managed.

"Please, don't call me sir." Benson smiled. "Benny is fine."

"Okay, Benny." Travis looked at Stephen. "Oh, ah, this is my roommate, Stephen."

"Nice to meet you," He reached out and shook Stephen's hand. "How long have you two been together?"

Stephen raised his eyebrows, and Travis blushed.

"Oh," Travis said. "We're just roommates, nothing more. He's not like that. Oh, I mean it's not that type of relationship."

Benson smiled and nodded. "Sorry, I shouldn't have asked that. It's really none of my business. It's just that…" An awkward silence hung in the air between them as Benson stopped his sentence short.

"HR would kill me if they heard this conversation right now." He laughed gently.

Stephen looked away, searching the room for something else to look at. Travis looked directly at Benson. "Well, I don't see any HR people here. Go ahead. Say whatever it was you were going to say."

Benson smiled at the younger man, an amused glint in his eye. "Okay," he said. "I was going to say that I thought you were out."

Stephen almost spit out the sip of the Heineken he'd taken. But Travis just smiled. "Yes," he said. "I am, actually."

Benson grinned, but he didn't say anything for a few minutes. He finished his drink and held it up in the air, clinking the ice cubes around the empty glass. "Time for a refill. I'll be right back." With that, he turned and walked away.

"He'll be back," Travis said as Stephen turned and nudged his friend in the shoulder.

"Sure he will. Just as soon as he refills that drink. In fact, I think I'll do the same."

Benson never did come back that night. Travis watched as he wandered off into the crowd to get his drink, and that was the last that they saw of him. Travis waited until almost the end of the night. The crowd had swollen to a bumbling mass of alcoholic fervor before dying down. Eventually, the waiters and bar backs began clearing the room and stacking the chairs. Stephen stood next to his friend until the end, nursing Heineken after Heineken and trying to make as much small talk as he could with someone he'd known all his life.

"Hey, look at them," Stephen said when they were almost the only two people left in the room. Three random couples were spread out around the place now; two of them deep in conversation and the third seriously making out. Stephen was pointing to the couple making out. "Who are they?"

"Oh God," Travis said. "I think that's the receptionist's boyfriend and one of the women from HR."

They both chuckled, the levity of it giving them each a second to breathe a little easier. But the laughter died off and faded into an awkward silence.

"He's not coming back, you know," Stephen finally said after a few minutes.

"I know," Travis said. "I was hoping he would."

"I know you were." Stephen put his hand on Travis's shoulder. "I have to ask—what's so special about that guy anyway?"

"Nothing, I guess." Travis shifted his weight. "He's just really, really hot and he's got it all happening. He's got the right job, he drives an amazing car, owns a great condo."

"He seems a little old for you?"

"Old?"

"Yeah, old." Stephen tried to soften his tone. "He's what, forty?"

"Thirty-five. But I don't really care about that. I kind of like that he's older. He's already been through all this."

"Why are we even talking about this? It's not like you're going to go out on a date with the guy? He's not even gay is he?"

"I don't know," Travis said. "I thought he was, but it's not important. Let's just get out of here. I'm bored with this place already. I feel like we wasted an entire night here."

"It's still early enough to get a beer at Cleary's."

"Sounds good. Let's go."

Travis and Stephen grabbed their coats and left Locke-Ober's through the front door. The frigid air immediately surrounded them as they stepped out into the Boston night, forcing them to hunch their shoulders and tuck their faces into their identical pea coats. They began the slow walk through the financial district, eventually emerging onto Boylston Street and trudging against the wind in the direction of home and Cleary's. The walk would be a cold and long one, but neither even brought up the thought of calling a taxi. The twenty dollars it would cost to get home would be much better spent on beer or groceries or a combination of the two.

2011

City Year

That winter, Stephen and Travis decided to economize. The splendor and generosity of the holiday party at Locke-Ober's was in stark contrast to what the firm actually paid Travis as an entry-level employee. Stephen made about the same income, and the two of them had spent so much at Christmas, they were nearly broke when they returned home from New Hampshire after the holiday.

While beer, rent, and food could only be cut so much, they decided to go without monthly commuter passes on the T for a while. Walking to work wasn't so bad in the warmer months, but December, then January and eventually February had been a parade of miserably cold weather in Boston that year. Every morning, they bundled up in their pea coats, scarves, woolen hats, and gloves.

Every morning Stephen and Travis would start out together down Boylston Street, the cold chasing at them, seeping in at their necks and at their wrists where the edges of their coat sleeves didn't quite meet their gloves. The entire city seemed like a grey silhouette on those winter days, the sidewalks the same color as the buildings which, in turn, were the same color as the cloudy morning skies. Some mornings, it snowed while they walked to work, the snowflakes highlighting and brightening the starkness of the morning, coating the streetscape in a blanket of fresh white powder. But the snow, for all its beauty and grace, always seemed to come on a ferocious wind that bit at their faces and swept into the creases of their boots as they walked.

The first sign of life along their walk was the group of one hundred or so City Year kids, most of them just out of college, gathered at Copley Square every day for their morning warm-ups and motivational speeches. Their bright red jackets formed a bouquet of color against the dull winter streets, and their calisthenics, while muted and unfinished and barely coordinated, seemed like a ballet against the stillness of everything else in the early morning city.

"I couldn't do it," Travis said one morning as they passed by Copley Square just as the group was beginning their warm-ups.

"They're the same age as us," Stephen said. He stared at the group as they walked.

"No. I mean I wouldn't want to do it. Ever."

"I don't know." Stephen continued to stare at them. "It's just a year out of their lives. I might be able to do it."

Travis shook his head. "It's like taking a vow of poverty."

Stephen looked down at his hands and laughed. "You know, we're walking because we're too cheap to buy T passes, right?"

Travis smiled, but his expression was devoid of humor. "Yes, Stephen Davis, I understand that. But at least we're getting a start at something. They're just sitting there, doing a year of I don't even know what. I can't wait to make more money. I don't want to have to worry about my next paycheck."

"They spend a year helping out with the schools in bad parts of the city," said Stephen. "It's a pretty good program from what I understand. They help tutor kids and spend time at the schools doing stuff."

Travis gazed at the group as they began a round of jumping jacks. "Yeah, but they're putting everything else on hold. I couldn't wait to start living on my own and working and making some money at least. I mean." He paused to let out a breath of white air. "It's not much now, but next year it will be a little more and then more after that. The last thing I would want is to prolong the beginning of everything."

"Well, I don't think it's like that for them." Stephen said. "It must seem like they're doing something good for the world—you know, giving back starting at the very beginning."

They walked in silence across most of the rest of the square, stopping for a second at the edge of the open space to look back at the group. They were at the corner of Boylston and Clarendon Streets, the edge of the square occupied by the brown brick Trinity Church with its gracefully pitched roof and wandering cloisters that stretched out into the square.

Travis shook his head. "Why do you always do that?"

"Do what?"

"Always turn things around so they're good." Travis looked at Stephen for a few seconds before turning back around and continuing their walk. "It's not a bad thing, I guess. But it always seems like you're just doing it to be obnoxious."

Stephen turned in time with Travis and matched his stride as they started up Boylston again. "I don't do it on purpose," he said. Then after a few paces in silence, "I guess I just like to see the world in a certain way."

"You like things to be nice," Travis said. "You always have. You want everyone and everything to be nice. No conflict, no evil."

"Travis," Stephen held his gloved hands out in front of him as they walked. "There is nothing evil about City Year. It's a great organization that helps out the schools in some of the worst parts of the country."

"It's not just City Year, it's everything. You always find…" He stopped, unable to think of the right words.

"The good in everything?" Stephen finished Travis's sentence with a question. "That's not a bad thing. It's a healthy, positive outlook on life."

Travis reached over and playfully punched Stephen in the arm. "Whatever, dork."

Stephen smiled. "You know you really should be nicer to me."

"Why's that?" Travis said, a real smile spreading across his face now.

"I'm the best roommate you could ever have," Stephen said as Travis made a face at him. "It's true. I look at the bright side of things, I make great conversation, and most importantly, I'm just as poor as you."

"We won't always be poor." Travis's smile faded a little. "Someday, I'll have boatloads of money, and I'll have a condo here and a big house back home and I'll drive a Maserati."

"And then you can join City Year after that." Stephen returned the punch with a gentle right hook to Travis's shoulder.

Travis just nodded and rolled his eyes. "Yeah, that's exactly what I'm going to do. Exactly."

The two of them were almost to the Boston Public Garden by this time, almost to the point where they would split off to head to their respective offices. The sun was just starting to peek through the dull morning cloud layer, letting a tiny bit of blue sky through and brightening the grayness of everything just a little bit. They walked the rest of the way together in silence and when they separated, they punctuated their morning stroll with a fist bump and a short, "Bye. See you tonight," each saying the words almost simultaneously as they headed off in their own directions.

Meeting Gabriel

"What are we doing here?" It was Friday evening and Stephen had been putting up with the cryptic messages from Travis all day. He had given Stephen an address to meet him at after work.

Travis was standing on the sidewalk in front of a long row of tall windows looking out onto the street. "I just wanted to try this place, you know, for a drink."

"What is it?" Stephen said, looking in through the windows.

"It's called The Raven."

"It's a gay bar, isn't it?"

"Come on, Stephen. I just want to check it out and see what it's like."

Stephen sighed and shook his head. "None of the hot guys from your office wanted to join you?"

Travis shook his head. "They're all straight."

"I've heard about guys like that." Stephen put his arm around Travis's shoulder and walked him toward the door. "Don't let them get you down. They obviously don't know what they're missing."

"Whatever," Travis said. "That office is so 1987. I'm practically back in the closet. I just needed to go somewhere where I can be out."

Stephen smiled at his friend. "You know, you could have told me where we were going."

Travis looked at him and shrugged. "I know, but I didn't want you to bail because it's a gay bar."

"Whatever. It's not like I would have said no. When have I ever said no to anything?"

"True. Still, I didn't want to take any chances. Plus I thought it would be fun to surprise you."

Stephen shook his head as they reached the door. "Come on," he said as they walked through. "You're buying."

Inside, the place looked like a sports bar more than anything else. It was dark with flat screen television monitors hung throughout the room. On one side was the bar and on the other, a room with three pool tables. The place had a slightly dingy feeling to it. Old photos of people in polyester sport uniforms hung on the wall. An actual softball jersey covered in scribbled signatures hung in one corner, and around the entire room, about two feet below the ceiling, ran a shelf full of trophies for softball, bowling, and a variety of other sports.

"You wanted to come *here*?"

"Yes, indeed, I did." He already had his eye on a tall redhead wearing a blue sweatshirt and playing pool at the corner table.

Stephen rolled his eyes at Travis. "What kind of beer do you want? I'll go to the bar. You obviously have a game plan."

"Sounds good, I'll take an IPA." He smiled. "I'll be by that table over there. I suddenly feel like a pool lesson." He patted Stephen on the back and made his way over to the pool tables.

Stephen walked over to the bar, keeping his eye on Travis as he ordered the two beers. He paid no attention as the bartender winked at him and the two guys on either side of him at the bar leered. He took the beers and headed over to Travis.

Travis was leaning against the wall behind the pool table with the redhead, next to a small round cocktail table. He was doing his best James Dean pose, leaning languidly against the wall, shoulders back, one leg bent, and a foot notched up right above the molding on the bottom of the wall. Stephen had to admit, the pose accentuated his looks. Travis had always been an athlete, and he was naturally well defined. His shoulders were broad and his waist narrow. His arms were bent enough to show off his biceps, and he had a cool, slightly disinterested look on his face that drew attention to his full, round lips and his dark brown eyes. Overall, he looked like quite a catch.

But despite the pose and the smoky looks, Stephen noticed the redhead wasn't paying much attention to Travis. He set the beers down on the table. Travis nodded to him as he picked up a beer and took a long, slow sip. Stephen shook his head slowly and looked around the bar again. Now that he was closer, he could see the redhead's blue sweatshirt was actually a Boston Police shirt, the big blocky letters stenciled across the back.

"There you go," Travis said under his breath. "He's about to look our way."

"How can you tell?"

"I can just tell."

The pool game was coming to a close in front of them and only a few balls remained on the table. The redhead only had the eight ball left. He circled the table slowly, his eyes intent on the green felt. He stopped and leaned over to survey the table from eye level as he prepared for his shot. He stood up and leaned over the table again, this time ready to shoot. He pulled the pool cue back and placed it between his fingers.

"And…he's going to look up…right…about…" Travis's voice was deep and low, barely a whisper. "Now."

He drew the cue back to shoot and, sure enough, just before he took his shot, the redhead looked away from the table and up at Stephen and Travis. He raised his eyebrows just enough so the guys knew he was looking at them, and he smiled. Then he shot. A loud crack broke through the air in the bar as the cue ball smacked into the eight ball, sending it directly into the corner pocket closest to Travis and Stephen.

"Wow, nice shot," Stephen said.

"Yeah, I'll say," Travis mumbled.

The redhead set his cue down on the pool table and shook hands with the guy he'd been playing with, and then he headed to the bar. Travis did a double take, but tried to hide his surprise at the redhead's lack of interest.

"Oh well," Stephen said. "It's totally okay. You'll find someone else."

Travis smiled, a tight-lipped fake smile. "You don't have to feel sorry for me, Stevie."

"I'm not feeling sorry for you. I'm just trying to soften the blow."

"Or lack of one."

"What?"

RALPH JOSIAH BARDSLEY

"Never mind." Travis took a sip of his beer and was just about to say something when he decided against it. Stephen was about to ask what was on his mind when he noticed the redhead walking back with a fresh beer in his hand. He walked directly up to the two of them and nodded, first at Travis, then, a deeper nod at Stephen, where his eyes rested as he took a sip of the beer.

"Hi," he said. "I'm Gabe. Up for a game?" He nodded over his shoulder toward the pool table.

"Uh, hi," Stephen said. He could feel Travis glaring at him, but he didn't turn his head to look. "A game of pool?" He immediately felt stupid.

"Well," Gabe said and flashed a perfect smile. "We could play basketball, but the pool table is closer."

Stephen laughed, easing the tension between them but doing nothing for the iciness happening with Travis.

"I'm not really much of a pool player." Stephen turned to Travis. "Travis is, though. Travis, why don't you play?"

The transformation was almost instant. Travis looked briefly at Stephen, took the hand off, and smiled a giant smile at Gabe. "Sure, I'm up for it."

Gabe glanced briefly at Stephen before meeting Travis's eyes. "Sure," he said, and turned toward the table. "You can break if you want."

The game took quite a while, Travis keeping pace with Gabe for much of the time. Travis tried to make conversation, but Gabe kept looking back over to Stephen.

"So," Gabe said, when one of his shots forced him over to the side of the table closest to Stephen. "I haven't seen you here before."

"Oh, yeah, well," Stephen said. "I don't usually go out that often."

"What he means," Travis said across the table, "is that he doesn't usually go to gay bars."

"Ah." Gabe nodded his head slowly, not taking his eyes off Stephen. "And why is that?"

"Well," Stephen started to answer, but didn't get far.

"It's because he's not gay. He came with me tonight because he had nothing better to do."

• 100 •

"Nothing better to do," Gabe said. He kept his eyes on Stephen for a few more seconds before he took the next shot. The cue ball flew across the table, snapping into the three and sinking it into the side pocket with a decisive thunk. "Well, I guess it's my lucky day." He stood up and looked at Stephen. "I mean, at pool."

Stephen found himself unable to take his eyes off the guy. He stood in front of Stephen, leaning casually on his pool cue, looking directly at him. He moved toward the table where he'd left his beer, leaving Travis standing on the other side of the table. Gabe picked up his beer and took a swig of it.

"So," Gabe said. "You don't play pool, you don't go to bars, you don't date guys," he said with a smile, "yet. What do you do?"

"I didn't say I don't go to bars." Stephen felt something weird in his stomach, something that didn't seem right.

"Oh, so you do go to some bars?" Gabe raised an eyebrow.

"Some, yes," Stephen said softly. He was suddenly disoriented, too.

"Like which ones?"

"Like," Stephen paused. "I don't know. He suddenly couldn't think of a single bar in Boston. "I guess I like the Pour House."

Gabe smiled. "Up on Boylston Street?"

Stephen nodded. He could feel his face starting to heat up, and he was horrified to realize he was blushing.

Gabe held Stephen's gaze and kept smiling for another few seconds. In the background, Stephen could hear the smack of the cue ball hitting something as Travis missed his shot.

"Your turn," Travis said from across the pool table.

"I'll be right back," Gabe said to Stephen. "Don't go anywhere."

Stephen nodded and looked across the room at Travis. Travis had a scowl on his face and simply glared at Stephen and shook his head. Stephen shrugged in response and shifted his eyes to watch Gabe. Gabe looked over the table for a few seconds, then grabbed his pool stick and slowly walked to the other side of the table. He leaned over and took the first of four shots, sinking ball after ball until he had cleared the table down to the eight ball.

Gabe glanced at Travis for a second, then over to Stephen. "Pick a pocket," he said.

Stephen looked blankly at him. "What do you mean?"

Travis tapped his pool stick on the ground, rolled his eyes, and shook his head slowly.

"Pick a pocket," Gabe repeated. "Which hole do you want me to get it in?" He pointed to the table with the tip of his pool stick.

Stephen could feel himself blushing again. "Oh." He stumbled over the words. "Jeesh, I don't know. Whichever one is easiest, I guess."

"Ah, come on," Gabe said. "That's the fun of it. You call it, I'll hit it. That's the challenge, that's what makes it interesting."

"Okay," Stephen said slowly. He stepped closer to the table and looked at it in detail. Travis had been stripes, and three striped balls were still spread across the table. The eight ball was almost directly in the center, about an inch away from one of Travis's balls. The cue ball was at the far end of the table from Stephen, between the bumper and another one of Travis's balls. From Stephen's limited knowledge of pool, he could see no clean shot. "How about this corner?" He pointed to the corner closest to him.

"Eight ball, left corner pocket," Gabe called, his lips pulled up to the right in a smirk and a twinkle in his eyes. "I was hoping you'd call that one." He leaned over the table and sent the cue ball flying in the exact opposite direction than Stephen would have thought. Stephen watched in amazement as the cue ball ricocheted off of the bumper, headed back toward the eight ball, and tapped it just hard enough to send it directly into the corner pocket Stephen had pointed to.

When the ball thumped into the pocket, Gabe stood up and nodded his head at Travis. "Good game," he said.

"Good game," Travis said. He gently laid his pool stick on the table. "I need another drink," he said. He headed to the bar, clearly avoiding eye contact with Stephen.

"Okay," Gabe said. His eyes seemed to light up at the prospect of having Stephen to himself for a little bit. He stepped back around the table. "So, how do you know each other?"

"Oh." Stephen realized Travis had abandoned him with this guy in the corner of a gay bar, not that he wasn't enjoying himself. That was the problem—the butterflies, the blushing. Something was obviously happening. Stephen was confused, but he felt a thrill and had to admit reluctantly to himself that he wasn't ready for it to end yet. "That's Travis. He's my roommate. We grew up together in New Hampshire and moved in a couple of years back when we both wanted to move to Boston."

"So he's your gay roommate?" Gabe took another sip of his beer.

"Yeah," Stephen nodded his head. "I guess you could say that."

"And you're…?"

"I'm the not-gay roommate."

"But you're curious." Gabe smirked. Stephen looked down. He suddenly couldn't feel his feet.

"I don't know what you mean."

"You know something?" Gabe leaned back and looked at Stephen from head to toe. "In my job, you get so you can tell a lot about a person, just by looking at them."

"Oh yeah?"

"Yeah."

A million things went through Stephen's head at that moment, but he could only bring himself to say one. "What can you tell about me, then?"

Gabe stared at him, silent for a moment. His hair had a brassy, golden sheen in the sunlight, and his blue eyes took on an almost mystical glow. "Are you sure you want me to say?"

"Go for it," Stephen said in a rush of uncharacteristic confidence. He wasn't especially braver than usual that evening, but he was wrapped up in the conversation by that point and there was no way out of it.

"All right," Gabe said. "I can tell you're normally shy. You don't like the spotlight, and you never volunteer to go first when you're in a group."

Stephen nodded. "Fair enough. You're right so far, but that could be most people."

"Nah," Gabe shook his head. "You're more shy than most people. You cling to Travis like he's you're safety blanket. But I can also tell that you're extremely smart."

"And handsome," Stephen added with a laugh.

"You're making fun of me now," Gabe said.

"No." Stephen brought a note of seriousness back to his voice. "I would never."

"You are also confused. You've only ever fallen for someone once, and you're not sure that was even love. You wonder if you're not normal in that way because no one has ever really pulled on your heart."

Stephen was silent.

"You've watched Travis fall in and out of love dozens of times, and you know you've never really felt that way."

Gabe waited a second, but still, Stephen said nothing.

"That is," Gabe continued, "until tonight."

Stephen's smile had faded.

It wasn't much of a game for him anymore. This guy, whoever he was, had gotten much too close to things for Stephen's comfort. "Does this work very often for you?" Stephen said.

"Don't get like that," Gabe said. "You were having a good time until just now."

Stephen pursed his lips. He felt as if he was being tricked somehow, but he couldn't put his finger on exactly how. He looked around the room and over to the bar. Travis was nowhere to be found.

"Maybe he went to the restroom," Gabe said.

"Sorry, what?"

"You're looking for your friend. You don't see him. I was suggesting that maybe he went to the restroom," Gabe said.

"What are you, a fortune teller?" Stephen said. He was standing up straight now, inches from Gabe's face.

"No," Gabe said. Stephen could feel the heat of his breath on his face. He smelled nice, a combination of cologne and chalk from the pool table mixed with the faintest whiff of beer. There was just enough space between them that there was no danger of them touching. "I'm a cop."

"Oh. I guess that makes more sense."

"So…" Travis was suddenly back beside them. He seemed to materialize out of nowhere. "Are you two going to kiss? Because if you are, Stevie, I can find a way home."

The silence between them was heavy, and Stephen felt the remarkable tension of the evening draining away, as if it was seeping into the ground at their feet and dissipating in to the earth.

"No," Stephen said. "We're not."

Gabe leaned back and looked away from Stephen toward Travis. "We were just talking."

"Just talking." Travis pulled a tight smile across his face, obviously struggling not to be snarky. "That's exactly what it looked like."

"Can I see your phone?" Gabe had looked back at Stephen and held his hand out.

"Yes, officer." Stephen wanted to pull the words back as soon as he'd said them. He didn't know why he'd said *officer*. It was clearly flirting, but he couldn't seem to stop himself. He pulled his phone out of his pocket and handed it to Gabe.

"Um," Gabe said, looking at the phone. "You need to unlock it."

"Oh, yeah, sure," Stephen said, entering the four digit number to clear his screen. "Here you go."

Gabe took the phone, entered ten digits and pressed send. He waited a couple of seconds, then pressed the end button. He added himself as a contact, and then handed the phone back to Stephen.

"Okay, straight roommate Stephen," he said with a smile. "Now you have my number and I have yours. Is it okay if I call you to hang out sometime?"

Stephen hesitated for a second. "Uh, I guess so."

"Good. You guys enjoy the rest of your night."

And with that, he walked out of the bar, turning briefly at the door to smile at Stephen one last time before he left.

WOULD YOU?

Travis didn't speak to Stephen for six days after they had gone to the Raven. He made it a point to leave the house early in the morning before Stephen even got out of bed. In the evenings, he came in from work and went directly to his room without saying a word.

Stephen knew he should resent the cold shoulder from Travis more than he did. Travis was being childish and petty about something Stephen felt hadn't even been his fault. But, in a strange way, Stephen was grateful for the space Travis's silence gave him. He couldn't quite figure out what had happened that night at the Raven and he wanted, even needed, some time to think things through.

It had been fun to meet someone new, and he had been flattered to be the object of someone's flirting. If he was honest with himself, it felt good to be chosen over Travis. Travis had always been the more vivacious one, the one that made friends easily, the one that everyone wanted to be around and to be like. To finally break that precedent felt, in some small way, as if it improved his own self worth.

Stephen had been so isolated and so alone for so long, he didn't know exactly how he should feel about Gabe. The last person he had been romantic with was in college, and the ending to that story had left him utterly broken. It wasn't even that Gabe was a guy, and he had only ever been involved with women before. He lived in a latter-gay world, after all. He should feel fine about experimenting along the spectrum, and those old rigid rules about gay and straight shouldn't even matter. Still, it was a little awkward for Stephen to imagine how things might progress with a guy.

While Travis avoided him, he sat alone in the apartment, wondering how things worked and if it was appropriate to hold the door for Gabe, or bring flowers on a date. In the end, he decided that a date, an actual take-someone-out-on-a-date date, was going to have to wait for a while. They could be friends, he told himself, but anything else would have to take a long time.

On the seventh day, Stephen decided he'd had enough of being avoided. He waited up late and intercepted Travis at the door as he came home.

Travis dropped his bag on the counter and was about to head into his room when Stephen said, quietly but sharply, "it wasn't my fault, so stop acting like it was."

Travis stopped and stared at him but remained silent.

"Come on, Travis." Stephen's tone was no longer sharp. "Why are you doing this? It was just some stupid guy at a bar. You're acting like it was some sort of competition. It wasn't. Now, come on and sit down and watch *Friends* with me, okay?"

Travis walked over to the couch and sat down facing the television. The two of them sat side by side for several minutes until Travis finally turned to him. "I don't care that he hit on you and not me," he said.

"You don't?" Stephen said.

"No, of course I don't care about that."

"Well, what is it then?"

"It's kind of weird."

"What's weird?"

"Well…that you were so into him," Travis finally said.

"Whoa, hold on." Stephen turned to face Travis full on.

"Don't deny it, Stephen. I was there. I watched the entire scene."

The two guys sat facing one another, neither saying a word for a few minutes.

"Anyway," Travis finally went on. "I guess I was just a little freaked out by it. I mean, why wouldn't you have told me first?"

"You think you were uncomfortable? How do you think I felt?" Stephen's eyes bulged out as he spoke. He tried to temper his voice, but he couldn't keep the underlying surprise out of his tone.

Travis put his hand on his friend's shoulder. "Stephen, I'm going to ask you something, and I want you to either answer me honestly or tell me that you can't talk about it."

"Travis, when have I ever not answered you honestly?"

Travis crooked his head and looked at his friend sideways. "That is what I'm wondering. Look, I know you didn't start things with that guy the other night, but it was difficult for me to watch it go so well with you. There was definitely chemistry there—lots of it. And it wasn't difficult because I was jealous. Was I a little envious he was all up into you and didn't notice me at all—even when we were playing pool? Yeah, sure, I'll grant you I was a little put off. But what really got me was that you were into him, and we'd never really even talked about that sort of thing."

"Talked about it? What do you mean?" Stephen folded his legs up underneath himself on the couch.

"Stephen, are you just a little bit gay?"

"Is that your question, Travis?"

"Well, yeah. That's my question." Travis sat and stared at Stephen as if he had nothing else to say.

"I don't know. I didn't really think about it until now, but I've been trying to figure things out for the last week."

"Oh, you thought about it before," Travis said. "I distinctly remember a conversation where you were mortified that my parents might have thought you were gay."

"I wasn't mortified, it just had never occurred to me."

"Never occurred to you or you didn't want to think about it because you were ashamed?" Travis's eyes had a strip of anger in them that Stephen had rarely seen.

"I wasn't ashamed. I would never be ashamed of something like that," Stephen said. "How could I be? You're gay, and you're such a part of me that we're practically the same person. If somebody said something bad or negative about gay people, I spoke up. You're my family and you're gay, so, by extension, it was part of my identity."

"Yes, Stephen," the fire in Travis's eyes had softened. "That's all nice and good, but it's really skirting a pretty important question, isn't it?"

"You mean am I attracted to guys?" Stephen's voice was low and gravelly as he finally said the words out loud.

"That would be the question."

"I'll be honest with you, I don't know. I'm not really attracted to that many people in general. I kind of think everybody just looks the same."

"What about the girl in college you were head over heels for?"

"Yeah, Melanie." Stephen smiled and leaned back in the sofa. "I guess I was pretty into her. I thought she was amazing, and it broke my heart when she transferred."

"Did you stay in touch with her?"

Stephen shook his head. "No, I didn't really want to do that. I thought it was too painful. I just wanted it to be over at that point."

"And what about now?"

"Now?" Stephen looked around the room. "Now, it's the same. I don't walk down the street looking at people thinking they're sexy or hot or whatever. I just don't."

"Hmmm," Travis said. "That's so strange. Everyone I look at— every guy at least—I think about what he'd be like in bed."

Stephen laughed, and soon Travis was laughing too. "No," Stephen said. "That's definitely not what goes through my head when I look at most guys."

"But this guy the other night?"

"Yeah…" The laughter had dissipated from Stephen's voice, leaving him solemn. "Something was different with him."

"Would you?" Travis nudged Stephen in the arm.

"What?"

"You know what," Travis said.

Stephen's face turned a bright shade of red. "I don't know," he said. "I've never thought about being romantic with…with a dude before."

Travis just smiled at his friend. "If he called you to go out, would you?"

"He already has."

"What did you say?"

"I didn't say anything." Stephen had a sheepish look on his face. "I didn't answer the phone."

"Did he leave a voicemail?"

Stephen nodded. "Yeah, he left a few."

"A few? And you didn't call back? You didn't even text him?"

"I didn't even listen to the voicemail."

"Why not? For Christ's sake, Stephen, at least have the courtesy to talk to the guy." Travis had a pained look on his face, his eyebrows knitted together underneath a scrunched up forehead full of wrinkles. "Give me your phone."

"No, Travis, I really—"

"Give it to me." Travis laid his hand out firmly between them, palm up.

Stephen dug into his pocket and reluctantly placed the phone in his friend's hand. "Don't call him," he said firmly.

"I'm not going to call anyone." Travis hit the voicemail button on Stephen's phone and entered the code. There were three new messages, all from Gabriel. The first one was from the day after they went out. Travis hit play and the phone's speaker came to life with the deep, smooth voice of the redhead from the other night.

"Hi Steve, I mean Stephen. It's Gabe. We met last night at the Raven. I just wanted to say I had a great time, and it was good to meet you. Anyway, I hope you got home safe. Maybe we can hang out some time."

He had a slight Boston accent, not like you heard in parts of South Boston, not the typical accent that people thought of as a Bostonian accent these days. It was longer and lighter in the consonants, more like a Kennedy voice. That accent came from the Catholic schools just outside of the city.

"Hmmph." Travis made a face. "That didn't sound so awful. Let's see what the next one says. It's from, let's see, two days later." He hit play.

"Hey Stephen, it's Gabe. Look, I was wondering if you might want to hang out this weekend. Maybe grab a beer or something. Nothing big, super casual. Just hanging out and maybe watching a game somewhere. The Red Sox are playing on Saturday. Let me know."

Travis looked directly at Stephen, and Stephen shook his head and then looked away without saying a word.

"Okay," Travis said. "Still not a stalker. Has a hot voice. Wants to do straight-ish things. Let's see what number three says. Oh, look it's from Friday, today…"

"Hi Stephen. It's Gabe again. Look, I'm not stalking you, I promise. Oh boy, even that sounds a little creepy. I, ah, I just wanted to see if…what I mean is that I really enjoyed meeting you. I won't keep calling, I promise. I just wanted to let you know that. So, maybe

I'll see you around at the Raven again if you're ever back there. Anyway, bye, I guess."

Travis stared at Stephen. "You at least owe him a text message."

"I know, I know." Stephen looked up at the ceiling. "I just don't know what to say."

"It's easy. I'll help you." Travis opened up the texting app on Stephen's phone. "Let's start with this short little, harmless text message—Hi Gabe. Sorry I didn't call back; been out of town."

"But I wasn't out of town," Stephen said.

"Yes, I know that, but what else do you think you can say to him about why you haven't been responding? 'My name is Stephen, and I'm not sure I'm into dudes yet, so I have been holding off on texting you or calling you even though you're super nice and just want to hang out?'"

"Well, I did tell him I wasn't into guys when we were out the other night."

Travis rolled his eyes and looked back down at the phone. "Shall we continue?"

Stephen clenched his jaw and leaned his head to one side, but when Travis raised his eyebrows and shot him a look, he reluctantly nodded.

"Sorry I didn't call back. Been out of town. I'm not that into sports, but hanging out sounds like fun. Let's meet at the Pour House next Friday for a few beers."

"Not that into sports?"

"Well, you're not," Travis said.

"I know, but you don't have to say it like that."

"Like what?" Travis made a scrunched up face.

"Like all elitist, like I'm above sports."

"That's not at all what I said in the text."

"Just say it some other way or take that part out."

"Too late. Already sent." Travis handed the phone back to Stephen. "I guess you're an elitist now."

Stephen sighed and laid the phone down on the couch between them. About ten minutes later, it buzzed.

A LITTLE RAZZING

Gabe sat on the locker room bench in his gym shorts. A sweaty tee shirt was draped over his shoulder and a pair of sneakers and damp gym socks lay on the floor by his feet. He had just finished a grueling chest routine with his coworker, Eric Ramirez. Ramirez had been his partner on the force for a few years now and the two of them regularly hit the gym late after work. Gabe had come back to the locker room and looked at his phone and now he couldn't put it down. Ramirez had been chatting away about something for the last few minutes, but Gabe missed everything he'd said. He was focused on a single text message notification that lit up the top of his screen. It was from Stephen Davis. He hadn't opened it yet. He hadn't dared.

Why a text message? he thought to himself. *Why didn't he just call me back? I left him a voicemail. Isn't it normal to answer a call with a call? Does a text message mean that he is blowing me off nicely?*

"What the hell is going through your head, Brennan?" Ramirez's voice suddenly penetrated his inner monologue.

"What's that?" Gabe said, still staring at his phone.

"What are you doing with that phone? You've been staring at it for the past five minutes, not listening to a word I said."

"Sorry," Gabe said. "It's nothing."

"It ain't nothing. I'll tell you that." Ramirez moved so swiftly, Gabe didn't even see him coming. Before he knew it, his partner had reached around him and grabbed the phone out of his hands. "Oh, no," he said, looking at the phone and then handing it back slowly.

"What?" Gabe said. "It's nothing."

"It ain't nothing. It's a text message. I can see that."

Gabe stared down at the still unopened message.

"Well," Ramirez said, looking down at the phone in Gabe's hand. "You gonna open it or just stare at it all day?"

"I guess I should," Gabe clicked on the text message and opened it. He read it and his face lit up in a smile as he did.

"What?" Ramirez stepped over the bench and sat down next to him.

"I got a date." Gabe said, and showed him the text message briefly before clicking off his phone and setting it down on the bench next to his gym bag.

"A date?" Ramirez said. "It's about time. Long as I've known you, you have never been out on a date. What makes this guy so special?"

Gabe stood up, threw his dirty shirt on the bench and shucked his gym shorts. "I don't know. I met him the other night while I was out shooting pool. Something about him just really stood out to me."

"Sweet," said Ramirez. "We're gonna have to throw a party— Brennan's about to get laid."

Gabe shook his head. "I don't know. We'll see. I got a vibe off him, but he said he's not into guys."

Ramirez arched an eyebrow. "What's that all about?"

Gabe shrugged again. "I don't know. He said he was at the bar with his gay friend, just to hang out or whatever. But, we had some real energy. He was so, I don't know…"

"Hot?" Ramirez said.

"Yeah, I guess. In a different sort of way. You know how when you go to bars everybody starts to look the same?"

"It's been a while since I've been out to a bar like that, but yeah, I know what you mean. All the girls are wearing the same exact dress, and they're all huddled up with their friends. Every time you talk to one of them, it's like you could be talking to any of them. They all say the same old shit."

"Yeah, same thing in the bars I go to. Except, it's guys, not girls. But yeah, they all start to seem exactly the same—the same conversations, the same jokes, the same games. This guy, he was different."

Ramirez let out a soft laugh. "But, Brennan, is it because he's straight? I don't want to see you get hurt or anything."

Gabe grabbed a towel out of his gym bag and walked over toward the showers. Ramirez stood up off the bench, grabbing his own towel and following him.

"I'm not going to worry about that," Gabe said. "Like I said, there was definitely some energy between us. He was totally into me." He paused. "And we're just meeting up for drinks. If there's nothing there, then that's fine. Maybe we just go out, have a few beers and then see where it goes."

Ramirez nodded and left it at that as he cranked the hot water faucet and stepped into the shower stream.

A Night at the Café

One of Travis's oldest memories from childhood was walking across his yard to Stephen's and seeing him standing by the edge of the river with three red balloons in his hand. The balloons were a couple of days old by that point, and Travis recognized them as the balloons from a party they had both been to earlier that week. Only now they looked puffy and wrinkled.

"Why do you still have those balloons?" he said to Stephen as he approached. But Stephen didn't answer at first. He was looking out toward the river.

"Stephen," Travis repeated as he got nearer to his friend. "Why do you still have those balloons?"

Stephen turned around, and Travis could see a big smile on his face. "Because I like them," he said. "I had a really good time at that party, and they make me remember it."

"But you don't need the balloons to remember it. Besides, they're starting to get all messed up now because they're old."

"The balloons remind me I was there, and they let everyone else know I was there too. If I let them go, then people won't know."

"Know what?"

"Know where I've been." Stephen clutched the balloons carefully in his little hand, but Travis noticed the strings had no loops or knots in them. All Stephen had to do was let them go, and they would sail lazily away, even in their half-inflated state.

Travis sat by himself in the bar at the Tremont Café, trying to push away the memory. He couldn't think of anything that would have caused him to recall it from the depths of his mind. He took a sip of his beer and tried to focus his attention on the room around him. This had become his Thursday bar. He had made it a point to tour the gay and gay-friendly bars of Boston every few weeks or so, and he liked this one because it was different.

It was a little cabaret bar with a piano in the corner and a group of tables with candles all around it. But Travis liked sitting up at the bar because he could see everyone in the place. Tonight, the crowd was the usual combination of older men and some younger, more flamboyantly-dressed men with loud designer tee shirts and usually carrying a man-purse of some sort.

Stephen loved watching the tourists who came in after a night at the Majestic or the Wang Theatre, the wives smiling at the "find" they'd just made, a cute little cabaret bar nestled in the corner of Boston's theatre district. The husbands always looked around carefully at the crowd and chose a table as far from everyone else as possible.

Travis was alone that night. He hadn't wanted to ask Stephen. He was still not quite over what had happened at the Raven. Not that Stephen would have come tonight anyway; he wasn't a fan of the Tremont Café. He still went out with him on other nights, more to the pub bars and the dance clubs.

He thought of his friend and the memory of the balloons came back. Travis had wanted to reach out and force Stephen to let go of the balloons, but he hadn't. He'd just nodded instead, and the two boys sat down along the river's edge. He couldn't remember anything after that. His mind kept playing over the words—*The balloons remind me I was there and they let everyone else know I was there too.* What had he meant? Had Stephen really even said those words, or was it some trick of his mind, a memory that Travis had somehow subconsciously fabricated?

"Buy you a drink?" The voice jostled him out of his trance. He looked up to see Benson sitting on the bar stool next to him. He was grinning, pink lips parted slightly, revealing a set of perfect, bleach-whitened teeth.

Travis smiled back at him. Benson hadn't so much as looked at him in the half a year since the office Christmas party at Locke-Ober's. In the weeks after the holidays, the weight of Benson's snub finally set in, and Travis's crush had begun to diminish. He stopped timing his trips to the reception desk to see him and eventually even stopped stalking him on social media. But here he was, six months later, smiling in all his blue-eyed glory.

"A drink?" Travis said slowly. "Hmmm, if I remember correctly, the last time you went for a drink you never came back."

"Ah, that." Benson's smile stretched out across his face. "Yeah, sorry about that. I got pulled away from the party."

"I'll have another beer, if you're staying now."

"I should explain," Benson said.

"About the drink or about ignoring me at the Christmas party?" Travis knew he was treading very close to a line he shouldn't cross. This was a senior executive at the company he worked for, and he could very easily imagine the unofficial consequences of something like this. He'd seen it a half-a-dozen times during the year he had been working there—hook ups or debates between different titles outside of work where people had the illusion of freedom. When they went wrong, it was usually the senior person who shut down, giving the impression the junior staffer had come out on the winning end, but days or weeks or sometimes even months later, that junior person was gone. But the risk didn't deter him. "That was kind of rude."

"Yeah, about that. I couldn't say what I wanted to say to you there."

"What you wanted to say to me?" Travis shook his head. "What does that even mean?"

"Travis, let's be real. You're an attractive guy. But we were at a company party, and the place was crawling with our coworkers, not to mention Human Resources. What was I going to do? Let you start flirting with me right there, in front of everyone? How do you think that would have looked?"

Travis nodded his head silently. He was shaking just a little bit but not ready to commit to saying anything. He took his hands off the bar to hide their trembling. "You thought I was flirting with you?"

"I think you were gearing up to, yes."

"Whatever." Travis rolled his eyes. "If anyone was flirting, it was you."

"I made polite conversation. I said hello to you and your boyfriend."

"He's not my boyfriend, I told you that. If you'd been listening to anything I said, you would have heard that."

"Anything you said? Really Travis? We spoke for all of thirty seconds. I said hello, and you starting acting strange about something. That was the end of the conversation."

"Yeah, because you left and didn't come back."

"We've already been through that." Benson put his palm down with a thud on the bar. "Now, how about that drink?"

"I don't know what you're waiting for. You know what I want."

Benson flashed a brilliant smile that was both cocky and charming. "I guess I do." He looked around and raised his hand to signal the bartender.

"The one thing that I don't understand," said Stephen, "is how you knew he was going to be there." It was Friday morning, and he wasn't looking forward to work that day. He poured a little bit of milk into his coffee cup and returned the carton to the refrigerator.

"I told you, that's what's so cool. I didn't have any idea he was going to show up." Travis sat on the counter in their tiny kitchen, his toothbrush in his hand. "It was like it was just meant to be."

"I thought you were over this guy." Stephen blew on his coffee and took a timid sip. "This is the guy who walked away and totally dissed you at your company Christmas party, right?"

"He explained all that."

"Oh, really?"

"Yes, really, Stephen. It was all about HR. He didn't want to look like he was hitting on me at a company event."

"And just talking to you would have looked like he was hitting on you? You don't think that's a load of shit?"

"No, it's not a load of shit." Travis hopped off the counter and walked toward the bathroom. "He's just extra cautious, and I kind of like that," he said over his shoulder.

Stephen took his coffee and sat down at the tiny table. He was already dressed for work. "I don't get the gays."

"I heard that—and it's ironic coming from you right now. Are you ready for your gay date tonight?"

"Ha ha," Stephen said. "It's not a date."

"Okay, if you say so," Travis yelled from the bathroom.

"I still don't get the gays."

"There's nothing to get." This time Travis's voice had an edge. "He just likes me. I can tell."

"Whatever you say. I still think he's a jerk." Stephen picked up an old *Details* magazine from the table and flipped through in search of an article he might not have read yet. "Hurry up and get ready for work."

First Date: Stephen

They sat near the front of the Pour House, rain pelting the windows at the end of their booth, making a rattling noise that sounded almost fake. Through the blurred wet glass, the street lamps of Boylston Street shone in on them and reflected the glassy blue of Gabe's eyes.

Stephen swallowed and looked out the window. Across the street, the Prudential building towered above the rest of the Back Bay. It looked positively intimidating that evening.

"I have a confession to make," Stephen said.

"No," Gabe interrupted before he continued. "Actually, I'm the one who should confess."

Stephen cocked his head to one side. "Huh?"

Gabe shrugged self-consciously, and the light from the street gave him an incredibly serious look. "I know I was pushy the other night when we met. I hope I didn't make you uncomfortable."

Stephen didn't know what to say. The guy across from him was barely more than a stranger, but his apology made Stephen want to reach out and put his hand on Gabe's face. He felt himself blush at the thought, and quickly put it out of his head.

"I'd had a few drinks, and I was feeling cocky because it was such a good night at the pool table. And you were just sitting there, so…"

"It was the first time I ever got hit on," Stephen said.

"You mean by a guy?" Gabe rubbed his hand across his forehead and looked up at the ceiling. "I know, I'm sorry, you said you were straight. I just couldn't help myself."

"Stop apologizing." Stephen smiled at him, and Gabe smiled back. "It's okay. It was just a little confusing for me at first, because…" Stephen let his voice trail off.

"Because why?"

"Well, mostly because I found myself, I don't know, let's just say I didn't hate it. And that's a little confusing for me. That's all."

"Should I go?"

"Go?" Stephen's face lit up in surprise. "Go where?"

Gabe laughed. "Nowhere. Never mind." He shook his head. "This is one of the first 'first dates' I've been on in a long time. It's a little uncomfortable for me, too."

"Oh," Stephen said.

"This is a first date, isn't it? Or did I misread the signals again?"

"I don't know," Stephen said. "I guess it's just that 'date' is such a strong word. I'm not sure we can call this a date."

"And why's that?"

"Yeah, well, to start with, if it was a date, I think I should have asked you out to a nicer place," Stephen said.

"A nicer place?" Gabe arched an eyebrow.

"Yeah. You seem like a guy who maybe likes to go on dates in nicer places than this."

"You're saying you think I'm a little bit of a princess?" Gabe smiled broadly.

Stephen smiled back. "Well, I didn't use that word."

"Really?" Gabe let out a gentle laugh. "Stephen, are you flirting with me?"

"Maybe." Stephen glanced down at his beer then back up at Gabe. "In all seriousness, I should have thought of a nicer place to meet." He looked out the window and watched the individual raindrops as they slid down the glass, morphing from drops into streaks.

Gabe nodded. "Well, that's the best news I've heard all night."

"Why's that?"

"Because that means you'll have to bring me someplace nicer next time," Gabe said. A smile stretched across his broad face.

Stephen laughed. "Yes, I guess I will."

"And that means," Gabe continued, "that there will have to be a next time, whatever we end up calling it. And that makes me extremely happy."

The two of them laughed softly, and they each sipped their beers almost at the exact same instant. Stephen watched this new friend, who was becoming more than a friend second by second. He took a deep breath and tried to get his head around everything that was happening to him.

"Can I ask you a question?" Stephen said.

"Isn't that what first dates are for?" Gabe tipped his glass toward Stephen. It was not so much a toast as a gesture to proceed.

Stephen winced at the word again but decided to ignore it. "You're gay, right? Like full on gay?"

Gabe smiled and nodded. "As full on as gay gets."

"How long have you known?"

Gabe took a deep breath. "Well, that's always a hard thing to say, exactly. I'm pretty sure I've known ever since I was a little kid. But I've only been out for the past ten years or so."

"My best friend, Travis—we grew up together. We were born a few weeks apart and we lived right next to each other. He's my roommate, the one you played pool with the other night. Well, he's gay. He's always been gay. So, it's not a foreign concept for me. It's not like it's something I have to come to terms with as being good or bad. It's just that it's the first time I've ever been attracted to a guy. I've only ever really been with one other person, and that was in school. But then, you pretty much knew that the other night."

Gabe nodded. "When you called me a fortune teller."

"Yeah," Stephen said. "You were right on the money. I'm really shy, and I've only been with that one girl. Her name was Melanie, and I was crazy about her. Things were good for a while, but then they sort of, I don't know, just fell apart, I guess."

Gabe gave him a friendly look but said nothing.

Stephen continued as if he'd been prompted. "Well, I mean I've made out with other girls, but really, I've only ever been-been with that one girl."

"You've never slept with anyone else? Just one person."

Stephen nodded his head. "Just the one."

"Wow," Gabe said. "That makes me feel like…" He held his breath.

Stephen looked up at him. "Feel like what?"

"Well," Gabe took a deep breath and looked up to the ceiling as if searching for the right words. "Let's just say that makes me feel like I've really been around the block."

"Oh," Stephen said.

"You're probably somewhere in the middle of things," Gabe said. "Lots of people are."

"In the middle?"

"Yeah, not everyone is one hundred per cent gay or straight." Gabe picked up his beer and held it in in front of him. "It's okay not to fit into a label. Labels, say, like the label 'gay' or 'date,' suck. They're the lowest common denominator, and they usually just screw things up."

Stephen nodded. "I couldn't agree more." He picked up his own beer and took a sip.

They laughed for a few seconds. But as the moment of solidarity between them passed, they found themselves staring at each other across the table again. The conversation had come to a halt, and they both started to fidget a little bit. Stephen forced himself to watch Gabe's face as he looked around the room.

"Is something wrong?" Stephen tried to reignite the conversation. Anything would be better than the silent path they were headed down.

"No, not at all." Gabe cracked a serious half-smile, raising the right side of his mouth and scanning the room quickly again. "It's just that I usually go here after work with coworkers. It's fine, really, I just keep looking around to see if any of the guys have come in."

"Oh, man. And you don't want to run into your coworkers…"

"No, don't worry about it." Gabe said. "Even if they do come in, there's nothing to worry about. For the most part, they're pretty good guys."

"You know," Stephen said, "you're the first police officer I've met, in Boston at least. Back home in New Hampshire, where I'm from, there are two cops, and my mom and dad know them. Well, everybody knows them really. They only had one police car. They would have to switch off if they were going to patrol, or if they got called out. And we'd always see them when we went down town for breakfast on Saturdays. They were always together, even when they were off duty." Stephen hesitated for a moment, stuck in his own thoughts, while Gabe sat patiently and watched him. "Anyway, I don't think they ever arrested anyone. It was a pretty small town, and we all knew each other. I'm sure I would remember if someone got arrested."

"That sounds like a nice place to live."

Stephen shrugged. "It's small." After a few seconds of quiet he continued. "What kind of cop are you?"

"Just a regular cop. Part of the A-15 unit, Beacon Hill station."

"Oh," Stephen said. "Is there a lot of crime in that part of town?"

Gabe laughed. "A lot more than you'd think. But not like Mattapan or Dorchester. Mostly break-ins, theft, some domestic disputes."

"Not a lot of gang warfare?"

He shook his head. "No, not a lot of gang warfare."

Stephen tilted his glass back and finished the last of his beer. The two of them stared across the table at each other. They had come to another awkward point. Stephen didn't know what to say, and Gabe apparently didn't know how to help him. Gabe looked down at the table, breaking the connection they had and Stephen looked briefly toward the exit.

Gabe finally broke the silence between them. "Is it weird for you? That I'm a cop?"

"No." Stephen shook his head. "Not at all. I guess I just don't know what to say. I'm sorry, I'm a little shy anyway and now…"

"And now you have to talk to a cop." He finished his beer and looked down in the glass as if he was searching for something.

"What made you want to become one?" Stephen tried to smile. "A cop, I mean. Why did you want to go into law enforcement?"

He let out a long breath. "Well, I guess if I had to trace it back to one thing, it would be that a cop really helped out a close friend of mine in high school. Kept him from going the wrong way in life. When I saw that, I knew I wanted to help people like that."

"Oh yeah? In Boston?"

"No, I grew up in a little town northwest of here. Watertown. This guy was with the Watertown police." Gabe's words trailed off and became softer. He seemed to withdraw inside himself.

"That's cool."

"Only my dad didn't feel exactly the same way at first. He didn't want me going into law enforcement."

"No?" Stephen said, grateful that the conversation had seemed to pick up again.

"No. He wanted me to go to college, get a white collar job. He was like that—still is. He wanted me to sit behind a desk practicing law or something like that."

"So what did you do?" He felt stupid the minute the words were out of his mouth.

"It wasn't a problem, at least not the going to college part. You can't join most police forces until you're twenty-one anyway. So I went to college. No skin off my back, my dad paid for it." He smiled. "I majored in Criminal Justice at Northeastern. Got out of school, applied to the BPD, took the civil service exam, and after twenty weeks of the academy, I was walking the beat."

"And your dad?"

Gabe smiled. "We're pretty close. He doesn't like what I do, but mostly because he's scared something is going to happen to me. It's not like he doesn't approve. He was very supportive when I told him I'd made up my mind. Besides, you can't do much else with a criminal justice degree other than go into some form of law enforcement."

"Are you a detective?"

"No, not yet. I'm just a patrol officer. But I'm shooting for detective some day. No pun intended." He smiled, and Stephen felt the same strange feeling in his stomach he'd felt the first night they'd met.

"You're different than anyone else I've met since I moved here," Stephen said.

"You too." Gabe held his empty glass up. "All gone. What do you say? One more here or should we try somewhere else?"

Stephen took the hint. "How about we try somewhere over on Newbury Street?"

FIRST DATE: TRAVIS

On their first date, Benson took Travis to Sonsie's on Newbury Street, a favorite spot among the hip and well-heeled of Boston's Back Bay. It was a warm late spring night, and the restaurant had its front windows open out onto the street. The noise of the shoperatti wafted in from the street: the click clack of trendy shoes hitting the sidewalk, the swoosh of boutique shopping bags, the bubbling chatter about which stores were having sales and which never did. They sat in a booth in front of one of the windows. For the first time in his life, Travis was at a loss for what to say. Luckily, Benson seemed to sense his discomfort and did his best to make Travis feel at ease.

"You're not saying very much," Benson finally said. He'd been chatting away, covering the silences between them on his own for most of the dinner.

"Sorry," Travis said. "I guess I'm just still trying to digest the fact that I'm out on a date with you."

"What?" Benson shook his head. "Why is that weird?"

"I probably shouldn't say this, but well, I've had a thing for you for a long time."

Benson smiled. "Yeah, I kind of knew that."

"You did? How?"

"You mean you didn't think always hanging around outside my office was obvious?"

Travis just looked at the broccoli rabe on his plate and didn't say a word.

"Mysteriously lurking at reception every time I left the building for lunch wasn't supposed to tip me off? All of the time on my LinkedIn page was a little bit of a clue."

"You could see that?" Travis laid down his fork and rested his hands of the edge of the table.

Benson smiled. "Of course I could." He paused and reached over to put his hand on top of Travis's left hand. "I thought it was really cute."

Travis shook his head. "I'm so embarrassed."

"Don't be. You shouldn't be." Benson tightened his grip on Travis's hand. "It was kind of a turn on."

Travis smiled.

"I'm serious," Benson said. "Look, at thirty five, you take what compliments you can get. Especially when they come from a young, attractive guy like you."

"Well, you have a point there. It was coming from a very young and very attractive guy who had the major hots for you ever since he first laid eyes on you. You must have been really scared about what people would think."

Benson leaned over the table and kissed Travis lightly on the lips. It was a quick kiss, but a kiss all the same. He did it without any regard for the people in the restaurant. "I don't care what anybody thinks about it anymore," he said.

Travis smiled. He could feel himself positively glowing. He swallowed hard and tried to maintain his cool, but it was already lost.

"So, tell me something about yourself," Benson said.

"What do you want to know?"

"Well, for starters, where did you grow up? What sort of things do you like to do? What's your favorite color?" Benson's face lit up with a huge smile. "I hardly know anything about you, whereas you seem to know a lot about me."

Travis smiled back at him. "I bet people tell you how charming you are all the time."

"Not exactly," Benson said. "Most of the time it's quite the opposite." He reached across the table and gently stroked a finger across the top of Travis's hand.

Travis heard himself take a deep breath, but he couldn't feel it. He looked down and watched Benson's hand on his. It looked like someone else's hand. He shifted slightly in his seat and realized he was uncomfortably hard, which was also a little bit of a surprise. How had he lost track of everything that was happening to himself? He shook his head slightly and squeezed his eyes shut. He pulled his hand back. "I'm sorry," he said.

"What?" Benson said. "Sorry, too fast? Ugh, I always do that."

Travis shook his head. "No, it's not that. It's just a lot to take in. I'm not used to…" He couldn't think of the right words to finish the sentence.

"…not used to moving this fast." Benson finished the sentence for him. "I'm such an idiot."

"No, no. I've definitely moved faster than this before."

Benson shot him a curious look.

Travis quickly corrected himself. "No, what I'm trying to say is that I didn't think you felt this way about me. It's taking me a minute to process it all."

Benson leaned over and kissed him again, this time much harder and more passionately. "Well, let's see what we can do to make it easier for you to process."

Travis smiled and kissed him back.

A Day at the Park

So." Melissa's well-manicured hand landed solidly on Stephen's desk, right beside the report he had been staring at for the last forty-five minutes. He looked at her hand for a few seconds and watched closely as she drummed her red nails once on the laminate top of his desk. They made four staccato clicking sounds, one after the other, as each fingernail hit the desktop, taking his mind completely off his work. "It's pretty obvious by now that you're not one for company drinks nights, right?" It was more of a statement than a question.

Melissa could always be counted on for a mid-day stop by. Stephen guessed she was referring to the after-work drinks session she had invited him to the afternoon before, just like she had almost every Thursday for the past year he had been working there.

"Well, not really."

"And why is that?" She lifted herself onto the corner of his desk, scooting the draft report that he had been looking at about six inches down. Stephen shifted in his seat and pushed himself slightly away from her, trying not to be too obvious about it.

"I just had stuff to do," he said. He tried to look back down at his work, hoping she would go away.

"Stuff to do, huh? It seems like you've always got stuff to do after work. What's the matter, Stephen? You don't like us?" She cocked her head to one side, almost pouting.

Stephen tried to smile. "No, of course I like people here. It's just that after work is hard for me. I like to get home. I've usually got a lot of things I like to catch up on. I read a lot."

She smiled and pulled an envelope out from behind her back. "Well, I have a not-after-work idea."

"Oh yeah?" He stared at the envelope and tried hard not to look annoyed. "What's that?"

She waved the envelope. "I have here, in my hand a bunch of tickets to the Red Sox game this Saturday. They're for the company's suite, so there will be catering, air conditioning, and an incredible view of the game. What do you say?"

"Oh, well." He stumbled to find the right words.

"Oh, well, nothing," she said. "I'm not taking no for an answer. None of the execs are using the suite this weekend, and we don't have any clients in town, so these are up for grabs. We have more seats than we could ever use, so a group of us are going, and I've earmarked one of these tickets for you."

"Can I bring someone?" The words were out of his mouth before he could even think about how they might sound.

She hesitated for only a fraction of a second before recovering. The smile on her face barely registered a blip. "Sure," she said. "The more the merrier."

"Okay, good. Then I'm in. I'll take two tickets."

"Who's the second?" she said. Then cautiously, she added, "Girlfriend?"

"Oh, no," Stephen laughed. "Just my roommate. He's a huge Sox fan."

Melissa's face seemed to lighten up a little when he said that. "Oh, cool. There're plenty of spots, so no worries."

"Cool," he said, nodding at her with a rather blank look on his face.

"Cool," she said back. She was still sitting on his desk.

"Cool," he echoed her again, unsure of what he should do next. But she sat on his desk nodding. "So," he finally said.

"So," she said back to him.

"What time is the game?" he said, struggling to fill the space in their conversation.

"Oh, yeah. I guess that would be helpful." She pulled one of the tickets out of the envelope. "Looks like it starts at two."

"Cool." Stephen watched as she folded the ticket in her hand without looking at it. She kept her eyes on him, which made him feel like squirming. He focused on remaining still.

"Cool," she said.

"So," he started again. "Do you want to give it to me now or should we meet up later?"

"What?" She blushed instantly. It was the first time Stephen had seen her startled.

"The tickets." He pointed to the piece of folded paper in her hands.

"Oh, right." She blushed even more. "I'll just…" She hesitated for a second, looking down at her own hands and realizing the mess she was making out of the ticket. "I'll give them to you now. Just two, right?"

"Yep, just the two of us."

"Here you go." She handed two of the tickets to Stephen.

"What's his name?"

"Sorry?"

"Your roommate? What's his name?"

"Oh, it's Travis. He'll be thrilled about this." Stephen offered her his best smile.

"And if you need any help…" She gestured down toward the report he had been going over. It was the same report he'd been doing every week since he had joined the company.

"I think I'm good, Melissa. But thanks."

She gave him a feeble smile, her lips barely pulling up at the corners of her mouth. "Right," she said. "I'll just leave you to it then."

"I can't go," Travis said. They were sitting on the couch in their apartment, staring at the television. They weren't watching anything, but they hadn't bothered to turn it off. Instead, they let the local news station play softly in front of them, each mindlessly glued to the screen.

"What do you mean you can't go? You love the Red Sox." Stephen looked at his best friend, who did not look back at him.

"I do love the Sox," he said. "And I guess, technically, I can go. But I don't want to."

Stephen watched as Travis remained nonchalantly fixated on the screen in front of them. A casual smirk played on his lips, but he remained aloof. He was clearly focused on not focusing on Stephen. Stephen knew this smug expression, this act. Travis had done it all throughout their childhood when he was trying to make a point. The only problem was that Stephen wasn't exactly sure what point he was trying to make now.

"Subtle," Stephen remarked.

"I don't know what you're talking about." Travis glanced very briefly at Stephen.

"Fine. Okay," Stephen said. "I'll bite. Why don't you want to go to see your favorite team play the Yankees, the most evil organization in the world?"

Travis suddenly propped himself up on his elbows and pried his attention away from the television to face Stephen. "You've been telling me nothing good about this girl for the past few months. You detest her. Or perhaps you're secretly lusting after her, which I think is more likely given your recent penchant for libidinous activities."

"Libidinous what?" Stephen scrunched up his nose. "Where did you even learn that word?"

Travis rolled his eyes and continued. "In either case, I can't imagine an afternoon with her is going to be anything other than torture for me, so no thank you. I don't want to go. I'll stay put on the couch and watch the game from here."

Stephen stared at Travis for a moment, then back at the television. He hated to admit it, but his friend was right. He didn't want to go either, and he wasn't sure why he had even bothered to accept the tickets.

"But on the other hand, since you accepted the tickets, you really can't back out of going without embarrassing yourself in front of your entire work crew." A twist of hope colored his words.

"Pretty much," Stephen said.

"I mean," Travis pondered out loud, "it could be a really good opportunity to socialize with your work group in a safe setting. It would help you get to know them all. And they'd get to see you with a friend from outside of work. They'd know you were normal and you had a social life."

Stephen nodded in blank agreement.

"Oh, shit," Travis said suddenly.

"What?"

"I forgot I have to work Saturday. There is this high profile research project I have to finish up tomorrow."

"Oh, well." Stephen tried not to sound let down.

"But you know what? I bet I know who might like to go with you."

Stephen froze. He knew instantly who Travis meant. The aloof act had nothing to do with Travis not wanting to hang out. He had led Stephen right down the path to inviting Gabe. Stephen looked back at the television and absentmindedly gritted his back teeth.

Later that night, Stephen sat up in his bed. All the lights were out, and only the lamplight from the street below and the blue glow of his iPhone illuminated the room. His room was still sparse, though he had lived there for over a year. He had never put anything up on the walls, and the few pieces of furniture—a lamp, a chair and a dresser, all from his parents' house—did little to create a lived-in feeling for the place.

"You up for a Sox game this weekend?" The words stared back at Stephen from the crisp, businesslike screen of his iPhone like a dare or even a taunt. *What was he doing? Inviting Gabe to a ballgame with his co-workers. Was he crazy? What would they think?* There was obviously chemistry between them, but they were just friends. They had been out for beers one night and had some good conversation, but that was it.

Of course, all that's a lie, Stephen thought. Gabe had made his feelings abundantly clear that first night they had met at the Raven, and Stephen had been struggling to categorize his own feelings for the past week or so, one moment avoiding the truth and the next giving in to fantasies about what it would be like just to touch Gabe's hand, to feel his breath on his face again, the way he had that first night by the pool table.

Of course, Gabe had mentioned a Red Sox game in one of his earliest voicemails to Stephen, so maybe this was a friendly way to extend a great opportunity to see a really good game. There didn't have to be anything more to it.

Stephen finally pressed send on the iPhone, and a wave of nerves crashed through his stomach. For a few seconds, he even felt as if he were going to throw up. "No, no, no," he said out loud to the dark and empty room.

It was barely half a minute before the iPhone buzzed with a text notification. "Sure. Sounds fun. Just LMK where and when to meet."

"OK. Tomorrow afternoon. 12:30?" Stephen prayed it would be too much of a last minute thing and that Gabe would have something planned already.

"Sounds good. I'm in. Meet on Landsdowne Street somewhere for a pre-game pint?" The text came back.

Stephen tried to contain the weird mix of excitement and fear that coursed through his whole body. "Sure. May be a bunch of my work colleagues there as well. Hope that's okay." He typed back.

The response came almost instantly. "Fine. I'll be on my best behavior. Besides, this is so not a date." The text message ended with a smiley face and the emoji forced Stephen's whole face upward into a giant grin. He placed the phone down, closed his eyes, and tried to go to sleep as his mind danced with a potent mixture of excitement and fear.

"This is a very cool...ah what are we calling this? Hanging out? Yeah, let's go with that. This is a very cool place to hang out," Gabe said quietly to Stephen as they sat in two reclining chairs watching the Red Sox score another run over the Yankees. "The plush seats, the free beer and snacks, the air conditioned glass-enclosed box...this is the ultimate luxury baseball fan experience. How did you score these tickets?"

"The advertising agency where I work keeps the box mostly for entertaining high profile clients, but it goes unused almost as often as it gets used, so a bunch of us decided to grab the tickets this weekend."

"Awesome," Gabe said.

Stephen nodded in agreement but didn't say anything. The two of them were alone so far. None of his coworkers had showed up, not even Melissa, which Stephen found hard to believe. Maybe she had been so offended or embarrassed by his asking to bring a roommate that she had just decided not to come.

Gabe grabbed a handful of popcorn but stopped before tossing it into his mouth. "Hey," he said. "What happened to the rest of them? Your co-workers, I mean."

"Not sure," Stephen said. "They're all probably just late or something. I'm sure they're still coming."

"So..." Gabe shot him a covert look, lowering his voice to a whisper. "I shouldn't try to kiss you, then?"

Stephen looked over at Gabe, and the two of them locked eyes for a moment. Stephen imagined the look of fear and dread he must have had on his face, because the smirk Gabe had when he'd said the words disappeared completely after a few seconds.

"Kidding, kidding. Sorry," Gabe said. "I was just...I don't know what I was thinking. I know we're just hanging out."

The two of them looked straight out at the game. Stephen kept his hands folded in his lap and said nothing for a few moments.

"Look, sorry for saying that kissing thing. Really, I didn't mean it. If you want me to leave..."

"No. Don't worry about that. It's me who's being awkward. It's just a lot to think about, you know?"

Before either one of them could say another word, a crack thundered through the air and the crowd below them erupted in cheers. Someone had just hit the ball out of the park. Stephen and Gabe both searched the sky for the ball. Gabe spotted it first and pointed to where the ball was, putting his hand right in Stephen's line of sight to help him locate it, and at the same time leaning in so their shoulders were pressed together.

Stephen forgot all about the ball as he felt the heat of Gabe's shoulder through his shirt. "Oh, yeah. I see it," he lied. He took a deep breath as quietly as he could and did his best to memorize the feeling of Gabe's body against his. Stephen didn't know if he would allow himself to be this close to him again.

Stephen could feel Gabe looking directly at him. After a second he allowed himself to look back. Their faces were so close, he could feel Gabe's breath on his lips. He smelled of salt and beer, and Stephen imagined for a split second what it would be like to lean in and kiss him.

"So, you must be the roommate." Melissa's voice came from behind them as she and a group of Stephen's work colleagues came rushing through the door to the box.

Stephen felt himself turning red but took a deep breath and faced Melissa with as nonchalant a smile as he could muster. "No, my roommate couldn't make it. This is my buddy, Gabe."

Out of the corner of his eye, Stephen could see a look of disappointment flash on Gabe's face. But it was barely perceptible and only lasted for an instant. Gabe rallied, standing up and shaking hands with Melissa and the other co-workers that tumbled in after her.

She smiled briefly at Gabe and then shot Stephen a knowing look. He was unsure how much she had seen, not that there had been anything to see. They had simply been looking at each other. So what if she decided to read anything else into it. It was none of her business, he thought to himself.

The Card

Normally, Travis kept his desk clean and well organized. He didn't decorate it very much. He had no pictures pinned to the fabric wall of his cubicle, like some of his workmates. He didn't keep a collection of little toys or birthday cards or sports team emblems around. Every evening before he went home, he filed everything that was supposed to be filed, threw away anything he didn't need, and put away any stray pens or pencils. The small tray with his business cards was the only indication someone actually worked at the desk. So, Travis noticed immediately when he came back from lunch one day to find a blank manila folder on his desk.

"Hmmmm," he sighed, picking up the folder. Inside it was a sealed envelope with his name written across the front. His first thought was that the Human Resources lady on their floor had mistaken his birthday with someone else's. He briefly contemplated taking it back to her office before he sat down and dove into the afternoon's work. But something stopped him.

Instead, he picked up the card and held it in his hands for a minute. He even lifted it to his nose and took a brief sniff, but it just smelled like plain paper. Finally, he reached for the scissors in his top drawer and gently poked one blade into the top corner of the envelope, slicing it open in one quick motion. He placed the scissors back in the drawer and closed it before taking the card out of the envelope.

It was a simple white card with red letters across the front that spelled out, "Thank You." He opened the card to find Benson's own handwriting. "Thank you for a wonderful evening. I'm looking forward to spending more time with you. Benny."

Travis closed the card quickly and felt himself blush. After a moment, he placed the card neatly in the front of his top drawer so he could easily see it if he opened the drawer just a little bit. He took a deep breath and turned to his keyboard and monitor to get back to work.

Figuring it Out

S o what, exactly, is going on?" Ramirez's voice caught Gabe by surprise. It was Monday, and Gabe had found himself unable to focus on anything at work. He had been so distracted, he hadn't even thought to wait for his partner before heading to the gym.

He had left the station as early as possible, trying not to think about Stephen and the baseball game. He focused on his workout instead. It had been a back and biceps day, but he hadn't stopped after his normal routine. He did legs, he did abs, and he finally finished up by pumping out forty minutes of cardio on the stationary bike. He watched as people cycled through their workouts around him, starting and finishing, but Stephen stayed firmly at the center of his thoughts.

Ramirez had finally caught up with him in the cardio room, and Gabe breathed a sigh of relief for the company as his partner got on the bike next to his.

"Oh man," he said, in response to Ramirez's question. "You don't want to know."

"You had another date?"

"Well, sort of." Gabe looked at his partner. "I don't think it was really a date. It was more like we 'hung out.'"

"Huh?" His partner adjusted the controls on the bike and started to pedal. "What do you mean?"

"Well, we had a beer at the Pour House a week and a half ago." Gabe stopped and looked over at Ramirez.

"I know," Ramirez said. "When you didn't say anything about it, I made a conscious decision not to ask you. But I was dying to know how it went."

"It was fine," Gabe said. But he looked over at Ramirez and hesitated for a second. "You sure you want to hear about this stuff?"

"Knock it off, man. Of course I want to know." He smiled. "Besides, you've been out of it all day today. Everyone noticed."

Gabe shook his head and forced himself to look straight ahead at the mirrors on the opposite wall of the cardio room.

"So," Ramirez prodded him. "This not-a-date-date...What happened next?"

"Well, we agreed to hang out again, but that was it. Just hanging out. So, he texted me last Friday inviting me to the Red Sox game on Saturday."

"So he does like sports. I thought you said he didn't."

"I don't know." Gabe wiped a bead of sweat out of his right eye. "It's confusing as hell. I know he likes me. I can feel it. But..."

"But what?" Ramirez slowed his pedaling down and lowered his voice. "Gabe, are you sure you're not going after the wrong guy here? If the dude's not gay, he's not gay. You're not going to change that about him."

"It's not about gay." Gabe slowed down to match Ramirez's speed and looked directly at him as he searched for the right words. "Do I think this guy is usually into other guys? Not really. I don't think he's into anything, but we have a connection. I know we do."

Ramirez shook his head.

"No, seriously," Gabe said. "I know it sounds delusional, but at the game, we were all alone up in this high-end suite before any of his coworkers got there, and we were this close to kissing."

"What?" Ramirez laughed. "He took you to a game with his coworkers?"

"Yeah, what's wrong with that?"

"Gabe, buddy, look." Ramirez started to accelerate again. "I don't want to piss on your parade, but if the guy says he's not into guys, and he invites you out to see a game with his coworkers, it's not a date. It's probably never going to be a date."

"Maybe not yet, but I know there's something there. I just know it."

"Well, then you should call him and ask him out again."

Gabe was silent.

"You've got the next move, so make it. Say something to him about how you feel."

Gabe looked at his partner. "I don't want to think about it right now."

"Well then how about we finish up here and get a beer?"

"Fine," said Gabe.

"But, Brennan…"

"Yeah?"

"It's just a beer." Ramirez punched his partner in the arm and laughed.

"Fuck you, Ramirez." But Gabe was smiling as he said it. He could always count on his partner to get his mind off things. They spent another five minutes on the bikes before heading into the locker room to clean up. They ended going out for beers at, of all places, the Pour House.

Post Date Glows

The date with Benson quickly turned into a second date and then a third, and Travis talked about nothing but Benson, providing details on what they did together, where Benson took him, what they talked about, the first couple of times that they kissed. But Stephen remained suspicious of the guy. He wasn't outwardly hostile, but he got quiet whenever Travis talked about him.

"Why don't you like him?" Travis finally said one day. The two of them were sitting at the upstairs bar at the Rattlesnack on Boylston Street.

"It's not that I don't like him," Stephen said.

"That's exactly what it's like. Every time I talk about him, you shut down and get all quiet. It's like I come home from seeing him, and I want to talk to someone about it but I know if I tell you, you're going to give me the Stephen face of disapproval."

"The what?"

"Oh, come on, you know it's a thing. The face you make when you think something isn't quite right. You're doing it now."

Stephen smiled. "I can't help it, I just don't like the guy. I haven't ever liked him since he ditched you at the Christmas party. Something about him seems slimy."

Travis took a sip of his beer to avoid looking at his friend.

"I just don't want some guy trying to take advantage of you," Stephen said. "That's all."

"He's not taking advantage of me. He's really nice, and he likes me a lot." He paused. "We haven't even slept together yet. It's not like he's pushing me or anything. In fact, I wouldn't mind if he did push a little more. He's super hot."

Stephen looked up at the ceiling for a moment as if searching for patience, then back at Travis. "Is that all you like about this guy? That he's hot?"

"Like that's not enough?"

"Seriously, Travis?"

"Okay, no. I don't just like him because he's hot. He's got all his shit together, he's successful, he knows what he wants out of life, and he has already accomplished so much. I like all of that stuff."

"But what about how much older he is? You're just starting out," Stephen said. "You have to do all of those things for yourself. Don't you think maybe it would be better to be into someone who isn't so much older than you?"

"So, first you didn't like that he ditched us at the Christmas party, which is somewhat understandable, even if it seems like you held on to that for a long time. Now you don't like him because he's older and successful? I don't get it." Travis had a look on his face somewhere between pleading and frustration.

"All right. You're right," Stephen said after a few seconds. "Maybe I'm being just a tiny bit overprotective."

"Just a tiny bit?"

"Yes, smart ass." Stephen took a sip of his beer and put the nearly empty glass down on the bar with a thud. "You're my best, and at this point, one of my only friends. So allow me to be a little bit protective of you. But fine, if you really, really like this guy, then I will try to like him too."

"Well, then, that settles it. We both like him." Travis signaled the bartender for another round of drinks. "Speaking of dates…"

"Were we speaking of dates? I don't think we were speaking of dates in general. I think maybe you were talking about your date specifically, but we definitely weren't talking about dates in general."

"Okay," Travis said. He gave Stephen just a little bit of space before he started again. "But if we were talking about dates in general, would it be all right if I asked how your date with whatever his name was?"

"It wasn't a *date*. It was just a couple of guys hanging out."

"You know, Stevie, I have a lot of respect for you."

"Why is that?"

"Well, here you are, in your mid-twenties, and you've dated women your whole entire life, although not many of them, granted." Their drinks arrived, and Travis took a long sip of his beer. "You've been dating women your whole life, and then presto, you're going out with a guy, and you've already been out on your second date in two weeks."

Stephen laughed. "It wasn't a date. Like I said, we were just hanging out. But you would like him."

"Really?" Travis said with a smirk. "Why is that?"

"Well, um, you've seen him. He's pretty handsome."

"So, you're saying he's hot."

"Jesus, Travis. You're a piece of work."

"What is his name again, anyway?"

"Gabe." Stephen rolled his eyes. "Don't pretend you forgot."

"Oh, right, Gabe. That's a cool name," said Travis. "What does he do?"

"I don't want to tell you."

"What?" Travis put his beer down with a thud. "Why not? What does that even mean, you don't want to tell me."

"Look, I know you'll just make fun of it if I tell you."

"No," Travis said. He put his hand on Stephen's shoulder. "Come on, Stevie. If you like him, I'm not going to make fun of him."

"He's a cop."

"A what?" Travis stared directly at Stephen.

"You heard me," Stephen said. "He's a cop."

"Ohhh, Stevie, I never knew you liked authority." Travis chuckled gently. But he stopped. "Seriously, that's cool. You're dating the Village People."

Stephen just shook his head and looked away from his friend.

GYM RAT

The next day, Stephen went to a gym for the first time in a very long while. He'd played basketball in high school, and he'd had to take Physical Education in college and there had been a weight room involved in that. But it had only been for one semester, and it had been an eight thirty class, so most of the experience failed to make it into his long-term memory.

He had picked the Boston Sports Club because it was next to his office. His logic was simple. He could work out at lunch, on his way to work, or on his way home from work. Most importantly, he could do so without letting Travis find out. He knew he'd tease him about it, distract him or, worse yet, want to join him. Working out with Travis would be a nightmare. He would get into it, really into it. He would have them working out twice a day and eating an all-protein diet.

He signed up for a year's membership at the counter, and then he went to the locker room to change. Stephen wandered around the machines and the weights, assessing everything and wondering what he should be doing. The different contraptions reminded him of the medieval torture devices he'd seen in history books.

"Need some help?" said a short Latino guy in gym shorts and a tank top.

Stephen could feel himself turning red. He didn't know the first thing about the machines or the dumbbells. Stephen reluctantly nodded but said nothing.

The guy smiled. "You look like you're trying to figure out where to start."

"Yeah, I guess you could say that."

"So, back and biceps or chest and triceps today?"

Stephen stared blankly at him.

"Maybe it's a leg day?" The guy seemed to search his face, but Stephen still had no idea what to say or how to respond. "You're brand new at this aren't you?"

"Yeah." Stephen let out a long sigh. "I'll be honest with you, I have no idea where to start. I just joined today, and I don't know the first thing about any of this."

The guy smiled and laughed. His laugh wasn't unkind, but it still made Stephen feel even more self-conscious. The guy seemed to notice this and stopped immediately. "My name is Jack," he said. "I remember having the exact same feeling when I first walked into a gym."

Stephen looked him over. His arms were well defined but not huge; Stephen could see the lines of triceps and biceps as he stood there in front of him. He had square shoulders underneath the tank top, and his pecs filled out the front of the shirt so it hung loosely at his waist. It had obviously been a long time since Jack's first day at the gym.

"I'm Stephen," he finally said, not knowing what else he could say.

Jack tilted his head to one side and grabbed his chin with his right hand. "You know, my workout partner bailed on me a few weeks back. Do you want to work in with me?"

"Work in?" Stephen didn't know what he meant.

"Yeah, I could use a workout partner. And it might be a good way to learn about some of this equipment."

"I doubt I could do your workout," Stephen said.

"Sure you can. We'll adjust the weights and reps for what you can do right now, but the basic exercises should be all the same. Come on." Jack walked toward a bench and a cluster of weights in the back of the room. "Let's start with a back and biceps day."

Stephen shrugged and followed him. The workout consisted of a series of lat pull downs, rows, bicep curls, and a few other things which made him feel like rubber by the time he left the gym. Once they started working out, the conversation flowed easily between them. Jack never asked Stephen why he had decided to join the gym. Instead, he talked about why he had started. His dad and his older brother had lifted. They were both in the Marines, and Jack had felt left out. He had started going to the gym on his own to try and catch up with them.

"Do you work out with them now?" Stephen asked between bicep curls.

"No." Jack half-smiled, which Stephen found difficult to read. "My dad's in Washington DC now, and my brother is in Japan. So, no, I don't really get the chance to see them much."

Stephen decided to let that line of conversation go. He didn't want to pry further and besides, it was getting difficult to speak between reps.

Before leaving, they agreed to meet again at the same time tomorrow.

"Great. We'll work chest and triceps then," Jack said.

"Is that going to hurt more than it did today?"

"Probably," Jack said, laughing. "See you later."

Stephen tried not to limp as he made his way down the front steps of the gym and walked toward the Copley T station. His home was only one stop away, but he couldn't possibly make it on foot today.

FIRST BLOWS

"Travis, come back here." Stephen couldn't help the sound of panic in his voice. He had been on the phone when Travis came rushing into the apartment and made a beeline for his bedroom, slamming the door. From the brief rush of color that Stephen was able to make out, he could tell something was wrong. Travis's clothes were disheveled, his jacket was half off, and his shirt was untucked, hanging sloppily out of his pants. He had been halfway through a call with his mom, updating her on the latest from his life in Boston. He ended the conversation as quickly as he could without alarming her.

"Travis." He walked over to his roommate's door. "Travis, what happened?"

Silence from the other side of the door. Stephen waited for a few seconds then knocked gently. "Travis. Are you okay?"

Stephen turned the doorknob just a little bit. It gave easily, and the door clicked open in front of him. He nudged it a little wider and stepped into the room. Travis was hunched over on his bed with his head in his hands. He seemed to be rocking back and forth slowly.

"Travis, what's the matter?" Stephen walked over and sat on the edge of the bed.

"Nothing." Travis turned away from him, toward the window. "Nothing. I just…" His voice trailed off.

"What's wrong with your face?" Stephen said after a moment. "Why are you looking away from me?"

Travis shook his head silently. Stephen gently put his hand on Travis's shoulder and pulled him around to face him. As he turned,

Stephen could see he'd been crying. His face was red and puffy, but it was more than just that. His left eye was swollen and purple with bruises.

"Travis, what happened to you?" Stephen tried to keep his voice controlled and quiet, but he couldn't quite hide the shock he felt at seeing his best friend like this.

Travis couldn't speak. He rocked and shook his head from side to side.

"Did you get mugged?"

Travis struggled to take a breath, catching the air in great huffs as he tried to inhale. "No," he finally managed.

Stephen moved in closer to him and put his arm around Travis's shoulder. He hugged Travis tightly and sat with him for a few minutes while he cried. After a while, he reached up to Travis's face and examined the bruise closely. "Come on," he said. "We had better get some ice on that thing before it blows up like a balloon."

As they sat in the kitchen, Travis holding a towel-wrapped bag of ice on his eye, Stephen spoke slowly. "Travis, I want you to listen to me," he said. "I need you to tell me what happened."

Travis shook his head. The bag of ice made a muted sloshing sound, but otherwise the room was deadly silent.

"Travis, look—"

"No!" he said. "I don't want to talk about it."

"Did Benson do this to you?"

Travis didn't respond. He sat, almost hiding behind the bag of ice.

Stephen shook his head. "He did." Then he suddenly slapped his hand down on the counter top. "That fucker."

Travis jumped at the sound of his hand. "Don't do that," he said, his voice raspy with exhaustion.

"Sorry," Stephen said. He placed his hand down gently on the surface of the counter. "Why did you let him hit you?"

"It wasn't like that." Travis took the ice off of his face for a moment and looked at his friend.

"Wasn't like what?" Stephen took the ice out of Travis's hand and placed it gently back over his eye. Travis tried to turn his head, but Stephen gently stopped him. "Come on, you need to ice it for a little bit longer. I'll hold it for you. Tell me if I'm putting too much pressure on it."

Travis smiled slowly. "Thanks." He took a ragged breath, and the sobs started again. Stephen rubbed his shoulder gently with his other hand as he held the ice to his friend's face.

"So, he hit you. I can see that much. Do you want to tell me about it?"

"It wasn't like that. He didn't know what he was doing."

Stephen scrunched up his forehead and inhaled sharply. "Really?"

"Really, Stevie. He was on something. I'm not sure what it was. I went over and he had been out with a couple of his friends and they were rolling or something. I'm not sure exactly what it was. But..." Travis's voice trailed off.

"But what?" Stephen prompted.

"I had just stopped by after being out for a few drinks with some of the guys from work. He had texted me earlier and told me to come by. And so I did. I knew something was wrong when I got there. I knew he was high or whatever. He wasn't acting normal. But you know, I'm crazy about him, so I thought, what the heck. I'll just go in for a little bit."

Stephen took the ice off Travis's face and examined the eye. "And then what?" He very gently touched the puffy area below the eye and put the ice pack back on.

Travis winced. "He made me a drink. We started making out a little bit, you know nothing serious, just a little kissing. And then out of nowhere, he started getting rough."

"Getting rough? What do you mean?"

"Just rough. I don't know." Travis hesitated. "He grabbed me by the crotch, then he grabbed my neck. I laughed at first, then when he got more physical, I tried to back away, but that only pissed him off. He tried to grab me by the throat again, and when I backed away, he punched me."

The room was silent and neither one of them spoke for a few minutes. In the distance, they could hear the hum of a T bus as it pulled away and lumbered down one of the side streets toward Boylston.

"And then what?" Stephen pulled the ice pack away from Travis's eye and walked over to the sink. He stripped the hand towel off the plastic bag and set it out flat on the counter to dry. He then emptied the bag of ice into the sink and threw the plastic bag in the rubbish bin beneath the sink.

"Then I left."

"I'm calling the police."

"Stephen, no. Stevie…"

"What? The fucker punched you. That's abuse."

"Stevie, no. Please, you have to understand."

"Understand? What's to understand? You're the one that doesn't understand. What he did was battery. He gave you a black eye."

"He was fucked up on something."

"Oh, so that's supposed to make it better? Travis, do you hear yourself?"

"Look, Stephen, you need to calm down. What happened tonight wasn't him. He was on something. It wasn't who he is. It was bad shit." Travis slipped down off the counter and walked over to where Stephen stood in front of the sink. "I know it's over. I know I can't see him again. It just kills me a little bit. I thought I had a chance with him, to have something real. A real relationship. Not just with some stupid twenty-something year old with an entry-level job and no money. Now it's over, and I hate that. I hate what that means."

"Travis…" Stephen shook his head slowly. "You're not feeling sorry for this monster, are you?"

"No, not for him. But I am sorry about the way it all turned out. I still think he's an okay guy, just with a few issues to deal with." He looked Stephen directly in the eyes. "I don't want you to do anything crazy like going to the police."

Stephen turned around and walked out of the kitchen. "Whatever you say, Travis. But he's not a good guy."

Weekend in New York

The following Friday evening when Stephen arrived home sore from his work out, Travis met him at the door with two packed bags.

"Where are you going? Are you going home? Why are you packed?" He tried to keep the edge of panic out of his voice as he ran through all the emergency situations that would require one of them to immediately go home.

"Relax, Stevie." Travis handed him one of the bags. Stephen recognized it as his.

"Wait. Why did you pack my bag?"

"We're going to New York for the weekend."

"What? I don't want to go to New York."

"Well I do," Travis said. "It's been a hell of a week, and I need to get out of town and have some fun."

"But where are we going to get the money to go to New York?" Stephen asked.

"Relax," Travis said. "My dad sent me a load of cash this week. He was feeling generous or something. He said I should use it to put toward credit cards, but what the hell? I can always pay those off later."

Stephen didn't have time to react. "Fine," he said.

"Come on. Our train leaves in half an hour, and we have to get down to Back Bay Station."

They made it to the train station, Travis galloping out ahead of Stephen and urging him on. Stephen's sore muscles ached under even the light weight of his backpack full of clothes. But once they were on the train, he relaxed and fell into a deep sleep that lasted the entire ride to New York.

When they arrived at Penn Station, Travis dragged them from the train to the hotel for a brief stop to check in, and then almost immediately out. It was Stephen's first time in the city, but Travis had been there several times throughout his college days. They stayed in Chelsea, hitting all the shiny bars and clubs Travis had hit during his school years—Therapy, The G Lounge, even Flaming Saddles, the gay country and western bar.

The first night, Travis and Stephen made their way to one of the bigger clubs that was having a gay night. But despite the night's label, it seemed like almost a quarter of the people there were straight women. Stephen watched the crowd gather around his friend. He smiled to himself and took a sip of his beer, placing it back down on the sticky railing he had been leaning on for the last forty-five minutes.

Another group of college girls tried to dance with him. They had made their way up to the box he was dancing on and surrounded him, waving their arms in the air and trying to grind to the Hex Hector dance mix the DJ was spinning. One of them had even tried to jump up on the box and dance with him. You could hardly blame her. Travis was young, and he was in excellent shape. He had his shirt off, and his skin gleamed in the strobe lights as he moved gracefully to the rhythm of the music.

But the moment she hoisted herself up on the platform, he turned his back and danced in the other direction. The girl tried to edge closer to him, but he was having none of it. He completely ignored her. After a few awkward moments, she jumped back down to join her friends, and they moved off in a different direction.

Travis turned and looked directly at Stephen, waving at him and gesturing for him to come up on the platform and join him. But Stephen shook his head and laughed. He'd been watching Travis up on the dance floor ever since they arrived together at the nightclub. Travis hadn't even waited for the floor to get crowded. He made a beeline for the platform as soon as they'd gotten their drinks. The club had been one of Travis's favorite spots to go when he had visited during college. It was a collection of three dark rooms, sporadically lit in neon or strobe or sometimes black light. The smells of dry ice, stale beer, and Drakkar Noir mixed together to make the place almost unbearable for Stephen, but he put up with it for Travis.

Stephen looked around, the crowd growing ever more dense as the night ticked on. Another Madonna mix faded into the room, something from *Ray of Light*, but Stephen wasn't sure exactly which track it was. The bodies in the room moved faster and faster, together in sync with one another. But not Stephen. He liked to dance, but only alone in the apartment when he was sure nobody was watching.

Stephen drained the last of his beer and left the railing to wait in the line building up in front of the bar. He would be waiting for ten minutes for his next drink. He did his best to look distracted in line, avoiding the glances of both guys and girls as he stood there, one of the few people alone in the club. He had fastened his stare to the bartender and shuffled slowly toward the counter as the music thumped in the background and everyone around him shouted at each other. When he was just a few steps away from the bar, he felt someone behind him grasp the corners of his white Calvin Kline tee shirt, pulling it gently up. He quickly grabbed the strange hands and plastered them to his sides, refusing to let his shirt come off. A familiar voice chuckled behind him.

"Come on, Stevie. You've got to loosen up a little, have a little fun, show a little skin."

Travis had come down from his perch on the dance floor. He was dripping wet with sweat. His hair glistened, and his grey tee shirt was tucked into the side of his Levis. His body was still that of the college and high school athlete he had been, slender and strong with well-defined shoulders and arms that were almost fitness-model perfect. The only thing that even hinted at the decrease in physical activity since he'd graduated was a tiny softening around the belly. You could still see the outline of his upper abs, but just above the belt line was starting to look more human.

"I am not taking my shirt off, Travis." Stephen smiled, though. He knew his best friend was just teasing him.

"You should, you know. You look good."

Stephen's smirk broadened. "Forget it," Stephen said. "There's no way this shirt is coming off."

"Well, how about at least joining me out there on the dance floor?" Travis leaned into his best friend. "This is a dance club, and we did come here, allegedly, to dance. Did we not?"

"*You* came here to dance."

"And you came with me to dance." Travis sounded as if he had just played a trump card.

"Correction. I came with you. Not necessarily to dance."

"Stephen, remember when they used to call you the ghost in high school?" Travis looked him straight in the eyes.

"Yeah." He had hated that name. "What about it?"

"Well you can't be a ghost. You're too young, too attractive. You have to get out there and have some fun, man."

Stephen edged closer to the bar. There was one more guy between him and another beer, and he wasn't going to let his conversation with Travis derail him on his mission. "Travis, don't worry about me. I *am* having fun. I just don't feel comfortable up there on a platform in the middle of the dance floor."

"We can move. We don't have to be up there on the platform."

Stephen just shook his head.

"Come on, Stephen. Don't be one of those guys who just lingers like fog on the edges of the world, never really taking a bite out of things, never really living."

"Travis, you can hardly say I'm not living just because I'm not up on a platform with you gyrating to a Madonna song. Plus, you know how I dance. I can't feel the rhythm of a song to save my life. I'll just end up doing the lawn mower or sprinkler or whatever they're calling it when the dorky guys get up there and dance."

"You're not a dork, Stephen."

The guy in front of him had gotten his drinks and moved on. Stephen slip-stepped up to the bar and immediately engaged the bartender, a topless gym bunny with flawless pecs and huge biceps. He was completely covered in glitter. "May I have a Budweiser?" Stephen said before turning to Travis. "What do you want?"

"I'll take a beer too," he said.

"Make that two Buds, please." Stephen pulled a twenty out of his wallet. The bartender placed two bottles on the counter in front of Stephen and popped the tops off of them with a church key before taking the bill from Stephen. But as Stephen reached out for his change, Travis moved quickly from behind him to grab both bottles of beer and step away from the bar.

"Hey," said Stephen, shoving a dollar bill at the bartender for a tip and then shoving the rest of the change back into his wallet. "Where are you going with my beer?"

"You want this beer?"

"Yeah, I want that beer. I waited in line for fifteen minutes to get it."

"Well," Travis said with a laugh. "If you want it, you'll have to come get it out on the dance floor." He started out for the floor a few steps ahead of Stephen.

Stephen shook his head in mock anger, following his friend out to the periphery of the dance floor. Only after he arrived did he start to move around to the music.

"All right, you win."

Travis nodded. "I usually do."

"Fine, now give me the beer."

"Uh-uh. Only if you promise to stay out here for a few songs."

"What's a few?" Stephen continued to move to the music. The Madonna song had finally played out and now something from Britney Spears flooded the room.

"Let's say at least five."

"Five? That will be the next hour at the rate these remixes are going."

"You want your beer or not?"

"Fine. Five songs."

Travis handed Stephen the Budweiser, and then he stepped back. The two men danced, staying a safe distance from each other, but gradually migrating in from the outer edges of the floor to the center. Stephen had been reluctant to get out on the floor, but he was glad Travis had forced him out. He loved to dance, once he overcame the fear of moving his body in front of a crowd. Travis, as his best friend for roughly two and a half decades, had, of course, known this.

They drank and danced until finally crawling into bed as the sun was coming up Saturday morning. Stephen was exhausted, but he didn't complain. It was good to see Travis forgetting about things.

Stephen knew without having to be told, that it was Travis's way of healing.

They slept for most of the day, then rolled out of bed with enough time to get dinner and start the ritual once again. They went to different clubs, but Stephen still stayed mostly in the background as Travis took center stage on the dance floor.

They ended the second night of the weekend very much like the first, finally crawling into bed as the early morning sun brought the day-dwelling city to life. They slept until late morning, then groggily made their way to the train station. They walked like zombies, and neither spoke much except to coordinate things like getting coffee and bagels. The train ride home was nothing less than a giant, rolling nap. When they arrived back at the apartment that evening, Stephen threw his bag on the floor and dove onto his bed. He didn't even check on Travis before turning his lights out and falling asleep.

PONDERING A KISS

The next few weeks passed in almost a daze. Stephen began to see more and more of Gabe. Those first, slightly uncomfortable meetings had set the stage for a more honest and fun experience getting to know someone than he'd ever had before. It wasn't that Stephen was a different person with Gabe, but their early conversations had been so candid, he really didn't have to hide much of anything from him. So all of the tension that normally goes into a series of early meetings was gone. Stephen didn't worry about impressing him with a fancy dinner. Instead, he texted him and asked him where he wanted to go. Somewhere along the line, Stephen had even started referring to their meet ups as dates, making Gabe smile every time he said it.

As the weeks went by, Stephen's trips to the gym had begun to change his body. Jack, his gym partner was the first to notice. He constantly watched Stephen, telling him how his delts were improving or how his lats were really starting to get a nice "V" shape.

Travis was the second person to notice. But he noticed the consistent shift in Stephen's schedule more than the change in his body. "Why are you always home late now?" he'd said one Wednesday after Stephen arrived home after a gruesome leg work out. Stephen simply shrugged. Whether the shrug flexed his growing shoulders or the angle was just right, Travis said something about the change in his shape. "You're working out. How come you didn't tell me?"

Stephen shrugged again. "Don't know," he said. "I guess I wanted to make sure I could stick with it before I told anyone."

"Wait." Travis picked up the remote control and paused the movie he'd been watching. "Are you working out to impress the cop?"

Stephen rolled his eyes and walked toward his bedroom without answering him. "I hate when you call him that. His name is Gabe."

Travis got up off the couch and followed him to his room. "Is that why you're working out? So you can be all buff and muscled up for him?"

Stephen began emptying out his gym bag, but he didn't respond to Travis.

"I think that's cool," Travis said with a straight face. "I mean it. I think it's cool you like him enough to do something like this. I didn't know it was so serious."

Stephen sat on his bed and looked up at him. "It's not serious. It's just..." He couldn't find the right word to finish his sentence. "I don't know what it is, but it's not serious."

"Okay." Travis sat down beside him. "Whatever it is, it sounds like it's going pretty well. I wouldn't actually know, because you never tell me anything about him."

"I don't want to jinx it," Stephen said.

"Well, you won't jinx it by talking about it." Travis put his hand on Stephen's shoulder. "That's not how you jinx it. You jinx it by getting cocky and changing the way you act around him." He waited a few seconds to let his words sink in before continuing. "So, tell me about how it's going."

Stephen hesitated for a moment before facing Travis. A smile finally spread out across his lips as he thought about Gabe. "This whole thing is still pretty new for me, but he's great."

"Yeah?" Travis matched his friend's smile.

"Yeah. Things are going well. We are going to go see a play this week."

"Wow, a play." Travis raised his eyebrows. "That's a pretty grown up thing to do."

"I guess..." Stephen hesitated for a second. "We've been hanging out a lot over the last couple of weeks. It turns out he's into much more than just playing pool."

"Hmmm." Travis watched Stephen closely. "Hanging out or seeing each other?"

Stephen shrugged. He could feel the weight of Travis's stare. He knew Travis wasn't officially jealous or mad at him any longer about whatever it was that was happening with Gabe, but he still didn't want it to sound too exciting. "I guess it is a little more than just hanging out."

"You don't seem to talk much about him."

"Well, the first few times I saw him were kind of rough, to be honest with you." He shook his head. "No, not rough. I take that back. It was just a little clumsy for me. I didn't know if I was ready for it to be a date, or if I wanted it to be something else."

Travis laughed. "Stevie, it was pretty clear from the way you guys met that he was after more than just a friendship."

"Well," Stephen said, his eyes brightening visibly. "I don't know. I'm still not sure exactly what it was at the time, but looking back on it, yeah, maybe it was something more."

"Tell me what you like about him now that you know him a little better."

"I don't know," Stephen said. "I know it sounds awkward, but just talking to him is exciting to me. He's funny, and he seems like he's really interested in what I have to say. He wants to know about what I think. I don't know…we just talk about everything. I really like spending time with him."

"Awww," Travis said with a sigh. "And you weren't sure you wanted to be anything more than just friends in the beginning."

Stephen smiled. "I guess I was pretty stupid about it. Maybe naïve is the better word. All that aside, it's still a little awkward for me. But he is really sweet."

"Sweet?" Travis echoed the word. "Definitely, not a term used when describing a drinking buddy."

"No, he's not turning out to be a drinking buddy." Stephen tried to hold in the goofy grin that spread across his face.

Travis nodded his head. "Have you…" He raised his eyebrows twice. "You know?"

"Have I what?" His tone grew defiant.

"You know." Travis nodded his head faster.

Stephen was silent.

"For Christ's sake, Stephen. Have you even kissed him?"

"Well, yeah," Stephen lied. "Of course I have."

Travis met Stephen's eyes and stared at him for a few seconds before reluctantly nodding his head. "Okay," he said. "So, how was it?"

Stephen stood up from the bed. "I'm hungry. Have you had dinner yet?" He walked out of his room toward the kitchen, leaving Travis sitting on his bed, smiling.

"You haven't kissed him, have you?" Travis followed him out into the kitchen.

"I don't want to talk about it." Stephen raised his voice a little. "Do we have anything to eat?"

"That depends on what you want," Travis said. "If you feel like tomato paste or salt and pepper, then yes. We have plenty to eat. If you were thinking of anything else, then no, we're out of everything." He hoisted himself up onto the counter. "You haven't even kissed him?"

"See, this is why I don't like talking about him with you. You're just going to make fun of me."

"Stevie, I'm not making fun of you. It just seems a little strange. You've been seeing him for a while."

"Yeah, I know," Stephen said. "But remember, this whole thing is new for me. Can we go out to get something to eat? I'm starving."

"But you haven't even kissed him." He looked like he'd been slightly electrocuted. "We're not in second grade."

"I don't want to talk about it anymore. It feels right. I'm not going to rush it." Stephen crossed his arms as he faced his friend. "I'm running down to the street to grab a burger. Do you want to come?"

Travis stared at him in silence for a few seconds. "Okay, sure." He hopped down off the counter. "A burger sounds good."

FIRST KISS: STEPHEN AND GABE

The first cold evening took everyone by surprise that year. It came early in September when the leaves were still green on the trees, and the grass along the Charles River was still lush and full of summer. An unexpected cold front pushed its way down from Canada and blanketed New England in a cloudy chill that brought temperatures down into the fifties.

Stephen and Gabe walked close to each other along the Charles, their shoulders gently touching as they moved. Gabe let his hand go limp by his side, his fingers brushing Stephen's from time to time. He would occasionally lock his pinky with Stephen's and then reach down and lace his fingers into Stephen's, one by one until they were holding hands. Stephen allowed this little trace of intimacy, just as he had slowly begun to allow others—Gabe's hand over his on a stair railing, his arm over Stephen's shoulder in a half-hug when they met now, or sharing bits of food from the same plate. All the things that unlocked between people as they became closer started to unlock between the two of them. These things happened at Stephen's pace, but Gabe was always there, always waiting for more, always shifting ever so slightly to accommodate the next tiny step forward.

Stephen looked over at Gabe that day on the banks of the Charles, his short hair tousled roughly by the wind. It caught the rays of the late afternoon sun, giving it a golden hue that set him aglow against the deep blue river. They slowed to a stop underneath a cluster of trees near the Hatch Shell amphitheater. Gabe leaned into Stephen and looked directly at him, so close Stephen could feel his breath on his Adam's apple. They had been talking about something, Stephen was sure of that, but he suddenly couldn't remember what.

"Hey," Gabe said.

"Hey yourself," Stephen said back to him, clasping his hands and slowly raising them until they were even with his chest.

"Do you have any idea how handsome you are?" Gabe said. "How truly beautiful you are?"

"Stop it." Stephen couldn't hold his gaze. He glanced down at the ground and then out at the river.

"I mean it," Gabe said. "I thought you were good looking that first night I saw you at the Raven. But you're beautiful inside and out. It just shines through you."

"Stop it," Stephen said, finally daring to look back at Gabe's face. "You're making me blush."

"I don't care. I like it when you blush." Gabe leaned in even closer to him. "I really like you, Stephen."

"I really like you, too."

Without giving Stephen the chance to say anything else, Gabe slowly pressed his lips to Stephen's lips and kissed him. Stephen tensed a little bit at first, but then he relaxed into the kiss, opening himself up to the rough stubble of Gabe's face and the force of his mouth. It was different than anything Stephen had imagined. Where there had been softness when he'd kissed Melanie, here was a hard, unyielding mouth. Gabe slowly moved his hands down around Stephen's waist.

"Wow," Stephen said, leaning back after a few seconds. "I'm...I...Wow."

"You're not such a bad kisser yourself," Gabe said.

"I've never kissed a guy before." Stephen looked up at Gabe, staring directly into his eyes. Stephen wanted to kiss him again, wanted to hold him tight and feel the pounding of his chest close to his. But he held back, cautious of this new territory they had just entered.

"And what do you think?" Gabe smiled as the embrace ended, and Stephen backed ever so slightly away from him.

"I think it's pretty nice." Stephen laughed, the wind gently gusting up as he spoke.

Gabe shook his head. "Nice? I get nice. I was at least going for something a little more sexy than nice."

"LOL. You're very sexy, Gabriel Brennan," Stephen said.

"You did not just say 'LOL.'" Gabe smiled and ran a fingertip along Stephen's bottom lip.

Stephen nodded. "I did. I probably picked it up from my roommate."

"OMG, that's too bad." Gabe leaned in to him, and they kissed again. This time, one kiss led into another and another. Stephen felt his body temperature start to rise and he forgot to breathe despite his best efforts to stay calm. The feel of Gabe's mouth against his ignited an instant, powerful hunger in him. Stephen wanted to devour him. He couldn't get enough of the feel of his lips, the feel of his face, the sheer electricity of the embrace. Stephen leaned into Gabe's arms and lost himself completely for a few minutes.

But Stephen heard a rustle behind them, and they broke their embrace to see another couple passing them on the little path. They both looked out at the river, avoiding any possible eye contact. After the couple had walked by, Stephen nodded, and they began walking again.

"So, what do you say we grab drinks over on Charles Street," Stephen said, nodding in the direction of the Beacon Hill neighborhood.

"That sounds good," Gabe said. "Then maybe I can walk you home?"

Stephen felt like his heart was alive for the first time in his life. "That sounds like a plan."

Later, when they sat across from each other at the Sevens, a quiet little bar nestled among the eighteenth century brick townhouses of Charles Street, Stephen said, "I like that we took things slowly."

"You do?" Gabe cocked his head to one side and ran a finger along the rim of his beer glass. "Why?"

"I like the making out part, don't get me wrong." Stephen looked down at the table for a few seconds, wanting to make sure the words came out right. "This was all so confusing for me, and that couldn't have been easy for you to put up with. But I feel like we got to be pretty good friends over the past few weeks and, I'm glad we had the chance to do that first. I feel like…" he stopped. "I feel like that makes this more special. God, that probably sounds so stupid."

"No!" Gabe reached over and took his hand. Gabe's smile sparkled like chrome. "Me too. I feel the same way." He leaned in across the table and kissed him lightly on the lips. Stephen felt like he had just landed on the moon.

❖

Gabe walked him home that night and they briefly kissed on the doorstep to Stephen's apartment before Gabe turned around and left. Stephen stood on the steps for a few minutes, watching his figure recede into the cool Boston night.

Stephen kept the news of this new experience to himself. He didn't tell anyone, not his parents, not his workmates, but most of all, not Travis. He knew Travis would want to talk about his relationship with Gabe, what the kiss meant, where things were going, was he officially gay yet, or was this just an experiment. And that's exactly what Stephen didn't want to talk about. He knew he would have to think more about it at some point. He'd have to analyze it and start thinking about what their future together would be. But for right now, he just wanted to remember the night.

Gabe and he had agreed to meet someplace on that Thursday. Gabe was going to be out of town for a police training thing the first half of the week, so Stephen was on his own, trying not to think too hard about anything at all.

Somebody New

Gabe's father seemed like he hadn't aged a day in the six years since he had retired. At least that's what Gabe thought when he looked over at the man walking briskly next to him. In the late summer dusk of sunset, the lines on his father's face had all but disappeared, and the orange glow of the dull and tired sun gave a tint of youth back to his skin. Gabe smiled to see his father this way. This perpetual vitality had been part of him all of Gabe's life.

The two men were circling the same quarter mile loop in Watertown that Gabe had run on as a junior high and high school kid. In retirement, it had become an evening ritual for his father—four laps around to make an even mile-long walk every day. As a pediatrician, he had gotten after people of all ages about the importance of exercise. It wasn't until he himself retired that he had the time to be fit too.

"What is on your mind, Gabe?"

"What makes you think there's anything on my mind?" Gabe let out a quick chuckle. But his father knew him better than anyone else on the planet, and there was no use pretending.

"Oh, I don't know." His father shoved his hands deep in his pockets and pretended to look around the park nonchalantly. "It could be the fact that you can't wipe that smile off your face, or perhaps it has something to do with the fact that you are practically bouncing."

"I'm not bouncing."

"Gabriel," his father had a tone of mock seriousness. "You are most certainly bouncing, young man." He shook his head. "What's going on?"

"I don't know for sure, Dad," Gabe said, gazing up at the sky.

"But it's good, I can see that."

"Yeah, Dad, it's really good."

They continued walking for another few steps. Gabe's father kept his eye on Gabe, but the younger Brennan wasn't budging.

"Gabriel, are you going to make me drag it out of you?"

Gabe blushed just a little "Well, if you're sure you want to hear about it."

"I'm your father, aren't I? Of course I want to hear about it."

Gabe pursed his lips and let out a deep breath. "I've met someone."

"Someone, romantic?" His father raised an eyebrow.

Gabe was silent, but he looked over at his father for some hint as to how the news was hitting him. His father had always been okay with the gay thing, but it wasn't something they talked about very often. Gabe had never brought a guy home, had never introduced his parents to a boyfriend. He hadn't ever had a boyfriend for any length of time anyway, so it really hadn't been much of an issue. There had been the one-night stands and a few weeklong hook ups, but nothing worth introducing to his family.

"Yeah, I guess you could call it romantic," Gabe said.

His father grinned. He seemed to be holding something back. "That's great news, Gabe. Tell me about him."

"Well," Gabe said, suddenly at a loss for words. "Um, his name is Stephen. He's from New Hampshire."

"New Hampshire?"

"Well, he lives here in Boston now," Gabe said.

"I kind of figured that might be the case, Gabe. How did you meet him?"

"Oh, well." Gabe reached up and scratched the back of his neck self-conciously. "Nowhere special."

"Met him at a bar, huh?" The grin had returned to his father's face, this time a little bit broader.

"Yeah. I guess I did. He was out with his friend, and I was playing pool."

"There are worse places to meet people," his father said.

The two of them continued around the track for another few minutes in silence.

"Well, it's good to hear you're interested in someone. I was beginning to wonder."

"What, that I wouldn't find anyone?" Gabe laughed.

"No, no, no." His father took a deep breath and let out a long sigh. "I knew you'd find someone."

"Then what were you wondering?" Gabe looked over to see that look on his father's face that was reserved for special concerns.

"I was beginning to wonder if I'd done something wrong, to tell you the truth." His father looked over and met Gabe's eyes for a minute before carrying on. "I was afraid I'd somehow given you the message that your life wasn't okay, that it was somehow something not to talk about."

"What? Dad, no."

"Don't sound so surprised, Gabe. Your brothers and sisters were always bringing people around, always talking about girlfriends and boyfriends. I know you were different. I tried," his father paused, searching for the right words, "to tell you in my own way that it was okay to be who you were. I wanted you to know that you were remarkable—handsome, smart, brave. I wanted you to feel like you could be yourself around us.

"I tried to say that and show you that your Ma and I love you, full stop, end of story. And then I sat back and told myself that the rest was up to you. I had to give you the space to be you. But I watched as you grew into yourself further and further. You never shared very much. You didn't want us involved in your life. You didn't have stories about love, about happy dates or sad breakups. I thought it must be lonely to feel like you couldn't share with us. But I thought that if I pushed, I would only push you away, and I didn't want to risk that."

His father stopped and faced Gabe. "I'm so happy that you've found someone, Gabriel. I don't care if it lasts a few days or for the rest of your life."

Gabe tried to hold back the tears, but it was impossible. He felt the hot streaks on the side of his face, and he choked back a sob. Gabe suddenly reached around his father's neck and hugged him, and his father held him.

"When do you want to meet him?" Gabe finally said.

Back with Benson

One Tuesday night, Stephen came home from the gym to find the apartment empty. Travis was out, and that was a little strange because he had been home, sitting on the couch almost every day since he had split up with Benson a few weeks ago. Stephen resisted the urge to text him and find out where he was. He told himself Travis was probably just out with some friends after work. He pictured his friend sitting at a bar with a couple of work colleagues, and the image put his mind at ease. He made himself a peanut butter sandwich and sat down in front of the television.

A couple of hours passed, and he finally gave in to his worries and texted Travis. But Travis didn't respond. He waited until about ten o'clock and then called. No answer. He sat on the couch watching reruns of the *Big Bang Theory* and waited. Finally at eleven, the lock on the apartment door rattled, and the door slowly creaked opened. Travis stumbled loosely in and turned around to close the door after himself, leaning on the doorknob a few seconds for stability. When he finally turned around, he was smiling from ear to ear. His face was flush and his eyes were rheumy from drinking.

"Looks like you had a good time tonight," Stephen said as Travis took a few wobbly steps over to the couch and plopped down beside him.

"You could say that." Travis smiled dreamily up at the ceiling.

"You look like you got laid." Stephen punched his friend playfully in the arm.

"Yep, I did." Travis giggled. "And it was amazing."

"Amazing, huh?" Stephen chuckled. "Who was he? Where did you meet him, and will you ever see him again?"

"Geeze, dad, listen to you with all the questions." Travis's voice suddenly seemed to soften, despite the flippant tone he tried to maintain. "It wasn't a one night stand, and yes, I'll see him again. It was someone from work."

"Oooh, someone from work?" Stephen smiled. "First Benson, now someone else. Travis, you are fishing off the company pier."

"Well," Travis hesitated. "It wasn't exactly like that."

"Exactly like what?" Stephen shook his head, confused.

"It wasn't exactly someone else." He waited a few seconds before continuing. "It was Benson."

Stephen's expression changed immediately. He creased his forehead, and his smile clouded over into a scowl. "What?"

"It was Benson."

"I know what you said. I just can't understand why you would do that."

"Look, Stephen, it's different now. He has apologized."

"Really? And that makes it all okay?"

"Stephen—"

"No. You can't be serious about this. The man punched you. What are you doing hanging out with him, let alone sleeping with him again?"

"I'm going to get back together with him."

"What?" Stephen almost jumped off the couch. "Travis." He tried to control his voice, taking a deep breath and closing his eyes before he continued. "Travis, please don't do that. He's bad news."

"Look, Stephen, I didn't want to tell you because I knew you'd react like this." Travis couldn't meet his eyes. He stared down at the couch cushions. "I really, really like him. He has some things he needs to work on."

"Things he needs to work on—" Stephen started.

Travis put his hand up. "Yes, he has some things he needs to work on. But he's seeing a counselor, and I'm going to try and make things work out with him. I like him, Stevie. I really do. He's handsome and successful, and he's the first guy I've ever really connected with. What I need from you now is support. I need you to be behind me on this, as my best friend. I don't need a lecture on domestic abuse. That's not what this is."

Stephen inhaled sharply but held his breath.

"Seriously," Travis continued. "It's not abuse." He kicked his shoes off and folded his feet underneath his butt on the couch. "It happened while he was high, and he's not going to do that again."

Stephen watched Travis beside him on the couch, his face a twisted combination of hope and worry, confusion and determination. Stephen tried to put himself in Travis's head, but he couldn't. He couldn't imagine ever hitting someone. When he turned the situation around in his mind and thought about what he would feel like if Gabe hit him, his emotions became even more clouded. Would he forgive him? Well, shit, he thought. It was hard to decide in the abstract. If Gabe had been out of his head drunk, somehow not himself, it would be one thing. It would be hard, but Stephen would probably give him a second chance.

"Okay," Stephen said slowly, articulating the word as if it were almost too difficult for him to say. "If that is what you want, I'll support you."

Travis let out a sigh. "Thanks, Stevie." He smiled. "That makes me really happy."

The two of them watched late night television for another ten minutes. Neither one of them said much. Stephen was still trying to get his head around the conversation they had just had. Travis sat silently, seemingly absorbed in whatever was happening. Stephen didn't even notice what show it was.

Finally, Stephen decided it was time for him to go to bed. "See you in the morning," he said as he held out his hand for a fist bump.

"Night, Stevie." Travis made a fist and gently crashed his knuckles into Stephen's. "Thanks for listening tonight."

Stephen tried to smile. "Anytime." But he had a bad feeling in his stomach as he headed to bed.

DATE NIGHTS AND SECRETS:
WHAT ARE YOU HIDING?

The squad car pulled up to where Stephen was standing on Boylston Street, across from the granite façade of the Boston Public Library. Boylston was normally crowded, but it was after rush hour and the throngs of people had thinned out to a trickle. Stephen had stopped on his way home from the gym to read a couple of emails on his phone. It was dusk, the daylight almost completely faded from the sky, and Stephen didn't notice the car until it had completely stopped in front of him and blared the siren for a second.

He looked up to see two officers in the car. The one in the driver's seat rolled down his window and smiled at him. Stephen looked directly at the officer's face, but it took him a few seconds to recognize him. Gabe looked so different in his uniform. His reddish-blond hair was completely covered under a hat, and he wore a Kevlar vest underneath his shirt, giving him a slightly barrel-chested appearance.

When Stephen did finally recognize him, he put his phone away and walked over to the cruiser. "Good evening officer," he said, a smile lighting up his face from ear to ear.

"Hey there," Gabe said. He was smiling too, but his tone was different. It sounded stronger than when he wasn't working.

"This is Officer Ramirez," he said, pointing to the guy in the seat next to him. He leaned across the front seat of the car slightly and waved.

"Hi there," Stephen said, a little unsure of the proper way to greet a police officer when you were just casually meeting one. He shifted his attention back to Gabe. "What's up?"

"Just finishing up some official police business," he said with a smile. "You know, high priority stuff."

"Yeah, high priority." Ramirez leaned back across the seat. "Barking dog on Marlborough Street. Old lady kept calling and calling. Finally they sent us out to secure the scene."

Gabe gently pushed Ramirez back over to his side of the car. Stephen laughed despite himself. He had never really had a conversation with an actual Boston cop before, except for Gabe. All of his expectations for what they were like came from the shows he'd seen on television. He'd never really thought they could be funny.

Gabe leaned his head out the window, closer to him. "We still on for later?"

"Oh yeah," Stephen's face glowed. "I can't wait."

"Me too," said Gabe. He smiled, but just as he did the radio inside the cruiser blared something, and the smile vanished from his face. Ramirez picked up the receiver and spoke into it, a garbled mess of words Stephen couldn't understand.

"You have to go," he said to Gabe.

"I do." He nodded. "See you in a couple of hours?"

"Count on it," Stephen said, backing away from the cruiser. Gabe gave him a quick wink and focused back on the street before taking off into traffic. Stephen stood watching the taillights of the cruiser for a few seconds before resuming his walk home.

At the apartment, Travis was lounging on the couch watching television and eating a microwaved burrito. "Home from the gym?" He looked up from the television as Stephen closed the door behind him.

"Yeah," Stephen said. "How'd you guess?"

Travis let out a snort of air. "You come through the door with a gym bag, and your arms are pumped up to the size of small pit bulls. It's not exactly a mystery Stevie."

Stephen shrugged. "Pit bulls, huh?" He did a single bicep curl with his gymbag in his right hand.

"Small pit bulls," Travis said, finishing the last bite of his burrito. "Puppies, actually. So don't get cocky."

"You staying in tonight?" Stephen said. Travis had been going out a lot in the weeks since he had gotten back together with Benson.

"Yeah. Just need to lay low for a night or two. I've been going out a lot."

Something was up. Stephen could tell from the tone in his friend's voice. "Everything okay?"

"Yeah, fine." Travis got up and brought his plate out into the kitchen. As he passed, Stephen noticed a giant bruise on his left forearm. At first he just stared at it and held his breath. He tried not to jump to conclusions, but he felt the rage beginning to build up in the pit of his stomach.

"Okay, what happened?" Stephen pointed at Travis's forearm and tried to keep his voice casual. "That looks like a nasty bump."

Travis shrugged. "It's nothing. Just a bruise. Something dropped out of the supply cabinet at work."

Stephen watched his friend with disbelief. He knew exactly when Travis was lying. What galled him now was the fact that Travis was afraid even to be honest with him. Stephen faced Travis as he scraped the remnants of the burrito off his plate and into the trash, then began running water over it in the sink.

"Something just fell out of the supply cabinet?"

"Yes," Travis said, keeping his eyes focused on the plate he was washing.

"And it left a bruise on your forearm that looks like someone's hand print?"

"Look, Stevie." Travis rinsed the plate and set it beside the sink to dry. "I don't know what you want me to say here."

"How about you tell me what really happened to your arm?"

They both stood staring at each other for a moment, neither one able to move. Finally Travis spoke. "He didn't mean to do it."

Stephen dropped his head, his eyes focused on the floor, he was unable to look at Travis at that second. "I figured it was Benson again," Stephen finally said.

❖

Later that evening, Stephen met Gabe at the Sevens on Charles Street. He was a little late, so he'd jogged the last few blocks. His cheeks were blotchy red, and his forehead had a thin coat of sweat on it. Gabe was waiting for him in a small booth up by the window in the front of the bar. He nursed a beer and had a fresh pint waiting for Stephen. He looked up the minute Stephen came through the door and watched him as he walked over to the booth.

But the Gabe Stephen saw sitting in the booth was markedly different from earlier that afternoon. The funny and easy-going mood had been replaced by a very serious, almost sullen expression on his face, and he had a small cut above his eye. He had showered, and his hair was still damp, but Stephen could see the bleeding had only recently stopped.

"Gabe, what's up?" Stephen sat down across from him. "Where did you get that cut?"

"Oh, it's nothing. The last call of the evening was a rough one," Gabe said. He tried to smile, but it did little to change the expression on his face.

"How so? What happened?"

"Ah, you don't want to know." Gabe waved his hand gently. "It was pretty bad."

"Tell me about it." Stephen reached over and put his hand on Gabe's.

Gabe looked at him for a moment as if weighing a decision, and then he shook his head. "You know that little sub shop over behind City Hall, back by the Farmers Market?"

"Yeah."

"Well, right after I saw you today, we had a domestic dispute in the apartment above that place."

Stephen shifted in his seat as he watched Gabe's face. "Go on," he said.

"Well, we got to the apartment. The cashier at the sub shop had called us. Reported a lot of screaming and loud noises—said it sounded like people throwing things and stomping around." Gabe pressed his eyes closed and took a deep breath.

Stephen rubbed his hand. "Was it bad when you got there?"

Gabe nodded. "You know that sinking feeling you get when you know something before you see it? Well, when we got there, the place was way too quiet. The sub shop had emptied out except for the staff. The cashier let us into the building, and everything was as still as a morgue until we got to the door. I could hear someone crying on the other side—deep muffled sobbing, almost more animal than human sounding. Ramirez knocked on the door, announced us, asked if we could come in. The guy just opened the door and walked back into the apartment. He was in his late twenties, and he wore a white Polo shirt with blood spattered all over it. The apartment stunk like it hadn't been cleaned in months—that smell of stale beer and filth that makes you want to throw up.

"As we followed him into the apartment, he sat down on the floor next to a bloody pile of clothes. He put his hand on top of the clothes and wept. Except," Gabe stopped to catch his breath. "Except that it wasn't a pile of clothes. I walked over to where he was sitting and looked down at the pile and noticed hair and some skin." Gabe took a series of shallow breaths, losing his composure for a fraction of a second before he seemed to pull back into an official sounding voice. "It was his wife and his baby girl."

Stephen swallowed hard. "Oh God."

Gabe nodded. "They weren't breathing, either one of them. When I reached down to pick the baby up, the guy went crazy. He started throwing things and screaming." Gabe pointed to his forehead. "He got me good with the edge of a broken beer bottle. We cuffed him and called for back up. The ambulance and the coroner came."

Gabe took a deep breath and continued. "He'd killed them. Drunk as you can imagine. He'd beat them both to death because the baby was crying, and he wanted to watch the baseball game."

"Oh my God," Stephen said. He leaned over the table and tightened his grip on Gabe's hand.

Gabe's eyes were glistening now. "I'm sorry," he said. "I know this isn't exactly date night conversation. I was trying to keep my shit together, but…" Gabe looked down at himself. "You can see I'm not always so great at that."

"It's okay. Sometimes you're not supposed to keep it together. Sometimes you need to open up and let yourself be sad. Especially when you see things like what you saw today."

"I just don't know why..." Gabe trailed off. "What switch flipped in his head? I don't get it." He took an unsteady breath.

Stephen looked at the man across from him. His blue eyes were cracked with streaks of red and dark circles beneath them.

"You know," Gabe said after a few minutes of silence, "there was no justice for that woman and her baby today. And there never will be."

Stephen nodded, staying silent.

"That guy will get locked up for the rest of his life or at least a very long time, but that doesn't mean anything to those two lying in a pile on the floor today."

Stephen nodded and gently released Gabe's hand. His thoughts went back to the bruises he'd seen on Travis's arm earlier that evening. "No." Gabe's words sank into his skin as he spoke. "No justice."

Flashback to Bruises

After Stephen went out, Travis spent the rest of that evening in front of the television, but he barely noticed whatever he was watching. He had a lot of stuff he needed to get straight in his head. The bruise, which he had tried to keep covered up, had actually happened the night before. He looked down at his arm for a second and then turned away. Most of the time, Benson was charming and caring, but then something would set him off, and Travis never knew what to do about it. It was like Benson turned into someone else.

Ugh, he thought, gently touching the yellow and blue skin on his left arm. "If I'd only handled the situation better," he said out loud to no one. "If I'd only knew how to react to him when he got like that." He tried to think back, looking for some pattern, some tell he missed that would have indicated Benson was having a bad time.

Travis replayed the memory again in his mind. Benson had gone home early after a meeting in the financial district. When Travis finished work, he thought it would be a nice idea to drop in at Benson's condo and surprise him. He let himself in using the key Benson had given him. Benson lived in part of a new complex in an area of town called Fort Point. It had formerly been artists' studios, but a developer had bought and renovated the building. Travis closed the door behind him and stood facing the huge wall of windows looking out over the waterfront.

"Hello," Travis said as he stepped further into the apartment. "Benny?" he called.

"Who's there?" He heard Benson's voice from the kitchen, followed shortly by the man himself, stumbling a little as he made his way out from the kitchen to the dining room. Travis knew Benson had been drinking. He wasn't staggering drunk, but his voice had a little bit of a lilt, and his eyes were glassy.

"Hi Benny, it's me," Travis said, taking a few more steps into the spacious living room.

"Me who?" Benson said, an edge to his tone.

"Me, Travis, that's who." Travis walked over to him and kissed him quickly on the lips. He smelled heavily of scotch. "Ooh, it must have been a cocktails and drinks meeting this afternoon. A little early for that," Travis added. But as soon as he'd said it, he knew he shouldn't have. Benson could be sensitive to any criticism about his work.

"So, now you're sneaking into my house and telling me how to do my job, huh?" Benson's steps echoed on the pine floor as he walked away from Travis toward the living room balcony. Along the way, he picked up a glass of scotch from the end table beside the sofa.

Travis smiled and followed a step or two behind him. "No, of course not," he said. "I was just noticing, that's all. How did it go?" He put a hand on Benson's shoulder, but Benson shrugged him off and turned around to glare at him.

"It went shitty, that's how it went. There are more of the same meetings tomorrow, which is just fan-fucking-tastic." His voice was almost a snarl. Travis wanted to back away, but stood still.

"I'm sorry to hear that," Travis said.

"What are you doing here anyway," said Benson. "Did you skip out of work early?"

"No, I left at the regular time." Travis felt a strange feeling forming in the bottom of his stomach. "I knew you were here, I thought I'd surprise you," Travis tried putting a seductive smile on his face.

"You did, did you?" Benson warmed up a little, a smile beginning to light up his lips. He downed his scotch in one swallow, and then he walked over to the coffee table and set the empty glass down. Travis followed him. When he turned around, Travis leaned in and kissed him again. This time Benson kissed back, grabbing Travis's shoulders and roughly pulling him into an embrace.

Travis pulled back and smiled. He ran a finger playfully over Benson's lips. "Now that's more like it."

"More like it?" Benson said. "What is that supposed to mean? Am I expected to be at your call? So you came over here and expected me to just light up for you?" His lips had curled back from a smile into a dark, twisted look. He backed out of the embrace and stood holding Travis's upper arms tightly.

"Benson, babe, I didn't expect anything. I was hoping just to come over and spend a little time with you." He leaned in to embrace him again, but Benson backed his head away.

"Don't give me that bullshit," he said, clamping down tighter on Travis's arms. "You think you're such a hot shit, don't you?" His eyes were wild now. "You think you're young and good looking and the world is just there for you, everyone falling at your feet. Well, you're not all that. You're a twenty-four-year-old twink. You're nothing special."

Travis blinked. Something was very wrong. Benson had been so loving and wonderful for the past few weeks, ever since they'd gotten back together. After the first incident, he'd promised it would never happen again. Now Travis found himself here with him, and it was happening again. "Benson, how much have you had to drink?"

"It's none of your business how much I've had to drink." His tone was deadly, and his words came out in short staccato syllables.

"Okay." Travis tried to back out of his hold, but Benson grabbed on to his left forearm. "I'm going to go. I think you need some time alone right now."

Benson tightened his grip on Travis's arm and shook him. "I'll tell you when you can go," he said.

"Benson, stop it. You're hurting me." Travis tried to back away again, but Benson was much bigger.

"Hurting you? Why are you such a little pussy?" Benson pushed him down onto the couch.

Travis fell hard, but the couch softened the landing. His arm throbbed where Benson had held him, and his heart pounded. He lay there looking up at Benson, who was unbuckling his belt.

"Benson, no," Travis said. "I don't want to do it like this."

"You'll want to do what I tell you you'll want to do," he said, pulling off his belt and throwing it aside. He pushed the coffee table away from the couch, knocking the empty scotch glass to the floor. It shattered and crunched as Benson stepped on it.

Travis decided to make a run for it. He rolled into a ball and sprang off the couch, but he was too late. Benson caught him by the arm and spun him around. They stood face-to-face, Benson staring into his eyes. Something switched off in Benson's face at that moment.

"Baby," he said, his voice soft and soothing all of a sudden. "Oh, baby, I didn't mean to scare you. I thought you just wanted a little adventure. Something a little rough." He smiled sweetly, his eyebrows raised in counterfeit surprise, his eyes radiating a look of false tenderness. "That's all. I never meant to frighten you." He touched his hand to the side of Travis's head, stroking his hair and cupping his cheek gently.

Travis looked up at him and then away. "I think I need to go now," Travis said. "I'm supposed to meet Stephen. I...I just wanted to stop in and see you." He struggled to control his breathing.

"Sure," Benson said. "I understand. I'm glad you came by. I missed you today at work."

"Me too. I hope your meetings go better tomorrow." Travis tried to make his voice casual.

Benson backed away, ignoring the crunch of glass underneath his feet. It sounded like bones breaking. Benson looked down at the mess and shook his head. "I should get something to clean this up." He walked back to the kitchen and returned a few seconds later with a dustpan and broom. "Meetings tomorrow? Oh, yeah, they'll be fine. It will all be fine." He knelt down and started to sweep the wet shards of glass up into the dustpan.

"Good, good," said Travis. "Well, I'm going to head out now."

"Sure," Benson said from the floor. "Travis?"

"Yeah?"

"I really hope I didn't scare you. I thought you might like it, you know, rough. I know a lot of guys do. I was just trying to spice things up."

"Yeah." Travis bit his lip. His arms still burned where Benson's fingers had clutched him like a vice grip. "I don't know, I'm not really into the rough stuff."

"Okay," Benson smiled gently from the floor. "I'll remember that. Tell you what." He paused for a second and looked up at the ceiling, as if searching for the right words. "This weekend, let's go out. There's a new restaurant in the South End I've been dying to try. I'll have my admin get us reservations. We'll have a nice dinner and a few drinks. Sound good?"

Travis nodded. "Sure, sounds great."

"Good. Let's make it Saturday."

"Okay, Saturday."

"Tell Stephen I said hello."

"I will," Travis said, and he headed out the door, closing it softly behind him. When he was finally out in the hall, he leaned against the wall for a few seconds to steady himself. His legs were shaking. In fact, his entire body was trembling. He needed to just get home and be by himself.

First Times

Stephen looked around the tiny apartment and tried to catch his breath. He was a little embarrassed by the fact that the walk up the five flights of stairs had winded him. He made a mental note to add more cardio at the gym. He exhaled deeply and tightened his stomach, aware that Gabe was just a few steps behind him.

The front hall of the apartment was barely more than six square feet of space with a bookshelf on one side and an umbrella stand and coat rack on the other side.

"Go ahead in," Gabe said as he stepped through the door behind Stephen and dropped his keys in a dish on the shelf by the door.

Stephen walked into the room and looked straight ahead to a great big bay window looking out onto the rooftops on the other side of Charles Street.

"Wow," Stephen said. "Great view."

"Yeah," Gabe said. "It's pretty small, but I love it."

The place was sparsely but neatly furnished with a dark blue modern couch and two red leather chairs. The walls on either side of the room were exposed brick. A small door to the right headed off to the bedroom, and an arch on the left led to a shallow kitchen and dining nook. The floors were hardwood, and Gabe had placed a white area rug in the living room under the couch and chairs. A giant flat screen television sat against one wall on a small white shelf stacked with DVD cartons.

Stephen dropped his bag onto the couch and tried desperately to look cool and relaxed. His hands were shaking, and he could feel the sweat starting to drip down in the corners of his shirt just underneath the armpits. *Oh gosh, what am I doing?* he thought to himself. Spending the weekend with Gabe had seemed like such a good idea when they had agreed to it early that week. But he'd never stayed over before, and this was very new territory for Stephen. He looked at Gabe.

Gabe took Stephen's shaking hands in his. "Why are you nervous?" he asked.

"I'm not nervous." Stephen smiled, and his stomach shook with butterflies. "Well, okay, that's a fib. I'm a little nervous."

"I'm glad you decided to spend the weekend," Gabe said.

"Me too."

"We get to spend the day together today, maybe go for lunch, then take a long walk." Gabe dropped Stephen's hands and wrapped his arms around his waist. "Then maybe we can see a movie or just sit and talk over a couple of cups of coffee. And then we can come back here and snuggle on the couch. How does that sound?" Gabe leaned in to Stephen and kissed him on the mouth, gently at first, then deeply.

Gabe had shaved that morning, but his chin was still stubbly, and it grazed Stephen's face, tickling him and taunting him at the same time. Stephen felt his entire body flush. What was it about this guy that drove him absolutely crazy? He didn't know for sure, but every time Gabe touched him, his skin felt like it was coming alive for the first time. Stephen felt himself start to harden as he kissed Gabe back. After a moment, he pulled back. "It's only Saturday morning."

Gabe chuckled. "That's okay. I don't feel any differently about you in the morning or the evening." He leaned in, and they kissed again.

"Gabe." Stephen backed out of the kiss for a second and looked around the apartment. "You know, I've never..."

Gabe followed Stephen's eyes and took a deep breath. He took Stephen's hand and sat him down on the couch. Gabe sat down a respectable distance down from him and pulled one leg up underneath himself. "Do you want to hear about my first time?" he asked.

The comment took Stephen a little bit by surprise. He had felt like he was going to have to awkwardly discuss his lack of experience, but

Gabe had completely changed the dynamic of the situation. Stephen nodded. "Yeah…"

"Well," Gabe took a breath and his face glowed with a smile. "It didn't actually happen until I was in my twenties. I was a little bit of a late bloomer."

"You mean with a guy?"

"With anyone." Gabe sighed. "I always knew I was gay, but I just couldn't deal with it. I tried dating a few women along the way, but I wasn't interested in them. I tried making out with a few in college, but it did absolutely nothing for me."

"I bet you broke a few hearts," Stephen said.

Gabe shook his head slowly. "I don't know about that. I mostly kept my distance from everybody. I didn't have a lot of friends, either. Having to hide so much about myself, I didn't like feeling like I had to lie to everyone. I just felt better being by myself."

"That must have been lonely," Stephen said.

"The summer after I graduated, I moved back home to my parents' house out in Watertown. I got a job on a work crew in one of the state parks out by Lexington and Concord, building new trails and cleaning up older ones. We built a lot of wooden bridges and planked walkways."

Stephen nodded, thinking of the trails through the national forests back where he grew up. He'd always wondered who built them.

"Sometimes we worked in big groups if we had a large job to do, but a lot of the time we split off in to pairs to take care of the smaller tasks—clearing brush or putting in a sign post somewhere. I always seemed to end up with this guy named Cabhan."

"You mean Kevin?"

"No. He was Irish, fresh off the boat. Cabhan is a Gaelic name. Well, like you, he was incredibly handsome." Gabe reached out and ran the back of his hand slowly along Stephen's cheeks. "He had bright blue eyes and beautiful skin. And his shoulders were big and broad, and he had these arms that were made of steel."

Stephen laughed a gentle little laugh. "Easy there, forest ranger."

Gabe smiled back at him. "Anyway, we spent a lot of time together, and I never thought that anything would come of my crush. I was still in the closet to everyone except a couple of `close friends.

One day, we were out in the middle of the woods clearing some trees that had fallen down during the last big storm. It was the middle of the summer and it was scorching hot out. Well, we got to a part of the path that ran along a pond, and we both decided we should cool off. I stripped down to my boxers, but Cabhan went full monty and took everything off.

"You're not going in your drawers, are you? You'll chafe like hell when you get out," he yelled out to me. I was a pretty shy guy at that time, but having been called out on it, I pretty much felt like I had no choice, so I took my undershorts off and left them on my pile of clothes on the bank of the pond and waded in after Cabhan."

Stephen watched as Gabe paused and looked out the window into the distance, as if remembering the scene he was describing. Stephen waited silently for him to continue. In the quietness that folded in around them, Stephen could hear the noises of the street below, the soft bubble of conversation as people made their way into and out of the antique and specialty shops along the street, punctuated by the occasional car.

After a moment, Gabe turned back to Stephen. "Sorry," he said. "I just got lost there for a second. Well, when we were in the pond, he swam over and just stood there looking at me. We were out pretty deep. I was standing on my tippy toes, and the water was up to my neck. Cabhan was just a little taller than me. He stared at me for about a minute, not saying a word, but his eyes had this glazed look to them, and I thought that maybe he was feeling the same thing that I had been feeling for him for most of the summer. Then all of a sudden, out of nowhere, he reached out and put one hand on my cheek and kissed me."

"Just like that?" Stephen said.

Gabe nodded. "Yup, just like that, completely out of the blue. Took me totally by surprise."

"But you had been crushing on him for a while, so it was a good thing, right?" Stephen was on the edge of the couch, intensely following the story.

"Oh yeah, a really, really good thing. We made out in the middle of that pond, and it was the hottest thing ever. It was the first time I'd ever kissed a guy. Hell, it had to be one of the first times I'd kissed anyone like that. I'd only kissed a handful of girls—women, whatever. And those had never been like what it was with Cabhan."

"What happened then?" Stephen prompted him to go on.

"Well, then he led me out of the water, we picked up our stuff, and we made our way up into a thicket of bushes without even getting dressed. Like I said, it was the middle of summer, so it was easy to find a spot that was hidden from view, not that anyone would have come down that path. It was a weekday, and we'd been working there for most of the day and nobody had passed. He cleared out a spot and spread his shirt down over the leaves and moss. Then he lay down and patted the earth next to him, looking up at me and smiling. I laid down next to him and he folded his arms around me, and, well…" Gabe's voice trailed off.

"And what?"

"And that was my first time."

"Right there in the woods? Outdoors? Seriously?"

Gabe nodded his head slowly.

"That's so hot," Stephen said.

"I know," Gabe said. "It was pretty special." He looked Stephen directly in the eyes. "The first time should be special for everyone. So, if you're nervous, or you're not ready, we can wait. There's no rush."

Stephen felt his heart beat through his ribcage. "What happened with Cabhan?"

"You mean after that?"

"Yeah," Stephen said. "Did you guys become boyfriends or anything?"

Gabe scrunched his face as if searching for the right words. "Boyfriends? No. We enjoyed each other's company. We worked together most of the rest of that summer, and we found quite a few chances to…well, you know. But after that summer, we each went our own way. Did I care for him? Yeah, I guess I did. But I was just figuring things out for myself, and I don't think I even knew what it really meant to be in a relationship. Looking back, I sometimes wonder if he did. We never talked about it. We talked about other stuff. I'm sure I talked a lot about wanting to be a cop, and he talked a lot about things in Ireland, and his family and different sports like soccer and hurling. But he was nice and kind and very conscientious, and I very much liked being with him."

"He sounds like a great guy," Stephen said.

"He was. Or is still, I'm sure. Wherever he is." Gabe put his hand on Stephen's knee. "But not as special as the guy I'm with now."

Stephen's face lit up with a smile.

"Not as special as my boyfriend," Gabe said.

Friends of Friends

W"ives and girlfriends night tonight," Ramirez said. He dried off, running the terrycloth over his legs first, then his torso and finally his arms. He threw the towel on the locker room bench and reached into his locker for his stick of deodorant. Gabe sat quietly on the bench across from him, sorting through his vanity kit with a blank look on his face. "They're all coming to the Pour House. I think it's dangerous, but hey, I only had one vote. I thought maybe someplace nice on Newbury Street or on the Waterfront, but nope. Vetoed."

"Mmmm," Gabe said, barely acknowledging him.

"They're going to end up picking on us, you know?" Ramirez continued. "They just want to get together and compare notes and commiserate. It happens every time we do this."

"Yup," Gabe said as he gently rearranged the contents of the kit one more time, trying to ignore his partner and wondering how he was going to get out of this conversation without causing it to erupt.

"Of course, I'm sure not everyone is going to be like that," Ramirez droned on. "My Lisa isn't. She's just coming because she wants to support me at work. I said, honey, you don't have to do that. But she said it was only the right thing to do. If the department was having a night to socialize with all of our significant others, she wanted to come along and show she cared about my work and she supports us. She says the same thing every time we have one of these deals."

Gabe had stopped messing around with the vanity kit and set it back into his gym bag. He couldn't do anything about this, so he just battened down the hatches. He knew the questions would be coming soon. But rather than rush them, he let Ramirez gradually get around to his point.

"In the end, I was really happy she said that. I know a couple of guys aren't bringing their significant others and everybody is kind of feeling sorry for them, you know. Like they don't really have a girlfriend or a boyfriend or whatever. Or maybe they do, but they're ashamed of them or maybe their significant others don't really have a supporting personality, where they'll show up for something like this."

"It's not an official event, Ramirez," Gabe finally said. "Everyone decided we should bring the girlfriends and wives out for a night of drinking somewhere every few months. It's not some departmental program."

Ramirez pulled a fresh tee shirt on over his head. "Man, that's what makes it so much more important. It's self-actualized team building."

"I don't think that means what you think it means," said Gabe.

"You know what I mean, Brennan. We all decided to do this on our own."

"You guys decided this. I didn't have anything to do with it," Gabe said. "Besides, what's the point of having a night where wives and girlfriends join us for beers? I don't understand."

"What do you mean? It's good for everyone to get together." Ramirez pulled on a clean pair of underwear, the waistband snapping against his pale brown skin. "You think it's a bad idea to get to know everyone's significant others?"

"You keep using that phrase—significant others—like something more is behind this." Gabe stood up putting on a button up shirt and pulling on a pair of boxer briefs. He slowly began to button the shirt as they spoke. "It's like you're saying it for a specific reason. We've always called it wives and girlfriends night before. Why this change now?"

Ramirez shrugged. "I don't know what you're talking about. We're trying to be inclusive."

"Forget it, Ramirez."

"Forget what?"

"I'm not inviting Stephen to wives and girlfriends night."

"Gabe, buddy, listen to yourself," Ramirez said. "Why are you being so homophobic? Are you one of those self-hating gays?"

"What? No." Gabe couldn't believe what he was hearing. "Are you serious?"

"What's going on here? Talk to me," Ramirez said.

"No. Ramirez, quit being weird. I'm not inviting him," Gabe said. "And that's that."

"Why? Because you're afraid people are going to talk about you guys behind your backs? Are you afraid someone is going to call him a name? What gives?"

Gabe stared at him for a few seconds, trying to decide the best thing to say to end the conversation quickly. "He's not going. End of story."

"Come on, man. It's significant others night." Ramirez shook his head.

"No," Gabe said. "It's not. It's wives and girlfriends. And I think Stephen would feel uncomfortable."

"He would? Or you would feel uncomfortable bringing him?" Ramirez cocked his head to one side and lifted an eyebrow.

"I'm not uncomfortable with anything," Gabe said.

"Oh, really? You're not embarrassed to bring your boyfriend to hang out with all your cop friends."

Gabe felt his face get hot, and he knew he was turning red. He said nothing.

"Because it sure seems like it to me," Ramirez continued. "It seems like you're avoiding having anyone see you with a boyfriend. So either you're ashamed of him or ashamed of us. Which is it?"

"I don't have to listen to this." Gabe buttoned the last button on his shirt, picked up his duffle bag, turned around, and walked toward the door.

"Hey Brennan," Ramirez shouted at him.

"What?" Gabe said without even turning around.

"Pants."

"What?"

"You forgot your pants."

Gabe looked down and shook his head. "I didn't forget them."

Ramirez doubled over in laughter, and Gabe eventually began to chuckle as he walked back over to the bench, unzipped his duffle bag, and pulled out his pair of jeans.

❖

Stephen had been strangely quiet when Gabe asked him about going to Significant Other's night.

"Is that really what you call it?" he asked as he played with a French fry on the edge of his plate. He had only finished half of his burger before Gabe had brought up the invitation. Gabe had tried to make it sound normal, just something the guys from the station did from time to time.

"Yeah," Gabe sighed, his own burger half-eaten as well. "That's what they call it now."

"What did they used to call it?"

"Well," Gabe hesitated, unsure what to say. "They used to call it Wives and Girlfriends night."

"I see," Stephen said. He put the French fry down, took a sip of his beer and looked around the restaurant.

They had agreed to meet after work for dinner. After a couple of suggestions of sushi or Ethiopian food, they had decided to be less ambitious and just settled on burgers at Emilio's, a Greek diner in the South End on Tremont Street. It was always busy, and Gabe liked it because it was family owned and run. He'd been going there for years, and the same group of brothers was almost always working when he came in.

"If you don't feel like it, I totally get it," Gabe said. "I know hanging out with a bunch of cops might not sound like a ton of fun."

"Do you want me to come?"

Gabe felt the heat rise around his collar. "Yeah, of course," he said. "If you want to go. I don't want you to feel like you have to."

"Who is going to be there?"

"A bunch of guys from the station."

"Ramirez?"

"Yeah." Gabe smiled, thinking it was cool Stephen had remembered his partner's name. "Ramirez will be there. He asked me if you were coming."

Stephen looked relieved and mildly surprised. "In that case, I think I'll go."

Gabe nodded quietly and looked back down at what was left of his own burger. He was contemplating finishing it, but it was a little messy at that point. He glanced up and noticed Stephen staring at him. "What?"

"Oh, nothing really," said Stephen. "I was just wondering what you're supposed to wear to something like this."

Gabe laughed. "I'd go with jeans and a tee shirt."

"Yeah, okay," Stephen said. "I figured it was something like that. But I didn't know if I should dress up or anything. I don't want to get there and have everyone in dress shirts and pants...or I guess, dresses and heels."

"Ha, no. Don't worry. The only ones who might be in dress pants are the waiters."

Stephen cocked his head to one side, which Gabe thought made him look like a little kid. "Where is it?"

"You'll never guess," Gabe said, picking at the burger.

Stephen looked at him for a second before he got it. "The Pour House?"

Gabe nodded his head slowly, and Stephen closed his eyes.

"I should have known," Stephen said.

"I don't know what the big deal is. You brought me to meet your work friends and that was only the third time I had ever seen you," Gabe said.

"That was to Fenway, in box seats to see a great game."

"Still," Gabe pointed at him across the table. "I hardly knew you and I had to face your girlfriend."

"She wasn't my girlfriend."

"Why do I have the feeling she thought there was still hope," Gabe said.

"Why do I have the feeling that being arm candy at a Boston Police event where I'm categorized with the wives and girlfriends is going to be a tad more intense than suite seats at a Red Sox game? By the way, isn't it a little sexist to call it wives and girlfriends night? Don't you hang out with any women from work?"

"Of course we hang out with women. That name is just a hangover from decades ago. We don't really even use it anymore." Gabe looked Stephen directly in the eye. "Listen, if you're uncomfortable we can leave." Gabe finally made the decision that the burger had passed the point of eating and placed his napkin on top of it. Stephen did the same thing.

"I know." Stephen's expression softened. "I'm actually looking forward to it."

"You are?" Gabe tried to keep the surprise out of his voice.

"Yeah, absolutely. I'm looking forward to actually meeting Ramirez, not just seeing his face in the patrol car, for one. And who knows? Maybe this will give me good karma for any potential speeding tickets."

Gabe shook his head. "I don't know about that. But what do you say we get out of here? It's a nice night for a walk on the river."

By the time Significant Others night finally arrived, Gabe had gone over every possible scenario in his head for how the night might play out. He had imagined the worst, his mind conjuring up images of his coworkers snickering and whispering under their breath as he and Stephen walked through the room, followed by situations that ended in knock-down, drag-out fights where everyone was kicked out of the bar and actual on-duty police had to be called to break things up. At moments like that, he would bite his lower lip, suck in a deep breath, and tell himself to try and relax.

Of course he also imagined much better scenarios, where Ramirez and Stephen chatted all night long and his other colleagues told him that it was really cool he brought Stephen. He liked the way those scenarios made him feel warm and like things with Stephen were permanent. In the days leading up to the event, he held on to those thoughts and kept them locked away in that spot in his heart-brain he reserved for special things.

The event itself was nothing spectacular. The night was crisp; cold enough to require a light jacket. Gabe and Stephen arrived later than they had planned because Gabe had met Stephen at his apartment, and the two of them walked across the Fenway and down the few blocks of Back Bay.

"I need a little pre-game," Stephen had suddenly called out as they walked down the beginning of Boylston Street, past the firehouse. He abruptly turned right just as Boylston crossed over the Mass Pike and headed toward Bukowski's, a tiny bar nestled in a cement parking structure perched above the highway.

"A pre-game?" Gabe said. "That doesn't exactly sound like you, Stephen." But he regretted it the moment he said it. Stephen gave him a look somewhere between desperation and slight annoyance. "But it sounds like a good idea," Gabe added.

Inside, Bukowski's was a long narrow couple of rooms set up shotgun style. A row of small booths with windows looked down over the Mass Pike on one side, and a long wooden bar on the other side stretched the length of the place. Gabe followed Stephen to the end of the bar, and they took the last two stools. Gabe didn't even get to speak before Stephen ordered two shots of Jameson.

As the bartender nodded and got their drinks, Stephen grabbed Gabe's knee tightly under the bar.

"I want you to promise me two things before we head over," he said.

Gabe felt his stomach start to seize up. Stephen was never like this. "Sure. What?" he asked.

"First, if I want to go, we go," Stephen said with a dead serious look on his face. "No questions asked. We just leave. If I'm uncomfortable, I'll get all weird and have a hard time talking to people and probably spill a drink and knock something over."

Gabe felt himself almost laugh, not out of cruelty, but out of some deepening fondness for this guy who was so unlike anyone he had ever met. "No problem," he said.

The bartender set down the two shots in front of each of them. Stephen stared at the shot for a moment, and then he looked up at Gabe but said nothing.

"The second thing?"

Stephen took a deep breath. "The second thing is that I want you to let me know if I say anything stupid. Just give me a nudge or a look or something. I've been wracking my brain all day about what to say to a room full of cops, and I can't really think of anything. So if I start talking about something I'm not supposed to, let me know, okay?"

"Stephen," Gabe said, putting his arm around his neck. He could feel Stephen tense ever so slightly. "You're not going to say anything stupid. You're an amazing guy, and I'm loving getting to know you and spend time with you." He paused for a second, suddenly unsure where his own words were coming from. "In fact, I think I'm falling in love with you."

And there it was, Gabe thought to himself, a feeling of vulnerability settling over him. Where had that come from? Why did he say that? Of course he meant it, but saying it now would probably only make Stephen more nervous. Gabe half-expected Stephen to get up right then and walk out of the bar.

But he didn't. On the contrary, Gabe's words seemed to have a calming effect on Stephen. His face melted, the hard nervy creases in his forehead softened, and he parted his lips in a bright, full smile. "Me too," he said softly.

The two of them were silent for the next few seconds, as a happy awkwardness engulfed them both. A few feet away from them, the bartender coughed and nodded at them, raising a glass of something in their direction. He had obviously heard them. He didn't say anything, but his face was full of a kindness and warmth that made Gabe almost want to cry.

"Well, let's drink up then, shall we?" Gabe said.

Stephen nodded, and the two of them raised their glasses in return to the bartender, then swallowed the whiskey in one gulp. When they had finished, they put the glasses down on the counter and Stephen reached for his wallet. But the bartender shook his head. "It's on me, lads," he said, a strong Irish brogue shaping his words.

"Thank you," they both said at the same time.

"Okay," Stephen said. "Let's do this."

They arrived at The Pour House well after everyone else, which only made Gabe more self-conscious. As they walked through the door and over to the set of four tables reserved for the group of them, Gabe felt like the entire world was watching. Stephen seemed to have put all of his nerves aside. He walked confidently next to Gabe, close enough to brush his shoulder while they moved through the room, a gesture that implied a certain amount of intimacy without anything as shocking or explicit as handholding. Gabe reached down and touched his pinky to Stephen's, and he saw Stephen smile.

"Well, well," Ramirez said, approaching them and putting a hand on Gabe's shoulder. "We were beginning to think you two might have gotten lost."

Gabe chuckled brightly. "No, we were just taking our time getting here," he said.

"Good to see you again, Stephen," Ramirez said, reaching out a hand to him. "I can't believe you're still hanging out with this guy." He punched Gabe's shoulder gently. "You must feel sorry for him or something." But Ramirez's face seemed full of pride as he spoke. "I mean, that's why we keep him around at the station—that and all the weird noises he makes in the squad car keep us entertained."

"Easy, partner." Gabe clapped him on the back. "Don't go telling any of my secrets. You'll scare him away."

"I doubt that," Stephen said, looking first at Gabe and then at Ramirez. "I'm all ears." Stephen laughed. "But first I think I need a beer."

"All right, that's what I like to hear." Ramirez steered them over toward the table he was sitting at. "Come on over to my table. I want you to meet my wife."

Gabe watched Stephen sail off into the crowd, with Ramirez eager to show him around. The group was remarkable only in how unremarkable a gathering it was. Gabe had imagined stares and snickers laced with comments of barely civil greetings and quick dismissals. He had expected the group of officers to keep a cold distance from him and Stephen. But he could not have been more wrong.

He watched as Ramirez introduced Stephen first to his wife, and then to a few others. As the evening progressed, Gabe and Stephen moved around the room, engaging everyone in conversation.

Sometimes Stephen stayed next to Gabe and sometimes he talked to Ramirez or someone else. Indeed, the evening passed in back slaps and laughter that almost overwhelmed Gabe with a feeling of gratefulness he didn't think he could feel toward this group. For the first time in his life, he felt truly accepted.

DINNER WITH THE PARENTS

Stephen finally decided to tell his parents about Gabe when he'd found himself unable to say very much during their weekly calls. They must have known something had been up with him for a while, because they kept asking questions about how he'd been spending his time and if he had been going out a lot.

Stephen had planned a variety of ways to share the information. In one scenario, he had them driving down to a meeting in Boston where he would surprise them with an in-person meeting with Gabe at a public place, like a restaurant or café. In another scenario, he wrote it in an email where he could explain everything all at once without having to see the reactions on their faces.

Travis listened patiently to all of Stephen's schemes, gently rolling his eyes at each and every one of them.

"Just call them up and tell them, Stephen. They're not going to care that you're seeing a guy," he said. "They're just going to care that you waited this long to tell them. That's what they're going to be hurt about."

Sure enough, Travis had been dead on.

When Stephen finally placed *the call*, his father answered the phone. After a few minutes of chitchat about work and the weather, Stephen said, "So, Dad, I'm kind of seeing someone."

"Oh yeah?" His father's voice gone a little higher, a tone of pleased surprise resonating from the other end of the phone. "Really? Well, Stephen, tell me about this person. No, wait." He abruptly stopped. "Let me get your mother. Hold on. We'll put you on speaker phone."

The phone went silent for a few seconds except for the rustling of his father's hand over the mouthpiece. Stephen waited, his stomach doing somersaults inside him. Finally his father pressed the button for the speaker phone. "Okay, Stevie," he said. "We're both here now."

"Hi Stephen," his mother said. "Your dad tells me you've met someone. We want all the details."

"Well, Dad, Mom…" Stephen hesitated for just a second before plunging forward. "Well, guys, his name is Gabe."

"Oh." His father's response was followed by a long few seconds of silence.

"His name?" His mother asked.

Stephen pictured them in their kitchen back in New Hampshire, leaning over the counter, practically on top of the telephone the way they always did when they used the ancient speakerphone.

"Yeah. It's Gabriel, actually…but everyone calls him Gabe." Stephen couldn't think of anything else to say just then. "He's…Well, he's a policeman." He put his hand to his forehead as he listened to his own voice.

"Oh, well…That's great, Stephen." His father let out a short laugh. "Now I guess we don't have to worry about you being safe down there in the middle of that city."

"A police officer?" His mom said the words with a little bit of awe in her voice. "Wow. What's he like?"

And then Stephen laughed too. Not because the question was funny, but because that had been the question. In one quick phrase, his mom and dad had confirmed that they didn't care Stephen was seeing a guy. They only cared about the person.

"He's great," Stephen eventually managed to reply. "I want you guys to come down and meet him soon."

A week later Stephen looked around the table of a small Italian restaurant on Hanover Street, at the faces of the people he loved the most. Except for Travis, they were all there, squished together in the tiny restaurant his mother had read about in one of her foodie magazines. It had taken forever to get seated, and the tables were packed as tightly as possible into the restaurant. But it had been worth it to see the look on her face when they sat down.

"So, how did you two meet?" Stephen's mom was the first to dive into the details almost as soon as they were seated.

Gabe reached over and put his hand on Stephen's knee under the table, patting it gently before removing back to his own lap.

"We—ah…" Stephen and Gabe spoke at the same time. Stephen looked up at Gabe and silently nodded at him.

"We met playing pool," Gabe said.

"Pool?" Stephen's dad looked first at Gabe, then back to Stephen. "I didn't know you played pool, Stephen. It seems like you've picked up a lot of new activities since you've moved here."

Gabe chuckled but seemed to realize too late that it might be inappropriate. An uncomfortable silence settled at the table, and the air felt like it had taken on a weight of its own. The four adults sat looking at each other until, a few seconds later, the entire table erupted in laughter all at once and Gabe turned a deep shade of crimson. At that moment any tension at the table had dissipated as a warmth set in and Stephen finally relaxed into the evening.

"Actually, he hasn't made a lot of headway in pool. He mostly went with Travis that evening to keep him company. The two of them showed up while I was playing after a tough shift, and we struck up a conversation while Travis almost ran the table on me."

Stephen chimed in. "He's being modest. He beat Travis by a mile, or whatever the equivalent in pool is supposed to be."

"I can't imagine losing made Travis very happy." His mom smirked and everyone chuckled.

"No, it sure didn't," Gabe said, a knowing tone in his voice.

"Stephen tells us you're on the police force."

"Stephen." Mrs. Davis addressed her husband by his first name, but both the father and son looked at her. "Let the boy order something to eat before we drill him with more questions."

"No," Gabe protested. "It's all right. I don't mind. I'd want to know a lot more if I were you, too." He arched an eyebrow sideways at Stephen.

Stephen's mom smiled and nodded, putting her menu back down on the table.

"Yes, I'm a police officer," Gabe said. "With the Boston Police Department. I'm a patrolman."

"That's wonderful," Mr. Davis said. "Is it something you always wanted to do?"

Gabe nodded. "Yes, sir. Ever since I was a kid. I got my bachelor's degree in Criminal Justice and applied to BPD as soon as I turned twenty-one."

Stephen's mom reached across the table to take Gabe's hand. "It sounds really dangerous. Do you ever get shot at?"

Stephen gave his mom a quick look.

"Oh, sorry," she said. "I don't mean to be morbid. We're so excited to meet you." She hesitated, seeming to search for the right words. "Let us know if we're asking too many questions. This whole thing is a little new to us, Stephen has never invited us to meet someone he's seeing."

"Yes, it is a little dangerous, but we're always very careful," Gabe said. "And it's quite all right. Ask away."

She looked over at Stephen and then back at Gabe and beamed the brightest smile she could at him. "In that case, tell us all about yourself. What do you like to do? What kind of music do you listen to? What are your favorite sports teams? We want to know all about you."

Gabe looked back at her with a glint of amusement in his eyes and let out a soft laugh. "Okay," he said. "But I don't know where to start Mrs. Davis."

"Please," she said as she patted his arm. "My name is June." She pointed to her husband. "And you can call him Stephen. Or Stephen Senior, if it makes you more comfortable."

"Okay Mrs.—June," Gabe said. "I love the Celtics, Bruins, Red Sox, and Patriots. When I'm not working, I am into exercise and playing pool. I like a lot of movies and…," Gabe searched the air above his head for other things to say. "Oh, and I'm technically Catholic, but I don't really go to church much. I come from a big family. My dad was a doctor. And I'm a cop because I want to make the world a safer place."

"That sounds wonderful," June said.

They ordered after almost twenty minutes of conversation, and the rest of the evening went pretty much the same way as the beginning of the night. By the time the meal was over, they had covered just about everything from Gabe's kindergarten years all the way up through his rookie year on the police force.

Stephen watched as Gabe sighed and put the napkin on his lap. Stephen felt a yawn start to come over him, and he tried unsuccessfully to stifle it. It was still early, but the combination of too much food and a couple glasses of wine had started to make him drowsy. He looked out the window onto Hanover Street. In the fading light of dusk, tourists were heading to and from dinner and a few grey old men and polyester bedizened women, trudged home with bags of groceries, getting ready for the Sabbath.

Later that evening, they left the restaurant and headed toward the parking garage where Stephen's parents had left their car. Stephen's father walked alongside Gabe, the two of them exchanging a few words about the Red Sox and their chances at the pennant. Gabe noticed Stephen's father's pace was slower than the rest of the group, and it wasn't long before they were behind Stephen and his mom by about ten yards.

"I hope we weren't too bad tonight," he said. "We pelted you with a thousand questions. I hope it didn't feel like we were giving you the tenth degree."

Gabe nodded. "It's okay. I know this must all be pretty much a surprise to you."

"No," Stephen Senior shook his head. "The thing is," Stephen's father continued. "It's not really that much of a surprise. We honestly thought that he was different as far back as high school. Then he had a thing in college with Melanie or whatever her name was…" he stopped. "But we don't care that he's seeing a man. We all went through accepting that a long time ago with Travis. I shouldn't say accepting, but…"

"I know what you mean," Gabe said, trying to ease the conversation a little bit.

"It's just that there is one thing I want to ask of you." Stephen's father stopped for a second and stood still on the sidewalk. Gabe stopped with him, and he could feel the weight of the situation increase.

"Yeah?" Gabe looked up at him.

"Don't do anything careless, please. Don't do anything to hurt him."

Gabe nodded. "I won't. I promise."

"He's still my little boy." Stephen Senior looked directly at Gabe as if he wanted to be absolutely certain he was heard. "He's the most important thing in the world to me and June." He paused again. "Just be careful with his heart, okay?"

Gabe continued nodding while Stephen Senior spoke.

"I mean it," Stephen Senior said. "Be good to him. Please..." The man's voice trailed off. Gabe could tell he wasn't used to making this kind of request.

Gabe nodded solemnly. "Don't worry, I'll have a careful heart."

MEETING BENSON

Travis, Stephen, their two sets of parents and Gabe walked in silence from Beacon Hill to the Financial District, or FiDi, as Travis liked to call it. They were heading to The Mint, an upscale bar on the waterfront, where they were meeting Benson after a late day at the office. Travis had orchestrated the meeting shortly after Stephen had his parents down to meet Gabe. But, unlike Stephen, Travis had expanded the group to include his best friend and Gabe.

Travis led the pack, and Gabe let his mind wander as he fell into step beside Stephen. He could hear Travis telling the story of how he and Benson had met. Travis was enthusiastic, but Gabe was picking something up in his voice. He couldn't put his finger on it, but it was off.

"I can't believe this," June said to Sarah, Travis's mom. "We were just down here a few weeks ago to meet Gabe, and now this. It seems like these two have done everything together."

"I know," Sarah said. "Burt and I have been looking forward to meeting this Benson character ever since we heard about him." She smiled and looked over at her husband.

Travis glowed. "You're going to love him," he said, and Gabe noticed his pace speeding up just a little bit.

Stephen was silent as they walked, and Gabe could feel the tension emanating from him the closer they got to The Mint. He nudged Stephen's shoulder a little bit. Gabe winked at him. Stephen smiled in return and seemed to relax just a little bit.

"Have you met him, Stevie?" June said.

"Oh yeah," Stephen said. "He's great. Very successful and handsome."

Travis looked back at Stephen with a thankful smile of approval and maybe something like pride.

The Mint had been an old bank before becoming one of the swankest bars in Boston. Whoever had done the redevelopment had kept much of the original building intact. Art deco columns arched up toward twenty-foot high ceilings. The columns themselves were gold, inlaid with stylized Greek or Roman soldiers trotting off to war with spears and chariots. Gabe noticed they had suddenly fallen silent when they entered the bar. Gabe found the forced elegance of the place oppressive, but everyone else seemed impressed.

"It's quite a nice place, isn't it," Stephen's mother whispered to him as they waited for Travis to locate Benson.

Gabe nodded and smiled, holding back what he really wanted to say.

Stephen leaned over and whispered into his other ear. "You hate it, don't you?"

Gabe just smiled and looked straight ahead, keeping his eyes focused on Travis as he wandered around the restaurant. He knew he would start to giggle if he looked at Stephen.

After a few minutes, Travis came back to collect them. He had located Benson, who had arrived ahead of them and was already sitting at a table by the bar. When they walked over, Benson stood up and leaned in to kiss Mrs. Gaines once on each cheek as they were introduced. He took Mr. Gaines's hand and gave it a hearty shake as he introduced himself. Gabe thought the greeting was artificial, but the Gaines ate it up hook, line, and sinker. The Davis's stood by and watched until it was their turn for handshakes and kisses. Benson then turned to Stephen and gave him a warm look, followed by a mechanical embrace that made Gabe's skin crawl just a little bit.

"This is Gabe," Stephen said as he emerged from the hug. "My boyfriend."

Benson reached out his hand "Gabe, good to meet you. Travis has mentioned you before."

Gabe took his hand and they shook. "Nice to meet you, too," Gabe said, trying to match the warmth in Benson's voice. But even as they shook hands, Gabe felt a tiny warning somewhere in the back of his mind. Benson was too smooth, too polished, too perfect; Gabe had the feeling someone else was behind the smooth exterior. But he pushed that out of his mind. Tonight was neither the time nor the place to make things awkward.

Benson finally let go of his hand and turned back toward the rest of the group. "Please, everyone, sit down," he said, his voice like silk. "I'm so glad to meet you all. Mr. and Mrs. Gaines, Travis speaks about you all the time. I love listening to him talk about his little hometown in the woods of New Hampshire. He makes it sound like you live in a Robert Frost poem."

"Please," Travis's mom said, "call us Sarah and Burt. Mr. and Mrs. Gaines sounds a little like we're in a parent-teacher conference."

Gabe mostly managed to stifle a chuckle, but he wasn't completely successful and Stephen shot him a deadly look across the table. Nobody else seemed to notice.

"So, what do you do, exactly?" Burt said. "Travis tells us you're in charge of one of the divisions at the company you guys work for."

"Yes," Sarah added. "Travis says you pretty much run the place."

"Well, I wouldn't say that exactly." Benson looked at Travis, and the two of them locked eyes, Benson smiling and winking at Travis. "I've been there for a long time. But let's not talk about work. Travis is lucky he doesn't have to sit in on a lot of the more tedious meetings."

"And when I do sit in on a meeting, it's usually to take notes or get coffee," Travis said.

Benson shook his head benevolently. "That won't be for very long," he said. "This guy is one of our rising stars. He'll be on the management team before he knows it."

The comment had the desired effect on Travis's parents. They cooed, almost in unison as Gabe looked on in tight-lipped silence. He felt Stephen's hand on his knee and Gabe tried to warm up his expression. The conversation was off to a syrupy start, but it felt wrong to him. He watched the faces around the table, the Gaines more alert and focused than they had been all night. And Travis was glowing as Benson won over his parents with the ease and grace of a lobbyist working a room full of politicians.

Oh well, Gabe thought, *this isn't so bad.* He sat silently and listened as the group ordered drinks, and the conversation played itself into a string of things that people want to say and hear. He nursed his beer and nodded his head when called upon to do so until the end of the night when Benson picked up the check and the entire party meandered slowly out through the art deco restaurant onto the street. They all shook hands and hugged and kissed, but Gabe was quietly eager to be going.

2012

Moving Out and Moving On

Another year passed, and with it went all the quotidian events that mark the cadence of time. The frigid winter finally gave way to a wet spring. Boston expelled a deep sigh of relief as the cold Arctic winds turned to warm spring breezes. Then summer was upon the city in all its sweltering brutality. Newbury Street was full of life. Tourists in tee shirts and tank tops crowded the street, and the restaurants all set up their sidewalk tables for the season. They showed outdoor movies on the Boston Common and had festivals in all of the parks. The Hatch Shell featured a spectacular season of concerts on the banks of the Charles River.

Stephen spent more and more time at Gabe's apartment. As they emerged from those early days of their relationship where a new couple spends time by themselves, Stephen grew to know Gabe's circle of friends.

Travis and Stephen spent less and less time together. The friendship that had been an almost twenty-four seven relationship for most of their lives, gradually loosened and evolved into a bond that existed more *in absentia*. They saw each other for maybe one or two nights a week and briefly for the occasional morning they were both in the apartment.

Every year at the end of August, all the apartment leases in Boston expire, throwing the city into a chaos of frantic transition and clogging the twisted web of roadways with moving vans and pickup trucks piled high with cardboard boxes, mattresses, bed springs, and various forms of IKEA furniture. After two years in the apartment together, Travis and Stephen decided not to renew the lease.

Gabe helped Stephen as he sorted through two years' worth of stuff at the apartment. Some of it they threw out, but most of it went into boxes. Gabe's apartment was small and he didn't have a lot of storage space. Stephen's parents had reluctantly agreed to store some of his things in their basement, so Gabe drove him up with a stack of boxes stuffed into the back of his little Jeep Wrangler.

"So this is where you grew up?" Gabe said as he pulled off the interstate in Northern Vermont. The Jeep shuddered a little as Gabe downshifted and let out the clutch.

"Not exactly," Stephen said. He had been staring out the window for the last few miles. The Jeep didn't have air conditioning, so they had driven most of the way with the windows open, getting wind-blown and buffeted. This far north, the air had cooled down a little, but it was still thick with the grassy smells of late summer. "It's about another forty-five minutes from here. Go left at the end of the off ramp and then go straight for ten miles."

"Ten miles?"

"Yeah," Stephen said, a smile on his face. "And then we'll come to a little town. Go through that, take a right, and drive another twenty miles. Then we're just about there."

"Wow. You really do live in the middle of nowhere."

"Told you."

The rush of the wind made it difficult to talk much, so they spent the rest of the drive in silence. Stephen was secretly glad for the quiet. It gave him the space to gaze out at the landscape of dairy farms and rolling hills with a slight twinge of nostalgia. He had left these hills and fields years ago for college, and he'd never truly been back for more than a few weeks here and there.

"You okay?" Gabe finally said.

"Yeah. I guess."

"Uh-huh." Gabe sighed. "What's on your mind?"

"Nothing really. It's just…that it's a big step, us moving in together."

"Oh, that." Gabe looked briefly at Stephen then back out at the road in front of them. "Are you having second thoughts?" Stephen thought he could detect the faintest edge in Gabe's voice.

"Well, don't you think it's kind of a big step?" Stephen forced a brighter tone as he continued. "I mean, I think it's the right thing to do. I'm happy we're moving in together. But we're not really moving in together. I'm moving in with you. Your place, your stuff. It's a little weird for me."

"Yeah, I guess I understand that," said Gabe. "But it makes sense. Beacon Hill is more central, and we both like it there more than we do in the Fenway. If we were to go out and look for a new apartment, it would be a lot more expensive." Gabe reached over and grabbed Stephen's knee playfully. "Are you nervous about bringing me home?"

"What? No. It's not like we've got anything at the house to hide from a police officer."

Gabe laughed. "That's not what I meant."

Stephen looked back out the window, and silence filled the cab again as the rode on.

"It's going to be okay, you know," Gabe said.

"What's going to be okay?"

"Everything. They're going to be fine with you storing a few boxes with them. And it's going to be okay moving in with me." Gabe looked over at Stephen, making eye contact for a few brief seconds before looking back to the road in front of them. "In fact, I'm really excited about it."

"You are?" Stephen said, a note of caution in his voice.

"Yeah, of course I am. And I'm sorry if I didn't let you know that," Gabe said. "I'm looking forward to sharing more of my life with you."

Stephen reached over and took Gabe's hand. He squeezed tightly for the rest of the ride, letting go only for the brief intervals when he had to shift.

❖

Travis's phone buzzed. He could hear it clearly in the silence of the apartment, even though it was all the way in the other room. He was supposed to be packing, but he hadn't really been into it. He filled about three boxes with books and clothes and basically anything he didn't want to throw out. He cursed himself for not going back to New Hampshire with Stephen. At the time, it hadn't looked like he had much stuff to pack, but looks had been deceiving. He was moving in with Benson at the end of the month. While Benson's sleek waterfront condo had three bedrooms, he really didn't have a place for Travis's fifteen boxes of stuff. He'd have to ask his parents to come down and pick some of it up.

The phone buzzed again, and he pulled himself off the bed and went out to the living room where he'd left his phone. "Hello," he said as he swiped the green arrow on the bottom of the screen.

"Hey handsome." The voice on the other end of the line was smooth and crisp with a hint of a clenched-teeth Back Bay accent to it.

"Benson," Travis smiled.

"What do you say about letting me in? I'm down here, but the buzzer doesn't seem to be working."

"You're here? As in, at my apartment?"

"Yeah," Benson said. "I wanted to surprise you. Come down and let me in."

"Okay. I'll be right down."

Travis walked down the stairs and out toward the tiny front lobby of the apartment building. But he stopped in his tracks when he rounded the corner and saw Benson on the other side of the clear glass door, down on one knee with a huge bouquet of long-stem red roses. Travis brought his hands to his face and stared for a few seconds. He could feel the tears starting to form in the corners of his eyes, and his stomach scrunched up with instant butterflies.

He took the last few tentative steps toward the door and swung it open. Benson looked up at him and smiled.

"I know this has been kind of an emotional time," Benson said. "Moving in together is a big step."

Travis nodded his head but didn't say anything.

"But," Benson continued, "I am ready for more." He stopped for a second, cleared his throat, and produced a small box from his pants pocket. He clicked open the box to reveal a diamond infinity band. "Travis, will you marry me?"

Travis stood there, stunned. His feet suddenly didn't feel like they were touching anything. He felt lightheaded, like he couldn't catch his breath. He couldn't say anything.

Benson stayed down on his knee. After a few minutes of the silence, he began to look around. "Travis?"

Travis's eyes suddenly blinked to life. He realized fully what was happening. This man who had everything, who he'd fantasized about was asking to marry him. Travis was twenty-six that year, and Benson was in his late thirties. Travis wondered for a second what the rest of his life would be like with Benson, or worse, without him. All of this flashed through his mind as Benson knelt on the stoop of his soon-to-be-vacated apartment. Somewhere in the back of his mind, the memories of a few times where Benson had lost it also flashed. He remembered the fists, the pain in his arms as Benson gripped his forearms, the fear he'd felt at the moment when Benson had exploded. But Travis pushed those memories to the back of his brain.

"Yes," Travis said. "Yes, I would love to marry you, Benny." He knelt down on the stoop and kissed Benson, letting the door close behind him and locking them both out of the building.

"Who is the Ghost?" Gabe stood staring at the corkboard over Stephen's desk in his childhood bedroom.

"What?" Stephen wasn't sure if he'd heard him correctly. He stood up from the bed, where he'd been sitting and sorting through an old box of toys. His parents had told him he could store his extra boxes in the basement, but he would also have to sort through his room and pack most of that stuff away.

"The Ghost? Who is the Ghost?"

"Oh," Stephen looked up to see Gabe reading one of the high school graduation cards that he'd pinned to his board years ago. "It's nothing. It's what Travis used to call me in high school. Actually up until about a year or so ago, really."

"Why the Ghost? Were you spooky or something?"

"No." Stephen laughed. "I was a wallflower. I was afraid to speak in groups. I was really, really shy. And, well, Travis was the complete opposite."

"So he called you the Ghost?"

"Yeah, because I was so quiet he said most people couldn't see me unless I spoke up."

"I never really think about you as shy…"

Stephen laughed. "That's funny. I almost didn't call you back that first time because of how shy I was."

"You didn't. You texted me." Gabe raised his eyebrows.

"Oh, well." Stephen shrugged. "That was an accomplishment for me. I'm usually petrified to even do that."

"How did you manage to outgrow it?"

"I'm not sure I ever did. I mean, I'm pretty quiet in general. You seem to have brought me a little out of my shell." Stephen stepped over to Gabe and kissed him lightly on the lips.

"I can't imagine what it must be like to have the same friend for your entire life," said Gabe.

"Oh, you mean Travis? Yeah, I guess it's not exactly your average friendship when you think about it from the outside, but it's always been important for me. I imagine it must be what having a brother is like. You don't have friends like that from Watertown?"

"No." Gabe shook his head. "Not really. I have a few friends I ran track and cross country with in high school, but we really don't stay in touch. I think we're friends on Facebook, but that's all." He looked out the window at the river and the woods beyond.

"What about from college or the Academy?"

"Well yeah," Gabe said. "But that hardly counts as long term." He smiled. "I'm not that old, Stephen."

Stephen's phone buzzed. "Speak of the devil," he said before tapping on the green button pulsing on the device's screen. "Hey Travis."

He cradled the phone against his face. "Wow. Oh…wow." Stephen held on to the phone but had to sit down. "No, that's great," he said, struggling to keep his voice upbeat. "It's…" He looked across the room at Gabe, thankful he just had to listen to Travis talk. "Are you sure?"

"Who's that?" Gabe whispered.

"Yeah, congrats Travis. That's great, I guess. It just seems so fast. Are you sure you want to do this? Okay, okay, okay. I'm not trying to be a Debbie Downer. I'd love to be your best man." Stephen kept his voice steady and artificially bright.

"What?!" Gabe didn't even bother to whisper.

Stephen covered the phone and scowled at him. "Okay, see you soon. No, it's fine. I know you have to go. Can I tell the parents?" Stephen paused. "Okay, I'll wait until I hear from you."

He clicked the phone off and set it down on the bedside table, a stunned look on his face.

"Tell me that conversation was not what I think it was about."

"That was Travis."

"I figured that much." Gabe stepped over to the bed and sat down beside Stephen. "And?"

"And Benson…He just proposed to Travis." Stephen felt a wave of nausea pass through his stomach.

Gabe put his arm around Stephen's shoulder. "That's good, isn't it?"

"He wants me to be his best man," Stephen said blankly.

"As you should be. Who else would he choose for that role?"

"He and Benson want to have us over for a dinner this week to celebrate," Stephen said. He looked up at Gabe and shook his head. "I hope this is going to be all right."

"What do you mean? Of course it's going to be all right." Gabe tried to sound upbeat. "This is a great thing. They both love each other, right?"

"I guess," Stephen said. He had never told Gabe about the bruises he'd seen on Travis, about the tears and the confused apologies. "I'm just worried about him."

Gabe raised an eyebrow. "You're worried? Why? Is there something going on there?"

"No." Stephen shook his head. "No, there's nothing."

"Look," Gabe said. "I know you're going through a lot. Moving out of that apartment with him has to be a little bit like moving away from home for the first time, but this sounds like really good news."

"I guess so," Stephen said. What he didn't say was that he suddenly felt helpless.

Gabe gently folded Stephen into a full hug. The two of them sat like that for several minutes until they heard Stephen's mom at the foot of the stairs.

"Stephen," she called up.

"Yeah Mom?"

"Dinner will be ready in a few minutes. You and Gabe want to come down?"

"Sure Mom, we'll be down in a little bit."

THE WEDDING

Benson Harvey and Travis Gaines were married on a crisp September morning over a year later, when the air smelled of the first hints of autumn and all of New England was just starting to forget the hot and humid days of summer. Since that dinner in the Financial District, Gabe had only seen the couple a few times. Stephen and Travis had arranged a couple of double-dates—once right before Christmas for drinks before Travis and Stephen headed home to New Hampshire for the holidays and a second time when they tried to make a Red Sox game work. On both occasions, Gabe and Benson just didn't seem to click. After the baseball game, Travis and Stephen decided their significant others weren't going to get along. It just wasn't going to happen.

The wedding took place at King's Chapel, filling the white wood-paneled church to capacity with friends and family. Stephen was part of the wedding party and stood up beside Travis as his best man.

The ceremony was blissfully short, and the reception afterward was at Locke-Ober's, the private club where Benson and Travis had had their first conversation at the company holiday party years earlier.

"What's the matter, Stephen?" Gabe said. They were sitting alone at their table after the meal had concluded and most of the guests were up on the dance floor. "You've looked sick to your stomach all night."

"It's nothing." Stephen shrugged and smiled faintly. "I'm just a little tired, I guess."

"Uh-huh," Gabe said quietly. He rested his eyes on Stephen for a few seconds. He looked as if he was going to pursue the line of questioning, but he changed the subject. "You know, I always wondered what it was like inside this place," he said.

"Oh yeah?" Stephen tried to judge the look on Gabe's face. He seemed far away, his eyes unfocused and his lips slightly parted as if he were almost asleep. "And what do you think now that you're inside of it?"

"I think it's like a lot of things in life. It looks like it's really something from the outside. It's all shrouded in mystery and allure, mostly because you can't get into it. But once you do, bam. You're met with the plain old bland truth of it."

"Yeah?" Stephen watched his face.

"Yeah. And that plain old bland truth is that there is nothing inside you couldn't find anywhere else. It was all the mystery that made it seem like something else. It ends up being a broken promise."

Stephen reached over and took his hand. "Come on, Gabe, it's not that bad."

"Tell me something, Stephen." Gabe squeezed his hand gently. "Is this what you would want?"

Stephen paused for a second before he spoke. "What do you mean? This place?"

"The whole thing." Gabe waved around the room, gesturing out to the crowd and beyond. "This type of ceremony, this type of reception, all the crazy over-the-top formality of all of this?"

Stephen took a deep breath. "Well, I don't think this is the kind of wedding I would want."

Gabe let out a long sigh. "That's a relief, because I would never, ever want anything like all this." He unpinned the boutonniere he'd had on his lapel since that morning.

"But if you're asking me if I want to get married, that's another question altogether, and I'm not giving you an answer until I'm properly asked." Stephen squeezed Gabe's hand in reciprocation. "And before you even think about it, it's bad luck to ask that kind of question at someone else's wedding."

"Who said I was thinking of asking that?" Gabe smiled and Stephen shook his head. "Seriously though," Gabe continued. "I hope it works out for them."

MIDNIGHT CONFESSIONS

Stephen, what's going on?" Gabe sat up in bed. It was quarter past two in the morning, and the soft light from the streetlamp outside his apartment cast a blue glow over everything in the bedroom.

"You're awake?" Stephen looked up at him.

"Of course I'm awake. You've been rolling around all night. What's the matter?"

"Nothing," he sighed. "It's nothing, just a bunch of stuff going on at work."

Gabe shook his head and got out of bed, pulling a tee shirt from the floor and putting it on.

"Where are you going?" Stephen said, sitting up.

"Come on. If we're not going to sleep, then we're going to talk. I'll make some tea."

"Tea?"

"Yes, Stephen, tea. I'm Irish. It's what we do when people need to talk. We make a pot of tea and sit across the table from one another until the one who needs to talk starts saying whatever it is he needs to say."

Stephen smiled sleepily. "I bet it works great as an interrogation tactic. No wonder your people got most of their island back."

"Quit trying to be funny. I'm putting the kettle on, and you're getting your ass out of bed."

"Gabe, babe, come on back to bed. It's two in the morning."

"It's two fifteen, and believe me, I don't want to be out of bed at all, but you're not going to sleep until you get whatever this is off your chest. That means I'm not going to sleep. So, you've got five minutes to make it out of that bed while I make a pot."

Stephen laid his head back down on the pillow and rubbed his face with the palms of his hands. "Okay," he finally said, rolling out of the bed and following him to the tiny alcove of a kitchen. He sat silently and watched as Gabe filled the kettle with tap water and placed it on the stove.

"It's herbal tea," Gabe said, as if reading Stephen's mind. "No caffeine."

Stephen nodded as Gabe pulled a tin canister down from the cabinet. He fished out two teabags, setting them into a white teapot. He made the tea, waited a few minutes for it to steep, then set the teapot and two cups out in front of Stephen on the kitchen table. Gabe sat down across from Stephen and poured.

"Now spill it," he said, lifting the cup up to his face and blowing gently on it.

Stephen smiled a sleepy smile. "Gabe, I wish I could, but I can't really talk about it."

"Okay," he said. "You can't talk about it. Talk about it anyway. I'll help. It's not about work, so let's cross that off right from the start."

Stephen shook his head. "No, it's not about work."

"It's not about your parents."

"How do you know it's not about my parents?"

"Because you come from the perfect little family, and you talk about them all the time. If there was a problem, it would be running across your lips like a deep breath."

He put a hand over his cup of tea, warming himself. "You're good."

"So you're seeing someone else?"

"What? No!" He almost dropped his hand into the tea.

"Then what is it, Stephen? We're supposed to be able to talk about stuff, and you keeping things from me like this makes me feel like something's wrong."

He hesitated for a moment. "Gabe, what if I needed to tell you something you might not want to hear? About Travis."

"Stephen, what is the matter?"

"Gabe, I need to tell you something, but you can't hear it like a cop." He hesitated before going on. "Can you promise me that?"

Gabe waited a few minutes. "I guess so," he finally said.

"It's about Benson," Stephen said. "Sometimes he gets rough with Travis when he drinks."

"How rough?"

"I don't know exactly. Travis won't talk about it anymore. Things got pretty bad a while back, and they broke up. A little over a month later, they started going out again, and then Travis came home with bruises on his arm. He told me not to worry about it, that he could handle things. I should have said something when they got engaged, but I just couldn't bring myself to disrupt things. He wanted so badly to be happy."

"Bruises? How bad were they?"

Stephen pursed his lips and tilted his head to one side. "They were pretty bad," he said. "I tried to talk to him about things, but he didn't want to discuss it."

"That's why you were so shaken up after the wedding." Gabe put a hand to his forehead. "Stephen, we have to do something about this," Gabe said.

Stephen shook his head. "No. He made me promise I wouldn't tell anyone."

"That's not the right thing to do, Stephen. If this Benson guy is hurting him, it's domestic abuse. How often has this happened?"

"Just a few times, as far as I know."

Gabe looked away from Stephen, a glazed look on his face. "Stephen, you know I am bound by law to report this."

"No," Stephen reached across the table and placed a hand on top of Gabe's hands. "You can't. You said you wouldn't."

"I took an oath," Gabe said. "I wear a badge, Stephen."

"You made a promise." Stephen took a deep breath. "You made a promise to me."

"What are we gaining by not helping Travis out here?" Gabe folded his hands around Stephen's. "I know you think the world of him, but if the guy he's just married is showing a pattern of this kind of behavior, it's not going to change by sitting on the sidelines and not doing anything."

"I'll talk to him tomorrow," Stephen said. "I'll try to get him to do something."

Stephen gave Gabe's hands a squeeze, then pulled them back and took a sip of his tea.

A Searching River Run

Gabe looked out over the Boston skyline, then across the Charles River at the spot where he and Stephen had first kissed. He focused on his breathing and consciously listened to each stride, the crushed stone trail crunching beneath his feet. He sprinted ahead and counted to ten, running as fast as he could, then slowing down again into his stride.

"Hey man, ease up," Ramirez called out as he trotted along behind him, gasping for air. "Why are you pushing so hard today?" He could barely get the words out.

"I don't know." Gabe jogged in place for a moment and waited for his partner to catch up. He had been pushing it for all eight miles of the run. His body ached, and his lungs felt like they were going to explode.

"You always do this when you got something on your mind." Ramirez caught up to him but kept the pace slow. "What's going on?"

Gabe shook his head. Even the pain of the run wasn't enough to clear his mind. He kept replaying the conversation with Stephen from the night before. "It's nothing," Gabe mumbled as they moved in step along the path. "Just some stupid conversation I can't stop thinking about."

"Well, go ahead," Ramirez said. "You know you're going to say it anyway, so don't make me drag it out of you."

"It's kind of a delicate subject."

"So?" Ramirez huffed out the word as he struggled to breathe and run.

Gabe paused to think about how he could put things without giving away any of the detail. "Well, what if you knew someone was being roughed up by their spouse?"

Ramirez looked over at Gabe, then down at the ground in front of them again as he kept moving. "Oh man, that's a tough one," he said. "Do you know her? Do you know what the situation is?"

"It's not a her, it's a he," Gabe said, lowering his voice as if conveying a secret.

"It's a same sex relationship? Two men?"

"Yep."

"I think I'd try to talk to the victim," Ramirez said. "I'd try to let him know what services are available. I'd want to help. I know we're supposed to report it, but you really can't do much until that person wants out of the relationship."

They jogged along in silence, looking out over the river as the sun sparkled on the water.

"The problem is," Ramirez continued, "these relationships usually fall off everyone's radar."

"These relationships?"

"Yeah," Ramirez said. "Abuse in any relationship is bad. But the truth is, it's way more common in gay relationships. Almost a third of people in same-sex relationships get roughed up by their partner."

"What?" Gabe unintentionally started to speed up again. "That can't be right."

"Whoa, whoa, whoa, no speeding up there Steve Prefontaine," Ramirez said. "And yeah, it's a high number. But abuse in straight relationships is pretty bad too. It happens in about a quarter of heterosexual relationships. The patterns are similar in straight and gay abuse cases though. It's both emotional and physical abuse, and the abuse is usually pretty hard to see from outside the relationship. A big part of the problem in gay abuse cases is that nobody takes it seriously, including the police. They figure two guys in a relationship can stick up for themselves. They're on even footing."

Gabe said nothing.

"Brennan, Stephen's not...?" Ramirez didn't finish the sentence.

Gabe stopped dead in his tracks when he realized what the question was.

"Because I'll kill the fucker," Ramirez said, his voice rising as he stopped and faced Gabe straight on, sweat dripping down his forehead.

"No, no, no," Gabe said, trying to stifle a laugh. "No, we're fine. Stephen is fine and he's not..." But Gabe couldn't say the words. "I mean, we're fine." He shook his head, finally letting out a chuckle.

"Why are you laughing?" Ramirez's voice was dead serious. "If there is something going on, you've got to tell me about it, Brennan."

"No," Gabe said, matching his tone. "I promise you, we're fine. And thank you, Ramirez. That means a lot to me."

They were still a few miles from home, on the Cambridge side of the river, but the run had already been a long one. Gabe turned off the jogging trail and approached a grassy area dotted with a few cherry trees, across the river from the Boston University Campus. It was autumn, but they were still green with leaves and they threw spots of afternoon shade. It had been too long since the last mowing, and it had an unkempt luster. Ramirez followed him, and the two of them sat down almost at the same second, landing on the soft grass. Gabe inhaled deeply, the scent of grass filling his nose as he pulled his left foot back against his butt and leaned forward to stretch.

"You seem to know a lot about this," Gabe said. "How come?"

"I had a case a few years back before you came along," Ramirez said. He sat with his legs out in front of him, but he didn't bother to stretch. "Two guys in an apartment on Hancock Street. One just about killed the other in a fight. Social services got involved, and the LGBT Domestic Violence Project stepped in. Everyone was trying to help these guys—well, at least the one who was getting beaten up."

"What happened?" Gabe asked.

"It was tough. He didn't want to talk to anyone really. He was embarrassed—actually, I think he was both embarrassed and scared shitless his partner would find him and kill him if he reported the abuse. But Brennan..." Ramirez shook his head, his words drying up.

"What?"

"Brennan, you do realize how lucky you are, right?" Ramirez looked over at his partner.

"What do you mean?"

"Well, you come from a normal family, and you've had a pretty easy road. But a lot of your community gets abused all the time. Bullies at school, family members, bad cops—there is a lot of violence toward the LGBT community."

"Yeah, I know." But his mind was already racing, wondering how he might be able to find out more without breaking his promise to Stephen. He wanted to kick himself for making that promise. He would never swear to non-interference again. The price was too high. He hadn't slept a wink after they went back to bed, and he couldn't think of anything else all day at work.

Gabe looked out across the water. The river looked more like a giant lake here, corralled off on either end by low stone-arched bridges and filled with crew boats slicing through the water. He watched as one of the long narrow boats slid under the Mass Ave. Bridge in the distance. The boat was speeding through the water one second, then it slipped out of sight, out of existence. He thought of Travis again. How long before he slipped completely out of existence himself? It was too much to think about.

"You would report something, if you knew about it, wouldn't you?"

Ramirez shrugged. "I guess that always depends on the situation. Technically, we're supposed to." Ramirez brought his knees to his chest. "At the very least I'd keep an eye on things."

Gabe thought back to details of the conversation with Stephen last night. Maybe it wasn't as bad as he was thinking. Maybe it had only been an altercation or two.

After a few minutes, Gabe sighed deeply and stood up. Ramirez hoisted himself up as well. "Well," Gabe said. "We should probably get back."

Ramirez agreed and they both stared at the path along the river for a few minutes before bouncing back into a slow jog toward home.

"Thanks for letting me vent," Gabe said.

"No problem," Ramirez said. "But whoever this friend of yours is, you better keep a close watch on him. These things can turn real bad real quick."

Apples and Honeymoons

That year, summer seesawed gently into fall. The first cool days started early, but they were scattered with warm, even hot weather into the first two weeks of November. The leaves held off on changing. Without a frost, the parks and gardens around Boston stayed green, but the plants took on a droopy, exhausted look.

Stephen sat in the passenger side of Gabe's 1990 Jeep Wrangler, trying to listen to Adele on the stereo, but the noise of the wind and the other cars on Route 128 was so loud, he couldn't hear anything of the song except a faint trace of drums. Even with the hardtop and the full doors on the Jeep, it was still one of the loudest vehicles he had ever ridden in.

He had mentioned something once about getting a different car, but Gabe would hear none of it. He'd had the Jeep since he was sixteen, when he'd inherited it from his father. The first time Stephen had ridden in it, Gabe told him the entire history of the vehicle. He had done every oil change on the vehicle since the time he'd gotten it, and he'd replaced the head gasket, several parts of the frame, the struts, and even half of two front fenders. In Gabe's eyes, it was a work of art and a demonstration of love. To Stephen, it was something out of a history book.

"Where are you taking me again?" Stephen said, almost yelling over the noise of the ride.

"Apple picking." Gabe smiled at him. "Don't act like it's a foreign idea. You're from New Hampshire, so you can't tell me this is the first time you've ever gone apple picking."

Stephen couldn't help smiling from ear to ear. Somehow, this guy had managed to make him happier than he'd ever thought possible and it was the little things, like his kooky idea to go apple picking that had showed his innocent and fun heart.

"Okay," Stephen said. "I admit it. I may have gone apple picking a couple of times as a kid."

"Did you love it?"

"It was a chore. We'd go picking at the local orchards in the fall for extra pocket money. I remember spending days out on a ladder to bring home about fifteen dollars. It was always cold, and the bottoms of my feet would hurt from standing on the ladder rungs all day."

"Well, it's not going to be too cold today," Gabe said. "And I'll hold the basket of apples so you can do all the picking. How's that sound?" He reached over and grabbed Stephen's leg, squeezing his knee.

"Oh, don't forget," Stephen said. "We have to be back in time for dinner with Travis and Benson tonight."

Gabe winced and looked straight out through the windshield. "I didn't forget."

"Look, I know you don't like them—"

"Not them, Stephen," Gabe said. "Him. I don't like Benson. I think Travis is great."

"Look, let's just make it through the evening tonight. This is supposed to be a dinner to celebrate their marriage."

"We already did that. That's what the wedding was for."

"I know," Stephen said. "But Travis and I have been trying to find a time that works for just us four to get together for dinner, and we haven't been able to get any time on the calendar until tonight."

"This is going to end badly, mark my words," said Gabe.

"Tonight?"

"No, not tonight." Gabe stopped to think for a second. "Well, yes, tonight will probably end badly, but I was talking more generally about their relationship."

"Oh, I hope not," Stephen said. "Travis seems to think he can make things work."

"The guy is abusive," said Gabe. "I don't know how you make that *work*."

"Maybe it has stopped."

"That kind of tiger doesn't change his stripes without a lot of therapy."

❖

Stephen and Gabe were late getting to the restaurant that evening. Traffic on Route 128 was at a standstill, and it took them much longer than they expected to get back into the city. Stephen texted Travis half way through the drive to let him know, but it didn't matter. The damage was done. The two of them walked into the restaurant thirty minutes behind schedule. Travis and Benson were sitting at the bar when they got there, and Benson gave them an icy nod as they said their hellos.

"I'm so sorry we're late," Gabe said to Travis. "It was such a nightmare on the ride back."

"No worries," said Travis. But Stephen noticed how he looked over at Benson, and he could tell that something had passed between the two of them. Travis looked cautious.

The restaurant was one of those ancient wood-paneled places that had been there long enough to see three centuries turn. It was dark and shiny with lots of brass and deep green and red carpeting. Stephen caught Gabe's eye, and the two of them smiled. Gabe nodded to a particularly dreary oil painting of a shipwreck and winked at Stephen. Stephen held his breath for fear of laughing out loud.

"So, tell me how was the honeymoon?" Stephen said to Travis after Benson had chosen a bottle of wine and the waitress had taken their dinner orders.

"Well, it was probably the most romantic trip you could imagine." Travis beamed. He looked across the table at his husband. "We spent the whole time at this beautiful old hotel in Waikiki. It was amazing."

Benson smiled, and Stephen looked back and forth between the two of them, then over to Gabe. Gabe's face was stony, and he was silent. "That sounds amazing," Stephen said.

The wine arrived and as soon as it was poured, Benson stood up and raised a toast. "To the most handsome, smartest and funniest man I know. I am so glad that you said yes to me." The three of them stood up to join Benson, and they all clinked glasses.

"To the grooms," said Stephen.

Gabe was silent as they all raised their glasses to a second toast, and he didn't look anyone in the face as they sat down.

Travis and Stephen did most of the talking during dinner, catching each other up on things that had happened at work and at home in New Hampshire. Though both received the same set of gossip from their parents, they hadn't had the chance to mull it over between themselves as they used to do on a daily basis.

"So, how are things with Boston's finest these days?" Benson said as he slowly cut his steak, taking a bite and chewing.

"Fine," Gabe said, taking a sip of his wine.

Benson swallowed. "I had lunch with the commissioner the other day. All he could talk about was the new gang task force. I can't imagine it's going to make much of a difference."

Stephen caught the conversation and glanced over out of the corner of his eye at Gabe. He knew the placid expression on his face masked a deep distaste for what was happening around him.

"Well, they have to do something," Gabe said. "I suppose the task force is at least a step in the right direction."

"They? Don't you consider yourself one of the police?"

"Yes, of course I do." Gabe smiled tightly. "I meant we. But of course, the strategic direction of the BPD gets decided well above my pay grade."

"Hmmmph." Benson frowned slightly. He looked over to Travis, abruptly ending the conversation. "How is your pasta?"

Gabe shot Stephen a look. Stephen knew he could count on Gabe to keep his cool, but the sheer dislike in Gabe's eyes made Stephen uncomfortable.

The rest of the meal went smoothly, but the two couples left the restaurant heading off in different directions. The idea of a nightcap briefly crossed Stephen's mind, but he quickly decided against suggesting it. Benson and Gabe were not going to be buddies, and the thought of adding more alcohol to the equation tonight was just not a good idea.

❖

"I don't know what Travis sees in him," Gabe said as they walked across the Boston Common. The night was clear with a hint of coolness in the air. The grass was still green on the fields of the Common and the browning leaves on the trees still clung to the branches.

Stephen shook his head. "I honestly don't know."

They walked for a few strides before Gabe shook his head. "I don't believe that, Stephen."

"What? You don't believe what?"

"I don't believe you don't know what Travis sees in Benson. You must understand, at least more than anyone else. You've known him forever. What gives?"

Stephen let out a long sigh as they walked. "I think," he said after a moment, "he sees Benson as a prize."

"A prize?" The shock in Gabe's voice was palpable.

"Yeah," Stephen continued. "Travis always wanted to be the best at everything—basketball, running, swimming. Whatever he did, he wanted to be the best. I think he sees Benson as the ideal catch—he's good-looking, older, established, makes a lot of money. Marrying Benson is like Travis winning at being gay. Or maybe just winning in life, scoring the best catch for a partner."

Gabe stopped and turned to Stephen. "That is unbelievable."

"You asked me what I thought, and that's what I think, based on knowing Travis and all the conversations we've had over the years."

"No," Gabe said. "That's not what I mean. I believe you, but it's just incredible Travis sees things that way. I mean of all the men in Boston, he falls for the one with no sense of humor and a tendency to beat him up."

"Maybe it has stopped, Gabe."

"Did he tell you that?" Gabe looked doubtful. "Or give you any indication that it had stopped?"

"He won't talk about it anymore."

"It will happen again, I know it will."

"Can we not talk about this any more?" Stephen raised his other hand to Gabe's shoulder, so he stood in front of him, holding him at arm's length. "Please, I don't want to say anything that's going to screw things up between them. Trust me, I know things could go wrong. And I've tried to talk Travis out of this several times. But he's made his mind up, and I want to try and support him. This is a chance for him to be happy. Maybe Benson has changed. That's all we can hope for right now. It's not our business."

Gabe looked up at the sky for a few seconds, then directly at Stephen. His eyes were sad, even resigned. "All right, if that's what you want."

Stephen said nothing.

"Okay." Gabe leaned in to kiss Stephen. "There is one thing I know for sure," he said after he planted a loud sloppy kiss on Stephen's lips.

"What's that?" Stephen said.

"That I ended up with the best guy in the universe," Gabe said.

"Knock it off, Gabe. Now you're just being corny." But there was a giant smile on Stephen's face even as he scolded him.

"I can't help it, I'm in love with you!"

"Well..." Stephen batted his eyelashes at him playfully. "You do know how to sweep me off my feet, mister."

"Oh yeah?" Gabe stepped forward and slid one arm behind Stephen's back and the other behind his knees, swooping him up into his arms.

Stephen laughed. "I didn't mean literally, but hey, this is kind of nice."

SOME PEOPLE

Travis looked at the blinking light on his phone. He had turned the ringer off, but he couldn't do anything about the light. The small screen on the Alcatel desk phone said it was a ring through from the front desk. He had been avoiding calls all day, but he had to re-engage with the rest of the working world at some point.

"Hello," he said, finally picking up the receiver. But he barely heard the voice on the other end of the line. It was somebody in marketing talking about the need for a couple of data sheets he had supposedly been working on.

"Sure, I've got them," Travis said. "I've got the printouts at my desk, or I can email you digital files."

Of course, they had wanted to come by his desk and pick up the hard copies. Travis cursed himself for being stupid enough to volunteer those. He had been doing a good job of laying low all day long. The only people he had seen were the receptionist and a couple of guys in the restroom. Other than that, he had remained securely tucked away in his cube, his face buried in the screen. Now he had to face some girl from marketing with a black eye.

He had tried to cover it up that morning. After Benson had left, he ran out and bought some concealer from the CVS down the street from their condo. But Travis had never worn makeup before, and he was unable to make it look like anything except a poorly covered up black eye.

He snapped open the small vanity mirror he kept in his drawer at work and looked at himself. Ugh, he thought. Why hadn't he taken a sick day?

"Knock, knock." A cheerful voice jolted him out of his thoughts. He looked up. "I'm Jenny from Marketing. They sent me over to pick up those data sheets."

Travis pulled two folders from the middle of a pile on his desk and handed them to her. He remained sitting and tried to keep his face toward the floor, hoping she might not notice him. But she took a sharp breath when he turned.

"Ouch," she said. "That looks like it must have hurt." She reached out and took the folders from his hand.

"Well, it didn't tickle," Travis said.

"What happened?" she asked.

He hated it when people asked about things like this—the bruises, the scrapes, the black eyes. It was starting to be too much to think about, and he felt himself getting numb to the pain and humiliation of what was happening to him. He was so used to lying now, saying he had gotten in a bar fight or he had dropped a dumbbell on himself at the gym, that it almost seemed like the truth. He made sure to stay clear of Stephen whenever he had any cuts or scrapes these days. The farther he went down this road, the harder it was for him to say—even to himself—that the bruising was the result of Benson's fists.

"Oh," he said, finally looking up to her and smiling. "It was nothing really. A stupid disagreement with an old high school friend at a bar."

"With a friend?" She had such an innocent and carefree face, he wanted to tell her everything. But he didn't dare. She was probably the kind of person who wouldn't know how to deal with the truth of what happened to him. He was doing her a kindness in telling her only what he thought she could handle.

"Yeah, well, sometimes we get pretty passionate when we talk about sports," he said. "He's from New York, and well, you know how it goes with the Yankees."

"Uh-huh," she said. But something had shifted as he spoke, clicking into place, and she looked as if she was reading below the surface of his words.

Travis mustered his best professional voice. "Anyway, I should probably be getting back to work here. Let me know if you guys want to go over the data in any of those sheets. I'm happy to jump on the phone."

"Sure," she said. "You know, I've seen you like this before."

Travis didn't look back at her. "That's not a surprise. I've been working here for a while."

"What I mean to say..." Her voice got lower as she spoke until it was almost a whisper. "What I mean to say is that I've seen you with a black eye before."

Travis cut her off. "It's nothing. It's just a little bump."

"You've tried to cover it up with concealer." She perched gingerly on the edge of the chair in the corner of his cube, putting her at his eye level. "And you did a really bad job."

"Whatever." Travis could feel the anger rising in his chest. "Are we through here?"

"It looks like bad drag queen make up."

"What's your point?"

"My point is," she said. "That I'll help you fix it up."

Travis finally took in the full scope of her face. She was pretty, and her quiet brown eyes were full of kindness. Her makeup, which he noticed because of their conversation, was done exquisitely.

When he didn't say anything, she took a deep breath. "Meet me in the handicap bathroom. I'll be there in a minute, and I'll bring my makeup kit."

"You've got a whole kit?"

"Nothing too elaborate, but enough to help you look a little more normal."

"Okay," he reluctantly whispered.

She rose and left the cube, bringing the data sheets with her. He watched her go and thought about the quickest route to the handicap bathroom. After a few moments, he got out of his chair and headed there. He carried an open folder, with his head down, buried to hide as much of his face as he could. His cheeks burned with a combination of fear and humiliation as he walked the fifty or so yards to reach his destination. The handicap bathroom was a separate single unisex room that almost nobody used. He had never really thought much about it, but today it was a safe haven he was grateful for.

He pulled on the doorknob of the bathroom, but it was locked. "Great," he muttered. But before he could even step back from the door, it creaked open. The marketing intern smiled out at him.

"Come on." She grabbed him by the shirt and yanked him into the bathroom, quickly and quietly shutting the door behind her and locking it.

The room was about the size of a small bedroom with more than enough space to maneuver a wheelchair around. There was a single toilet in the corner with railings on the walls around it.

"Sit," she said, pointing to the closed lid of the toilet. She had a small bag of makeup resting on the sink and a compact and a small triangular sponge in her hand. Travis did as he was told and sat down slowly in the corner of the room on the hard plastic lid of the toilet. She stood back and looked at him for a second before putting the sponge down. She pulled a long strip of toilet paper from the roll and wet it at the sink. "I'm going to take some of this shit off your face first," she said. "Then we're going to fix you up right."

"Okay," Travis said, thinking his voice sounded distant and alien. She washed his face, gently rubbing away the base layer of makeup he had applied that morning, and then patting his skin dry with another wad of toilet paper. She was careful not to press down hard, but as gingerly as she moved, his face still hurt where Benson's fist had crashed into it.

"So, do you want to tell me what happened?" she said, her voice smooth and gentle as she worked.

"I told you—"

"What you told me was a crock of shit," she said.

Travis bristled, but he said nothing, and they sat in silence for a moment while she worked.

"You know," she started again, her voice as smooth as before. "I used to have a boyfriend. Back when I was in high school." She paused for a moment as she stepped back to the sink to grab something in her bag of makeup. "He was, I don't know how to say it really..." Her voice had changed a little as she spoke. Where it had been smooth and polished before, he began to hear a slight crack in her tone. "He used to say the sweetest things, really nice and always complimenting me. Except when he got mad."

She dipped another triangle-shaped makeup sponge into her compact and swirled it around. "I'm guessing this is the right shade of base for you. We'll know in a moment, although this light is shit, and it might be a little hard to tell. Anyway," she continued. "When he got mad, he sort of, I don't know, lost control, I guess you could say." She swallowed hard and took a deep breath. "And, well you can guess the rest."

In the absence of her voice, the room was so quiet he could hear her breathing as she stood above him. He let out a long sigh. "Yeah," he finally said. "I guess I can imagine the rest." After another moment of silence, he added: "It sounds like maybe we have similar taste in men."

She pulled out another compact and a brush. This time it was powder. She dusted the brush in the compact and tested it on the back of her hand before gently dusting over his face.

"There," she said. "That looks a little more normal. You're lucky. This one isn't that bad. Looks like it should heal up in a couple of days. Want to take a look?" She gestured toward the mirror over the sink.

But Travis stayed where he was. He had never admitted even this much to anyone except Stephen, and he had to take a deep breath in order to stay calm. He could feel the nerves in his stomach, and he knew that if he moved or even opened his mouth to say anything else, he might completely lose control.

"I finally left him." She leaned against the railing along the wall. "The boyfriend. I never told anyone about it, though. Not even my mother. I..." She rolled her eyes toward the ceiling as if searching for something. "I guess I was embarrassed. Or maybe just worried about what people would think of me. I didn't want people to feel sorry for me."

Travis remained silent.

"It's okay if you don't want to talk about it," she said. "I get it. But if you do, I can listen if you want."

Still he said nothing.

She moved back toward the sink and packed up her makeup bag. "Well, that makeup job should get you through the rest of the day. Wash it off tonight and meet me in here tomorrow morning before work, and I'll fix you up again. You probably won't need anything after that."

"You're not going to tell me to leave him?" Travis had to speak slowly to maintain his composure.

"I can't tell you that. If you don't want to leave him, you're not going to. Doesn't matter what I say. I know what that's like. It didn't matter what was going on. Nobody was going to tell me who I should and shouldn't see."

"That's sounds familiar." He managed a half-hearted grin.

"Just make sure you know what you're getting yourself into." She zipped up the makeup bag and put it discreetly under her arm. "I kept telling myself it was going to get better. But I knew it wouldn't. I refused to listen to my gut for a long time."

He nodded silently.

"I'll see you tomorrow," she said and unlocked the door. She gave him one last look as she left, closing the door quietly behind her.

CHRISTMAS PARTY AT BENSON & TRAVIS'S

I hate parties," Gabe said as he shoved his hands into his pockets. It had been impossible to find a cab, so they had made the unwise decision to walk all the way from their apartment to Benson and Travis's place. The December night wasn't especially cold, but the wind had picked up once they'd gotten to the waterfront, and Gabe was miserable.

The newer glass and steel buildings twinkled in the nighttime, set back among the older brick and limestone buildings. Fort Point had been a forgotten backwater of Boston for centuries, a commercial area housing garment factories and shipping docks. In the latter part of the nineteenth century, its cheap rents made it a haven for artists and musicians. After Boston's Big Dig project took the major highway that cut through the city and buried it in a tunnel beneath the harbor, Fort Point suddenly became attractive. It was relatively central to all the new waterfront developments and close to downtown. A new courthouse and a convention center made it a place to actually go. It took almost no time at all before luxury condominiums started going up all over the place, crowding out the artists and anybody else who had been there for any length of time.

"You don't hate parties," Stephen said. "You just don't feel like going to one tonight."

"I don't feel like going to *this* one tonight. We're going to have to sit there and pretend to be interested in whatever that pompous ass is spouting on and on about. He really drives me crazy."

"I know," Stephen said. "But let's do this for Travis. I know he really wants us all to be able to socialize together. And it feels like he's more and more alone these days."

Gabe pressed his lips into a tight grimace. He knew how important it was for Stephen and Travis. "Okay, fine," he said. "I'll behave."

"Good," Stephen slipped his arm inside of Gabe's. "Maybe I'll make it worth your while later on tonight."

"Really? I like the sound of that," Gabe said.

They approached the front of the building and Gabe went for the door when Stephen pulled him along the sidewalk.

"What? This is the address."

"I know," Stephen said. "But Travis told me to go around to the back. The front door doesn't really work that well. The buzzer is broken, and they can't let people in without coming down to the actual lobby.

"Doesn't work?" Gabe was astonished. "How much did this place cost? And the front door doesn't work?"

Stephen shook his head. "I know, right? Come on, its just around here."

Stephen led him around to the back of the building. It was abutted by a shallow parking lot that ended abruptly at the wharf. The parking lot and surrounding area had been forgotten by the developers, and it looked much the way it probably had in the 1960s—a blank space with nothing but pot-holed tar all the way to the water's edge.

"Wow," Gabe said as he stared out to the harbor. "They really should put something a little more sturdy down there." He pointed to a crude fence constructed from two two-by-fours. It was all that stood between the harbor and a driver who might not be paying attention to what he was backing in to. "Between that and the front door, they really need to get a few things straightened out here."

"Come on, Mister Fix-It," Stephen kissed him on the nose. "Although I love it when you get all butch, we're going to be late." He dragged Gabe under the awning above the back door and pushed the buzzer for Benson and Travis's condo.

❖

Gabe suppressed the urge to turn and run as soon as Travis opened the door and let them in. Instead, he stared straight ahead and gave Travis a hug as he welcomed them into the apartment.

The apartment was decorated in red and white satin ribbons. The entire place was strung with garlands of pine and holly from wall to wall. Against the huge windows looking out onto the harbor stood an eight-foot tall Christmas tree decorated with bows of the same red and white satin strewn across the rest of the apartment. The lights were low, and Frank Sinatra's "Have Yourself a Merry Little Christmas" played in the background.

"You made it," Benson bellowed from the other side of the living room as soon as he saw Gabe and Stephen. "I'm so glad you did."

"He's drunk." Gabe leaned over and whispered into Stephen's ear, making sure to keep a broad smile plastered across his face. "I'll bet you anything."

"Keep it together, Gabe. Just keep it together and be polite," Stephen whispered.

"Polite…what an interesting choice of words, only one letter different from police," Gabe said through closed teeth.

Stephen grabbed his arm and pinched him as they glided toward Benson. "Merry Christmas, Benny," Stephen said as they reached their host.

"Do you like the place?" He gestured around the room with two open arms.

"It's beautiful," Gabe said, doing his best not to clench his teeth when he spoke.

"It's all Travis," Benson said. Travis had emerged beside his husband, and Benson slid an arm around his shoulder and squeezed him tight. "He did a beautiful job."

Travis smiled and pecked Benson on the cheek. Gabe watched closely, looking for anything that might give away a crack in the veneer of their relationship. But as hard as he looked, all he saw were two men standing side-by-side smiling and proud of their home.

"Hey, Gabriel." Benson suddenly broke their perfect little moment. "I want to introduce you to someone, come with me." He gestured for Gabe to follow him. "We can let those two catch up."

"Okay." Gabe tried to veil the skepticism in his voice. He looked back at Stephen for a split second, and Stephen just raised his eyebrows and shrugged his shoulders.

"Have you ever met the Commissioner? I've been telling him all about you," Benson said as he guided Gabe through the crowded living room toward the balcony.

Soon after the introductions, Benson disappeared and left Gabe with the Commissioner. The Commissioner was warm and even funny during the brief conversation with Gabe. He asked all the right questions—how did he like being an officer? What would he do differently? What was his take on morale on the force these days? Gabe answered all the questions with polite and interested responses. He found himself actually liking the Commissioner and he was starting to relax, when he saw something out of the corner of his eye. The Commissioner had been standing with his back to the room, looking out over the harbor with Gabe facing him and the crowded room when he saw Benson grab the flesh on the back of Travis's arm. Travis twisted in pain, and Benson tightened his grip. A look of fear flashed across Travis's face for an instant before he managed to breathe in and put the façade back into place. That was it, Gabe thought to himself, the crack in the veneer that he had been looking for.

He finished his conversation with the Commissioner and then quietly excused himself. He got another drink and waited until he saw Benson standing alone, then made his way slowly over to him.

"You know," Gabe said quietly, leaning into his ear. "You have a wonderful husband. He's really an incredible person."

"I do indeed," Benson said, slugging down a sip of what appeared to Gabe to be whiskey.

"That's not something you want to take lightly. Some people wait all their lives and never find the right match."

"So true. Love favors the fair, is that what they say?"

"Love." Gabe paused for a moment. "I'm not sure who it favors, really." He took a sip of his own drink. "But when you find it, you really need to take care of it."

"Mmm," Benson nodded quietly. "Gabriel, what are you saying, exactly? Your words sound wonderful, all soft and pretty. But I'm not sure I understand what you're getting at."

"What I'm getting at, Benson, is that you don't want to abuse the things in your life. You could lose them or worse."

"Abuse them? Are you accusing me of…"

"I'm not accusing you of anything." Gabe's words were quick and steely. He was being careful, but he was not backing down. "What I am saying is that I saw the way you grabbed and twisted Travis's arm just a moment ago, and it didn't look much to me like the way people in a loving, respectful relationship touch each other."

Benson glared at him. "That was just a squeeze—a love tap."

"A squeeze?" Gabe nodded doubtfully.

"I hardly think I need to defend the way I deal with what's mine," he said.

"With what's yours? Benson, do you think you own him?"

"I think you should leave." Benson's eyes held a growing rage. "Now."

Gabe quietly set down his drink. "Certainly," he said, and he turned away to find Stephen.

2013

The Dull and the Flashy

Travis sat with his legs curled up underneath him on the silver Hughes mid-century modern couch. It was a piece of art, and it looked phenomenal across the wall of windows that overlooked Boston Harbor. Travis had loved the cavernous feeling of the place since the first moment he'd seen it, but it had never felt like his home. A chic, white ceramic fireplace took up an entire wall on one end of the open floor plan, and the kitchen of white marble and stainless steel made up the other end of the space. In addition to the couch, two Soto chairs and a glass topped coffee table worked together to establish the living room area.

As Travis flipped through the messages on his phone, he heard the bed creak down the hall as Benson began to stir. Last night had been a late one. The two of them had gone out with one of Benson's friends, a famous state Senator who had been at the forefront of the fight for gay marriage in Massachusetts back in the early 2000s. He had made a name for himself during a famous speech when he came out of the closet and talked about his partner of twenty years.

The four of them had gone to dinner at one of the posh restaurants in the South End where very expensive entrees came in spoon-sized portions on giant plates drizzled with colorful sauces and garnished with exotic flowers. What little food there had been was over-salted and not very interesting. The conversation, like the food, was also boring. Benson and the Senator talked about politics for the entire evening. The Senator's husband had looked equally bored, but he was a good twenty-five years older than Travis and had no apparent interest in making small talk. At one point during the night Travis considered the fact that this guy might be trying to snub him, but Travis didn't even care enough to be snubbed.

But Travis was aware enough to notice everyone else in the restaurant was watching them. From the moment they sat down they had been the center of attention—the subject of quiet whispers and discreet stares. He had to admit to himself he liked the attention. He smiled as he looked around the room and realized the status he had attained by being a part of this dinner party.

But the night seemed to drag on forever. Everyone drank—lots of wine at dinner, followed by brandy and then some sour nightcap after that. Travis paid as much attention as he could muster, participating in the conversation when it was appropriate. The Senator's husband did the same, sulking into whatever drink he happened to have in front of him at the moment.

The dinner finally ended around eleven, and the four of them took the Senator's car to one of the gay bars in the South End. They stood at the end of the bar watching music videos on gigantic flat screens and continuing to drink. Travis looked around at the other people in the bar. He noticed more stares and whispers, but not nearly as many as in the restaurant. Instead, most people ignored them. The room was full of beautiful young people dressed in tight tee shirts and jeans, moving to the music and gyrating into one another.

Travis sipped his vodka martini and put his hand around Benson's waist. Benson reciprocated, then let his hand drop to Travis's butt, where he squeezed so hard that Travis wriggled away slightly, not enough for anyone to notice, but enough to loosen Benson's grip on his ass. Benson turned away from his conversation with the Senator to look at Travis, surprised and slightly angry. But it seemed to be gone in less than a second. He continued the conversation with the Senator, his hand moving back up to Travis's waist and staying there.

The night finally ended around one thirty as the bar was clearing out for closing. Benson and Travis took a cab back to their condo. The ride home had been silent, and even as they were getting ready for bed, Benson didn't say a word. Travis tried to start a light-hearted conversation with a simple comment about how cute the waiter had been at the restaurant.

"Is that all you could do all night? Stare at the servers?" Benson said gruffly as he stood in front of the bathroom mirror and unbuttoned his shirt.

"No, of course not," Travis said, trying to maintain an even tone in his voice. He stood in the bedroom watching Benson, and he could sense something wasn't right with him.

"You were bored out of your skull, weren't you?"

Travis hesitated. "No, not bored, exactly, but sometimes I have a hard time keeping up with all the politics and everything you guys talk about."

Benson frowned. "You should try to learn more, maybe read more. It's a little embarrassing for me when you can't participate in a conversation."

"What did you say?"

"You heard me." Benson finished taking off his shirt and walked into the bedroom, throwing it at Travis as he walked over to the bed. "It's embarrassing. It makes you look stupid."

Travis stood there, unable to move, Benson's shirt hanging over his shoulder. He couldn't believe what he was hearing. But he let it go. He let the shirt drop to the floor where he was. He took his own clothes off and went to bed, shutting the light off as he crawled in.

That morning as he sat on the couch, he flipped through messages from friends and checked out the Boston gossip sites to see if Benson and the Senator were in any of them. Sure enough, on the home page of the most popular site was a picture of the four of them sitting at dinner. The caption read: "Boston Socialite Benson Harvey and Senator spotted out with hubbies for a night on the town." The gossip sites had always posted a lot of stories like that about Benson, and now they included Travis more and more, but seldom by name. He thought back to the days before he had really met Benson, when he was just silently crushing on him at the office. In those days he had fantasized about seeing just this kind of post. He wondered if it was worth it now, but he quickly put the thought out of his head.

Back in the bedroom, he heard the sounds of Benson getting into the shower. Travis thought briefly about their exchange at the end of the night and wondered if he should bring it up. He decided it would probably be better not to.

2014

The First Sick Day

The first time that Travis actually gave in and called out sick for a black eye was on a Monday over a year after their wedding. He sat in his bathrobe at the marble-top kitchen counter all day. Benson had left for work early that morning, before Travis was even awake. Not that Travis would have noticed him getting out of bed. Benson had slept on the couch.

The night before they had been out late, but they hadn't meant to be. They thought they'd go out to one of the early Sunday Tea Dances put on by several of the gay clubs. But the Tea Dance had led to an after party at an expensive townhouse in Boston's exclusive Back Bay neighborhood. Sometime toward the middle of the party, Benson had slipped off to the bathroom. When he returned, his eyes were red and glassy. Travis could tell that he'd done something.

Benson was silent on the cab ride home and Travis could sense something was very wrong. The minute they were in the door, Benson pushed him up against the wall, pressing his face into the sheetrock, and started groping his ass.

"Benson, stop it, you're hurting me." Travis tried to turn around, but Benson suddenly grabbed him by the scalp and slammed his head into the wall. "Benson, what the hell?" He felt light headed, and his head throbbed where it had hit the wall.

"Shut up," Benson barked at him. "I'll tell you when you can speak. You little shit. You live in my house, live off my money and you think you can parade around like a little slut all night and then not give it up to me when we get home." Benson ripped angrily at the back of Travis's jeans, but his hand slipped and he stumbled back a few feet. Travis took advantage of the stumble and got away from the wall, headed for the kitchen.

"Where are you going?" Benson was starting to slur his words.

"I'm going to put ice on my head where you slammed me into the wall," Travis said without turning around to look at him.

But it was a mistake for Travis to take his eyes off of Benson. Before he got to the kitchen, he felt an iron grip on his shoulder. Benson spun him around and threw him onto the floor. As wasted as Benson was, he quickly had the advantage over Travis, pinning him down on the ground and sitting on his stomach with his legs on either side of Travis's body. "You don't leave a room until I tell you to leave a room, do you understand me?" He slapped Travis hard across the face, making a horrible smacking sound as his hand met the soft tissue of Travis's cheek. Travis's entire face stung from the blow. He tried to free his arms, but he couldn't get them out from underneath Benson's legs.

Travis was stunned. He couldn't speak. He could barely breathe. Most infuriatingly, he couldn't stop the tears from coming. He lay trapped beneath Benson, his head and his face throbbing. Then, just as suddenly as it had started, something switched off in Benson as he stared down at Travis. Benson stood up and backed away from him. "I'm going out. Go clean yourself up and cry yourself to sleep, you little faggot. You disgust me. You're so ugly when you cry."

Benson turned around and walked out of the condo, slamming the door behind him and leaving Travis lying on the floor. As Travis crawled to his knees, he noticed the room was remarkably undisturbed for all the violence. An end table was a few inches out of place where Benson had knocked into it on his way to pin Travis down, and the wall had a smudge where Benson had slammed Travis's head into it. But other than that, the room held an eerie peace. Travis slowly got to his feet and went to the freezer for an ice pack. He thought about calling Stephen but decided not to. He couldn't bear to tell him what he had let happen to himself tonight.

Travis sat at the kitchen counter all day the next day. He stared out the window at the view of the harbor, watching ships come and go. He didn't look at his phone, and he didn't turn on the television.

He sat and wondered what he was going to do about the situation he had gotten himself into. He knew he didn't want to go to the police, and he would rather die than tell his parents.

At five thirty, he heard a key in the lock and the door opened. Benson walked slowly into the apartment and threw his coat on the couch. He walked over to Travis and wrapped his arms around him. Travis could hear the sobs emanating from his chest.

"I'm so sorry baby," Benson said through his crying. "I don't know what happened to me last night. Somebody must have spiked my drink with something."

Travis felt his body go numb. He sat on the stool as Benson held him and cried. He couldn't think of anything to say. Besides that, he was scared to say anything at all.

"I will never, ever hurt you again, Travis." Benson stood back from him and put his hands on Travis's shoulders, looking at him and shaking his head. "I'll stop drinking altogether, I promise."

Travis stared at him. "That might be a good idea," he said slowly.

"I will, I promise." Benson looked down at the floor then back at Travis. "I will be better about this, baby. I love you so much."

"I love you too, Benny," he whispered.

How Come You Get All This?

How come you get all of this?" Travis sat across from Stephen at the kitchen table of the tiny apartment that Stephen and Gabe shared in Beacon Hill. "You didn't even want this. You weren't even supposed to be gay. How come you end up with the gentle, caring, loving guy and I end up with…with a monster."

It had been a few days since the incident, and Travis's black eyes had faded. He'd covered up the remaining bruises with some foundation Jenny from Marketing had given him, but his lip was still split where Benson had backhanded him. He had called in sick for a second day in a row because he was too bruised and swollen to go in to work. Somebody would ask him what was wrong, and HR would have come by and asked him if everything was okay. As if he could say anything. As if he could just bare his soul and admit one of the leading executives of the firm had beat him up again after getting high.

Stephen was silent. He sensed the anger and the fear in his friend. It had changed him. It had turned him into something different than the confident, extroverted boy Stephen had grown up with. He had no words. He reached over and touched Travis's face, gently putting his thumb on Travis's lip and leaning toward his friend until their foreheads were touching. "Travis," he said, "you have to do something. You have to leave."

"And go where?" Travis let out a humorless laugh. "And do what? Can't you see this is what I've done with my life? I wanted the hotshot boyfriend with lots of money. I wanted not to have to worry about anything. I wanted to be taken care of. Now I'm married to someone who does this to me, and you're with fucking Prince Charming." He shook his head. "Don't worry about it. I can handle it."

The two men looked at each other across an empty space and neither knew what to say. Stephen had told him enough times he should leave, and Travis had refused to do anything for whatever reasons. In the silence of the apartment, they heard the front door open and close, followed by footsteps and Gabe's voice. "Hello!" he said as he came into the apartment. "Oh, hey Travis," he said, before doing a double take to look at him again.

Travis lowered his head, not bothering to hide the busted lip and the bruises. "Hi Gabe," he said in a low voice.

"What the hell?"

Stephen got up and reached over to him. "Gabe, don't. Just… leave it."

"Travis, what happened to you?"

"It was nothing, it's nothing. I don't really want to talk about it."

"Travis," Gabe said, sitting down at the table next to him, where Stephen had been. "Travis, you have to tell me what happened to you. You have to get help."

"No, Gabe, I don't," Travis said.

"Was this Benson?"

"Look, Gabe, I appreciate you're trying to help me here." Travis paused and looked up at Stephen. "But I really don't want to talk to the police about anything. I'm a big boy, and like I just told Stevie, I can handle this. He's not really that much trouble."

"Oh no, Travis. You're wrong. He's big trouble," Gabe said quietly. "You don't have bruises and cuts like that when there's no trouble."

Travis looked from Gabe to Stephen and back again. He stood up and shook his head. "Again, I know what you're trying to say, and I appreciate it, but I'm fine." He smiled a tight-lipped smile and turned to go. "I have some errands to run today. I'm going to head out. Stephen, I'll call you this week."

"Okay, sounds good." Stephen looked down, then called Travis's name, waiting for his friend to stop and look back at him. "Come back here if you need to—for anything."

Travis paused for a second and then headed out to the foyer. A few seconds later, they heard the door close and Stephen sat down where Travis had been. He took Gabe's hand and looked at him directly in the face. "I don't know what to do," he said.

Gabe shook his head slowly and squeezed Stephen's hand gently. "I hate that man," Gabe said. A deep rage burned in his eyes, as if it was barely kept in check by the day-to-day rules Gabe had to follow. "I don't often wish bad things on people, but that guy is an animal. This is just not right."

"I know." Stephen patted Gabe's hand.

"No, Stephen, I don't think you realize what's really happening here." Gabe took a deep breath. "Forget about the fact that this is morally appalling. We're accomplices to a felony. All of us who see this happening—you, me, his parents—we're all sitting on the sidelines watching. I'm a cop, Stephen, and I'm watching this happen right in front of my eyes and not doing anything about it."

"Please, Gabe. Nobody can do anything until Travis is ready."

"You keep saying that, babe." Gabe's voice was soft now. "And I think it's because you care about him, but I don't know if that makes it the right thing to do."

DETECTIVE

Stephen sat on a park bench a few yards back from the Frog Pond in the center of Boston Common. It was a beautiful sunny weekday, and the park was full of people playing hooky or making the most of extended lunch hours. Gabe had called Stephen earlier that day and asked him to take the afternoon off and meet him in the park for lunch. Gabe hadn't said specifically why, but he said he had a surprise that was pretty spectacular.

"Do you want me to bring anything for lunch?"

"No, don't worry about it. Meet me on the benches behind the Frog Pond around twelve thirty today," Gabe's voice was so full of excitement Stephen could feel the phone practically buzzing.

Stephen had gotten to the benches a little early and sat down. He looked around and breathed in the smell of the freshly mown grass and listened to the kids splashing around in the cement-lined pond.

He felt a hand on his back. He spun around to see Gabe in a pair of kakis and a button-down shirt, holding a shiny new badge out in front of him. Stephen, startled at first, stared at the new badge. It looked very similar to Gabe's old badge, which typically lived in the same dish on the shelf by the door that Gabe's keys landed in the second he got home. Stephen had looked at the old badge before. He had taken it off the shelf to see what it felt like, how much it weighed. This new one was different, but he couldn't quite put his finger on it.

"You got a new badge?" Then it dawned on him. "You got a new badge!"

"Yes," Gabe was beaming, "I certainly did."

"Oh my God, you made detective!" Stephen shouted at him. "That's amazing, honey, that's really amazing! Congratulations. I'm so proud of you."

Gabe produced a bag from behind his back. "And to celebrate, I brought sandwiches from DeLuca's."

"Oh, sounds amazing," Stephen said. DeLuca's had become a tradition of theirs for special occasions since it was one of the early places they had gone for a lunch date.

Stephen and Gabe sat down on the bench and Gabe began unpacking the lunch bags, setting the sandwiches, chips and a couple of Diet Cokes out between them.

"Gabe, listen," Stephen said, his voice suddenly somber after the wave of excitement.

"Yeah?"

"Look, I know what this means for you—more responsibility, more people looking up to you..." He paused, trying to figure out exactly how to say what was on his mind. "And this thing with Travis...I'm sorry I asked you to keep it quiet. I know it's going to be even harder now."

Gabe picked up his sandwich and held it in his hand. He looked at Stephen, and then out across the park. "I made you a promise," he finally said.

"I know."

"And I'll keep that promise until you change your mind," he said. "But Stephen, you know staying quiet isn't going to help him."

Stephen didn't say anything.

The Missed Drink

Stephen was supposed to meet Travis out for a drink after work later that week, but Travis never showed up. They had agreed to meet at the Sevens, the bar close to Stephen and Gabe's house. Stephen texted him, then called him, but no response. Finally, after an hour, Stephen went home.

"You're home early," Gabe called from the couch as Stephen closed the door behind him. "I thought you were meeting up with Travis. I didn't expect you for another couple of hours."

"Yeah, so did I," Stephen said. "He never showed up."

"Is everything all right?"

Stephen took a deep breath and shook his head. "I hope so. I tried texting him and calling him a few times and nothing. No response."

"I'm sure he just forgot."

"I hope so," Stephen said. He slipped his sneakers off and padded back into the living room and curled up next to Gabe. They watched television for an hour or so and went to bed.

At eleven thirty, the doorbell buzzed. They so seldom heard the sound they didn't recognize it at first. Stephen sat up in bed and nudged Gabe. Gabe waited for a second until it buzzed again.

"It's the doorbell," Gabe said, the sleepiness vanishing quickly from his words. "It might be just a bunch of kids pranking us. But we better check."

Stephen was up like a shot. Something in the back of his head told him it wasn't a prank. He rolled out of bed and stumbled as quickly as he could to the front hall as the doorbell buzzed again. He reached up and pushed the ancient talk bell. "Hello?"

"Stevie." Travis's voice crackled through the speaker, barely recognizable.

"Travis? Is that you?"

"Yeah. Look, Stevie, I need a little help." Travis's voice was shaky.

"I'll buzz you up."

There was a brief pause before Travis spoke again. "Can you come down and help me?"

"What's the matter? Are you okay?" But even as Stephen asked the question, he knew the answer. He didn't wait for a response, "I'll be right down."

He sprinted to the bathroom and grabbed his bathrobe off the hook on the back of the door. Picking up the keys from the dish by the door, he trotted down the five flights of stairs. When he opened the front door, he thought it was a homeless person at first. Travis leaned on the side of the entrance, barely able to stand on his own. He was huddled in a ball with his head down and a blanket pulled around him. Blood was crusted all around Travis's face and throughout his hair, like a gory Halloween mask where Travis's face had once been.

Stephen held back a retch and forced himself to swallow the feeling of nausea that hit him like a wall of concrete. He gathered Travis under his arm and walked him through the front door and up the steps to the inside lobby. He knew he couldn't get Travis all the way up the five flights of stairs to the apartment, so he settled his friend on the bench in the lobby of the apartment building. In the full light of the inside, Stephen could see more of the injuries. His face was yellow and purple and swollen everywhere. A cut ran the length of his face from his eyebrow out around his temple and down to his lip. He had several other cuts, most of them still seeping blood.

"Oh my God, Travis," Stephen mumbled under his breath. "We need to get you to a hospital. Wait here." He turned quickly and bolted up the five flights of stairs at full speed, not stopping until he got to his own apartment door. He fumbled with the keys, the growing sense of panic making him clumsy. He opened the door, ran to the bedroom and grabbed his phone out of its charger on his nightstand, dialing 911. While the phone rang, he slipped on the pair of pants he had been wearing earlier in the day.

"What's the matter?" Gabe was already up and pulling his pants on. "Stephen, who are you calling?" He sat up. "Is everything okay?"

"No." Stephen could hear his own voice crack. He listened to the recorded message of the 911 dispatch center, as his call was routed through to an operator.

"I'm calling 911. I have to go back downstairs. It's Travis."

"What happened?" Gabe said, but Stephen had already bolted out of the room and headed back out the apartment and down the stairs.

Stephen was halfway down the first flight of stairs when he heard the door shut again, Gabe's footsteps pounding after him. "What happened?" Gabe repeated as he caught up to Stephen on the third flight down.

"What is the nature of the emergency?" The female 911 operator's voice was calm and collected, with a thick South Boston accent to it.

"I need an ambulance, quickly," Stephen shouted into the phone. His voice was shaky, and he was out of breath as he reached the bottom of the stairs and ran over to kneel down in front of Travis.

"What address are you at?"

But Stephen couldn't answer right away, as he looked up at Travis the full weight of what had happened beginning to set in.

"Sir, what address are you at?"

"Sorry," Stephen said softly, taking Travis's hand. "We're on Charles Street." He gave the operator the street number and mentioned the Sevens as a landmark.

"What the hell?" Gabe had reached the bottom of the stairs and walked over to the two of them. "Did he do this to you?" His voice was a violent whisper of rage.

Stephen shushed him as he finished up with the 911 operator. He was still kneeling down in front of Travis, holding his hand.

"Travis," Gabe said, kneeling down in front of him, next to Stephen. His voice was gentle now, and he put a hand on Travis's knee. "You're going to be alright, we're going to get you to a hospital. Can you tell me what happened to you?"

Travis shook his head.

"Was this Benson?"

"He's high." Travis's voice was an exhausted whisper, raspy with a combination of fear and pain. "He chased me out of the apartment. I think he's coming after me." Travis shuddered violently.

"It's okay, you're safe now," Stephen said.

"He said he was going to find me and kill me." Travis's voice was small and shaky.

"You're safe now," Stephen said. "You don't have to go back there."

Travis drew a ragged breath and a sob emanated from him, but his eyes were too swollen and damp already for Stephen to notice the tears. Gabe looked down at the floor, his face a mask of stone. Stephen knew how Gabe looked when he was enraged.

"Gabriel, look at me," Stephen said as softly as he could. "I'm going to the hospital with him." Gabe started to speak, but Stephen shook his head quickly. "No, I'm going with him." Stephen looked up at Travis. "Do you have your keys?" Travis nodded and Stephen gently fished them out of his pants pockets. He handed the keys to Gabe. "I want you to go to his place, pack a bag with his things. Just the important stuff."

"I can't enter his apartment, I'm a cop," Gabe protested.

"You're also his friend, and he's given you permission to enter. Gabe, he can't go back there. Just go and pick up his stuff. If you have to deal with Benson, keep it as cool as you can. Okay?"

Gabe stared at Stephen for a long time. "Okay, I'll go," he said, taking the keys and standing up. "But if I see Benson--."

"You won't do anything if you see Benson, Gabe." Stephen stood up so he was facing Gabe. "You won't do anything that will jeopardize your position at work." He looked down at Travis or the shell of what had been Travis. "Just go. We'll talk about this later, okay?"

Gabe left, and Stephen stayed with Travis until the paramedics arrived. But the minutes seemed like days. Stephen sat on the bench next to Travis and gently put his arm around his shoulder. Travis leaned in to him. Stephen thought back to the days when they'd been kids and Travis had looked out for him, always taking him under his wing when he was too shy to speak or to make friends at school. Travis was always the strong one, always the brave one. What had happened to this magnificent creature? When had everything changed inside of him, and how did he let himself get to this?

The two paramedics arrived a few moments later. Stephen opened the door for them as they set up the stretcher. Stephen watched as they went to work with the unruffled efficiency of people who are untouched by tragedy, yet see it every day.

They focused on Travis, asking him questions about what he could and couldn't feel. "How did you get here?" one of the paramedics said.

"I walked," he mumbled. Stephen felt his legs almost give out beneath him when he heard that. In the rush of everything that evening, he hadn't stopped to think about how Travis had gotten to his house. He had just instantly been there, outside his front door. Stephen felt so stupid. Had he thought Travis had hopped into a cab, all rolled up and bloody inside a woolen blanket?

After they had him packed onto the ambulance, one of the paramedics turned to Stephen. "What relation are you to the victim?"

"We grew up together," Stephen said.

The paramedic looked at Stephen. Stephen thought that he might give him a hard time about not being a blood relative, but he couldn't have been more wrong. The paramedic didn't seem to care anything about that. "Are you riding with us?"

"Yes, if that's all right." Stephen realized he was wearing pants, a tee shirt, a bathrobe, and sneakers with no socks.

The paramedic nodded and motioned for Stephen to climb in next to the stretcher. Stephen sat in the back of the ambulance, his hand on Travis's knee as the paramedic went about hooking up various tubes to Travis's arms.

"You're lucky you called when you did," the paramedic said without looking up.

"Why's that?" Stephen said, although something told him he didn't want to know the answer, whatever it was going to be.

"He's got a lot of injuries. Whatever happened to him, he probably has some significant hemorrhaging, his breathing is unsteady, and he is slipping into a coma."

"Is he…" Stephen could barely bring himself to ask the question. His lips were trembling and he felt numb. "Is he going to be okay?"

The paramedic felt for Travis's pulse. "Too early to tell for sure."

Stephen bowed his head and said a silent prayer as he felt the tears well up in his eyes.

Accidents Happen

G abe revved the Jeep's engine as he sat at the stoplight. His heart raced, and his jaw was clenched tight. He could feel his teeth grinding, but he didn't care. He was as angry as he'd been in a very long time. The light turned green, and he popped the Jeep into first gear and sped away from the intersection. The images of Travis's bloody face kept coming back to him. If he didn't know who it was, he would have been unable to identify him. *And how did he get there?* Gabe wondered. *He must have walked all the way from the waterfront.*

"God damn it," Gabe shouted out loud to the open Boston sky above him. He sped through the streets of downtown and headed up Summer Street across the channel to Fort Point. The ride passed in a blur, the fluorescent office lights streaking by like lightning as he sped past old warehouses, artist studios, and office buildings.

Gabe sneered as he pulled into a parking spot behind the building where Benson and Travis lived. He cut the engine and looked at the keys Stephen had given him. One was marked back door. *Right. Let's make this quick*, thought Gabe.

He got out of the Jeep and headed toward the building, turning briefly to look down the length of the parking lot and out onto the water. The narrow strip of asphalt was one of the few undeveloped parcels left in the new Fort Point, a straight corridor that ran directly behind the building from the street on one side and clear out to the water on the other. Gabe had always thought it was preposterously dangerous. If you didn't know where you were going and weren't paying attention, you could turn off the street and drive right out into the harbor. All that stood between the parking lot and the water was a rickety wooden fence with two rails, probably a safety measure put up during construction years ago and never replaced.

As he headed to the door, something in the shadows over by the edge of the water caught his eye. At first it looked like a large pile of clothes, but the pile began to move. Gabe realized it was a person hunched over by the rickety old fence.

"Sir, are you okay?" Gabe shouted across the parking lot at the man. The man tried to rise to his feet, but he stumbled and grabbed out for the fence with one hand as a bottle dangled from the other hand. The fence wobbled as he put his full weight on it.

"Sir!" Gabe called out to him again and jogged over to where he was. "You can't lean on that fence."

As Gabe approached, he realized, with a twinge of nausea, who it was. "Benson."

Benson turned toward him and squinted. As his bloodshot eyes struggled to focus, he gathered his weight and stood straight up, facing Gabe. "What the hell are you doing here?" His voice was raspy and coarse.

Gabe swallowed the bile that threatened to come up, his neck muscles tightening as he fought against the urge to run into Benson and push him off the edge of the wharf. "Benson," he said, "Come on, back away from the water. You're drunk." *Why am I trying to help this asshole?* Gabe thought to himself.

"Fuck off," Benson snarled. He looked out over the water. "Where is Travis? Did you take him?"

"No, I didn't take him. But he's not here."

"You know, I'm going to find him and kill him," Benson said.

"No, you're not." Gabe's voice was steady but he was seething behind the calm tone. "You're not ever going to see him again."

Benson laughed, and Gabe's blood boiled.

"He's safe now," Gabe said. He walked a few more steps until he was facing Benson, standing almost a foot away. The man stank of booze and stale sweat. There was a small streak of blood on his left cheek and beneath his stained jacket, his white dress shirt was unbuttoned almost to the navel. "He's at the hospital, and I'm going to make sure he knows he doesn't have to ever see you again."

Benson's laugh grew louder. "You think he's going to listen to you?" he said. "He won't. He'll just come back to me. He always does."

Gabe clenched his fists and tried not to think about the Travis he'd seen earlier that evening.

"Oh, look at that." Benson's lips curled back in a hideous smile. "You're getting mad about it, aren't you? Why do you think what happens between me and my husband is any of your business?"

"When you put him in the hospital because you nearly kill him, it becomes a matter of police business, actually, not just my business."

"The police don't care about one more little twink who likes to get knocked around a bit."

"You're sick, Benson. You need help, and Travis needs to get the hell away from you."

Benson's face froze. His limbs went rigid and Gabe could see his grip on the bottle tighten. "Fuck that," Benson said. "He's not going anywhere." Benson smashed the bottom of the bottle on the pavement and lurched forward clumsily, swinging the broken end of the bottle at Gabe's face. Gabe easily ducked out of way, except that he hadn't moved quite far enough and a jagged end from the bottle grazed his forehead. The cut wasn't a bad cut, but it was deep enough to draw blood.

Gabe stood back, lifting a finger to his forehead to wipe away the droplets of blood forming there. Benson stood in front of him, the bottle still in his clenched fist. "Benson, put down the bottle. What are you doing?"

"What I should have done a long time ago." His face was a mask of bright red anger. "Putting you in your fucking place."

Gabe watched him carefully, his eyes following the bottle. "You're drunk, Benson. Put the bottle down and go sober up."

Benson lurched at him a second time, but Gabe was ready for him. Benson led the charge with his right hand. Gabe blocked him at the wrist with his left and landed a blow to the gut with his right. All of the anger from that night and the years of hating Benson landed with that blow, and the sheer force of it sent Benson crashing into the rotting wooden fence. Gabe watched in disbelief as the top two-by-four bowed slightly under Benson's weight. He flopped backward over it and flew out over the edge of the wharf. The last thing Gabe saw on Benson's face was the look of shock as he seemed to realize what was happening to him.

A second later, there was a splash and Gabe was left staring out over the dark harbor in absolute silence.

Gabe walked slowly over to the edge and looked down. The ripples of current caught the moonlight in their creases and pockets, shining back up at him like shards of glass in the deepest black of night. He took a sharp breath, unable to fill his chest. The air was thick, and his lungs felt tight, as if the salt of the sea was rising up and clinging to him, pulling him down to the surface of the water and out of the harbor with the tide, to the open ocean. He let out the breath. It was done. There was nothing more to think about, and he could never, ever, tell another soul.

He burned deep inside. His stomach sank into itself, and his gut started to ache. The full realization of what he had just done hit him like a pile of bricks. He rubbed his forehead where the bottle had clipped him. It had left just a tiny cut.

He turned around and walked back to the Jeep. He started the engine and after sitting for a moment, he texted Stephen to find out what hospital they had gone to. When the reply came, he put the car into gear and drove to Saint Elizabeth's Hospital.

SAINT ELIZABETH'S

The Saint Elizabeth's waiting area was a bright and airy room with large windows and soft yellow walls. Stephen had turned one of the chairs around and sat staring out at the night. Gabe walked up and turned another chair around next to Stephen. A faint smile crossed over Stephen's tear-stained face as he looked up at him. Gabe sat down and put his arm around Stephen and Stephen leaned into him.

"What did they say?"

"Blunt force trauma. Contusions, lacerations, and abrasions everywhere. Three fractured ribs. They're running a CAT scan on him right now."

"Oh," Gabe said. "I'm so sorry Stephen, I'm so, so sorry."

Stephen shook his head as more tears streamed down his face. He swallowed and took a deep breath. "I called his parents. I told them he was in the hospital, but I couldn't tell them what happened. I tried, but I couldn't get the words out." Stephen rested his head on Gabe's shoulder.

Gabe pulled Stephen in tighter and they stared out the window for what seemed like eternity. The doctors checked in with them a few times over the course of the early morning hours, and Travis's parents arrived just as dawn was breaking. Travis was admitted to a hospital room at seven that morning, his injuries severe but not life threatening. He was listed as in critical but stable condition.

Stephen and Gabe finally decided to go home around ten that morning. Stephen turned to Gabe as they started out of the room. "Where is his stuff? I'd like to leave a few things with his parents."

"Oh, right." Gabe paused. "I couldn't figure out which key it was."

"What?"

"The keys you gave me," Gabe said, fishing them out of his pocket. "I couldn't get any of them to work. I couldn't really see anything and none of them seemed to fit, so I just came here. I figured it was more important for me to be here."

"Okay," Stephen said in a sleepy voice. "We can always go over later today and get a few things."

"Yeah, it might be better that way anyhow," Gabe said.

"Yeah. Benson will be at work."

"Uh huh," Gabe couldn't think of anything else to say as they walked out of the building to the Jeep.

All Travis knew for sure when he woke up was that he was thirsty.

"It's okay." Stephen held his hand and stroked it gently. "You're okay now. You're safe."

"Where am I?" Travis's voice was scratchy, barely more than a whisper.

"You're at Saint Elizabeth's Hospital." Stephen tightened his grip on Travis's hand. "You slipped into a coma on the ambulance ride. Don't try to talk right now. You're okay. That's what's important right now."

Travis didn't say much of anything that first day after he woke up. He mostly just lay in bed. Occasionally, Stephen would see tears in the corners of Travis's eyes. He would lean over and gently brush them aside.

Travis was extremely lucky according to his doctors. He sustained no brain damage. His injuries would eventually heal, though he'd have several scars for the rest of his life. On the day after he woke up, Gabe came into his room dressed for work in a pair of khakis and button-down shirt. He was accompanied by another detective.

"What's going on?" Stephen said. He glanced over at the other detective. "I thought you were at work?"

"I am," Gabe said. "I'm here about Benson."

Travis looked up at him from the bed but said nothing.

"Gabe, I think maybe we can talk about Benson later. Travis isn't ready to talk about him. Can't you get a statement or whatever later?"

Gabe glanced over at the other detective, a man similar in stature to Gabe, but with dark hair and olive skin. The other detective raised his eyebrows, and Gabe nodded. "Look," Gabe said. "I thought maybe this might be better coming from someone Travis knows."

"What?" Travis's voice was weak and scratchy. "What happened?"

The dark-haired detective stepped forward. "Hello, Travis. My name is Detective Luotta. I know it's hard, but can you tell us the last time you saw Benson Harvey?"

Travis rolled his head to the side and stared up at the detective. "The last time I saw him? Are you from Social Services?"

"No sir," the detective said.

"There was an accident," Gabe said. "It's too early to tell, but we think it may have been suicide. Benson's body was found in the harbor a few days ago. It looks like he jumped off the wharf...or fell into the water...by your condo."

"What?" Stephen looked at Gabe, his eyes wide.

"Suicide?" Travis said, his voice barely audible.

"Benson's dead?" Stephen could not contain the shock in his voice. "Are you sure? Did you find the body?"

"Yes," Detective Luotta said. "As we mentioned, we found him a little over a day ago."

"Toxicology reports indicate he was high on methamphetamines, and he was likely drunk," Gabe added.

"Is there anything you can tell us about the last time you saw him, Travis?" Luotta said.

Travis stared out beyond the people by his bedside, his eyes blank. "No, not really. I saw him the night he did this." Travis gestured to his face. "He came home after going out with a couple of his friends, I guess. I don't know who. He was high, I could tell. Really high. I was sitting on the couch. He walked past me and went to the bar cabinet and pulled out a bottle of scotch." Travis swallowed painfully.

"Travis, this can wait. You don't have to do this right now if you don't want," Stephen said.

Travis waved a hand at him. "It's okay, Stephen." He looked directly at the detective. "He sat drinking for about thirty minutes, talking about the night he'd had with his friends, telling me how it was such a shame I wasn't smart enough to keep up with them. But he was erratic." Travis coughed, and Stephen lifted a cup of water to his lips. He took a sip before going on. "He was going on about things that didn't make any sense, things that had never happened or people that I'm pretty sure neither one of us knew."

"Had he ever been like that before?" The detective asked.

Travis looked back out beyond the detective and slowly nodded his head. "Yes," he finally said, "but he got worse after we got married." He took a lethargic breath. "I knew it was drugs. He was always very sneaky when he would take them, but I'm not an idiot. I knew what was happening."

"It's okay, Travis," Stephen said.

Travis shook his head slowly. "I should have gotten out, gone away, but I didn't want..." Travis's eyes were glassy, and a tear ran down his left cheek. "I thought I could handle it. I didn't want it to be a failure, me and him."

"And he beat you up like this?" Luotta said.

"Of course he beat him up. What do you think happened?" Stephen suddenly shouted. Luotta turned his head quickly and looked at Stephen with a compassionate frown on his face.

Gabe stepped forward and put his arm around Stephen. "We have to ask these questions, Stephen. We need to hear it from Travis."

Stephen shook his head and stared at the ceiling.

"Yes," Travis said. "He came after me when I came out of the bathroom. In the past I'd been able to get away, but I didn't see it coming this time. He threw me against the wall. I lost my sense of balance, and the last thing I remember was him punching me. When I woke up later that night, I was lying on the floor by our front door. He had taken some of my clothes off, but not everything. I grabbed the blanket from the back of our couch, wrapped myself up and snuck out the door. I think he heard me because he yelled as I got to the elevator. I slipped into the stairwell and heard him approach as the elevator doors opened and then shut. He said he was going to find me and kill me.

"I tried to get a cab, but the first one I saw slowed down until he got a look at me, then he sped away. That's when I knew I must be in pretty bad shape. I don't remember much of the walk. I just remember seeing Stephen and then passing out." Travis grabbed Stephen's hand. Then he looked directly at the detective. "I'm sorry he's dead, I really am. But honestly, if he didn't kill himself that night, he probably would have killed me. So, I guess I'm not that sorry after all, am I?"

"Did he seem suicidal to you at all lately?" Luotta said.

Travis shook his head. "Not suicidal, no. But he was so fucked up that night, nothing would surprise me."

"Yet he was sober enough to do this to you?"

"It wasn't a precision operation, Detective," Travis said.

Luotta nodded gravely. "Thank you for your time," he said. "Come on, Detective. We can go now."

"I'll be out in a second," Gabe said. "I just want to speak with Stephen."

Luotta nodded and left the room. As soon as Stephen was sure the detective was gone, he turned to Gabe. "How long did you know about this?"

"About Benson?" Gabe looked straight into Stephen's face. "They just identified the body today."

"And you had no idea that some one had jumped into the harbor at that address?"

"Stephen," Gabe said quietly. He glanced down at Travis, who now had his eyes shut. "No, of course not."

After a moment, Stephen raised his forefinger to Gabe's forehead and gently traced the scab that was left from the cut. He leaned forward and kissed Gabe silently on the lips. "You should get back to work," he said. "That detective is waiting for you."

Gabe took Stephen's hand in his and kissed it gently. "I'll be back tonight."

2015

Another Kind of Forgiveness

"What's wrong, Gabriel?" His father put down his steak knife and looked across the table at his son.

Gabe shook his head and swallowed the piece of broccoli he had been slowly chewing. This dinner had been his father's idea. His mom was away for the week with her sisters on a trip to New York, but she'd left a meal for every night she would be gone.

Gabe had been avoiding his parents ever since the accident. In the beginning, it hadn't been hard to do. He had explained that Stephen needed him right then. With everything that had happened to Travis, things were in a state of chaos, and he wanted to stay beside Stephen to be a stabilizing force.

But as the weeks went by, his father became more insistent. At first he suggested Gabe come out to the house, then he offered to come in to Boston to visit with him. Gabe started to dodge their calls on his mobile, but Gabe's father began calling him at work. He immediately resumed taking their calls on his cell phone because he couldn't stand the thought of people at the station wondering about his family life.

He had finally agreed to meet his father at their house for dinner while his ma was out of town, but he almost cancelled. He stared at himself in the locker room mirror after work, thinking of various excuses he could use to get out of going. But every one of them only led to his father showing up in person at his apartment or, worse, at work.

"Gabriel." his father's voice pulled him back out of his thoughts. "I know you and I know when you need to talk."

"I'm fine Da," he said. He heard his own voice as if it was some distant, disembodied noise coming from across the room.

His father folded his napkin and backed away from the table. He stood up and picked up this plate, and then slowly reached over and picked up Gabe's plate as well.

"Dad, what are you doing?" he said as his father stacked the plates on the counter next to the sink. "I wasn't done."

"You weren't started. Come on now, let's go for a walk."

"A walk, Dad? Now?" It was well after dark.

"The lights will be on down at the track for a little while longer," his father said. "It might do you some good to get some air. I haven't seen you this pale in a long while."

His father had equated pale with sick for as long as Gabe could remember. In the Brennan family, the word pale had become a good enough excuse to stay home from school. He knew it was useless to resist, so he grabbed his jacket and followed his father to the front door. But as he walked the length of the hallway toward the door, the weight of the last few weeks overcame him, and he stopped to take a breath.

His father faced him. "Gabriel, son…" he stopped for a moment. "Please tell me what's going on."

Gabe couldn't speak. He tried to, but his throat was dry and the more he tried to form words, the more he couldn't. He moved his mouth in silent gasps as that night came back to him. He could hear Benson's voice, he could smell the stench of liquor on him, he could feel the burning anger that had welled up in his stomach. He wanted to tell someone, anyone. He wanted to let someone else know he had done something so bad, he didn't think he would ever be able to forgive himself.

"Is it the thing with Travis? Did something else happen?"

Gabe dropped his head, unable to look at his father in the eyes. He kept his eyes cast down, looking at the floor. After a few seconds he slowly whispered "yes."

"Something bad? Is Stephen all right?"

Gabe suddenly shuddered and took a gulp of air as he lurched forward, a surprise cascade of sobs wracking his body. His father put both arms around him, folding him into a deep embrace.

"Oh, Gabriel," he said, pulling his son close.

Gabe at last let himself go. The tears streamed down his face as he buried his forehead into his father's shoulder. He tried to speak, but he couldn't catch his breath for the long wailing sound he barely recognized as his own voice. He felt himself go limp in his father's arms. Gabe's father held on to him and lowered both of them gingerly on the wooden bench in the front hall.

Gabe gradually got his breathing under control, and the giant huffing sobs began to slow and soften. As he sat in his father's arms, he told him everything about that night. He stopped when he began to describe seeing Benson hunched over by the edge of the wharf, but his father had tightened his embrace and gently rocked him as if he were a little kid again.

"It's all right, Gabriel," he whispered. "Take your time and get it off your chest."

And Gabe continued with the story. "I knew," Gabe said, leaning his forehead into his father's shoulder. "I knew what I was doing when I punched him."

"You couldn't have known for sure."

"It doesn't matter, Da." He started to sob again. "It doesn't matter. I killed him, and I can never undo that. It will be on me for the rest of my life."

"Gabriel Brennan." His father leaned back and grabbed Gabe by his shoulders. "Now I want you to look at me. No, shhh." He looked directly into Gabe's eyes. "Quiet now. Take three deep breaths." He had used that trick to get Gabe to stop crying when he was a child. Gabe shook his head. "I mean it Gabriel, three deep breaths, with me now."

His father inhaled deeply and Gabe looked at him for a second and then did the same. They breathed in three times deeply together, exhaling a loud sigh each time. And, miraculously, it still had the same calming effect it had when he was a child. He tried to smile at his father, but he couldn't. Merely moving his mouth threatened to send him into tears again.

"Gabriel," his father said again, looking directly at him now that the tears had stopped. "Have you told anyone about this?"

Gabe shook his head.

"Good." His father let go of his shoulders and gently stroked a lock of hair that had plastered itself to his forehead. "I want you to promise me something."

"What, Dad?"

"I want you to promise me you won't judge yourself for this."

"But, Da, I killed him."

"No." His father shook his head. "I know you Gabriel, and I know how full of good your heart is. Right now it may feel like you killed him, but you didn't."

"Dad…"

"No, son. Don't speak until I'm through." The look on his father's face was stern now. "He had been killing himself for a long time, taking a road that brings down others with him. What he was doing wasn't fair, and it's not fair his final moments should bring down someone else who has done so much good in this world."

"But Dad, that doesn't make it right."

"I think, Gabriel, you're looking at a very small view of what is wrong and what is right. Things happen in this world for a greater reason than we can understand sometimes."

Gabe sat silently looking into his father's eyes. The two of them didn't speak for a while. Gabe finally went to the bathroom to blow his nose. When he looked in the mirror, he saw his face was red and puffy from crying. He ran the tap and leaned over, splashing himself with water. When he looked up in the mirror again, he held his own gaze and wondered if what he had done would destroy who he was.

FLY AWAY

When Travis was eventually released from the hospital, his parents wanted to bring him home to New Hampshire, but he wouldn't let them. He went home with Stephen and Gabe and stayed for several months.

The police investigated Benson's death, but quickly ruled it accidental death. Gabe was not involved in the investigation after that first visit to the hospital. When Gabe eventually spoke about those couple of days after Benson's death, he said he had been in a haze and had not paid much attention to what was happening until someone had mentioned Benson's name. He thought, at the time, that it might be easier for Travis if he came along with the detective assigned to the case.

Benson's death made the front page of all the local Boston newspapers and several of the news stations ran short segments about him. The newspapers seldom mentioned more than Travis's name. Travis laughed bitterly to himself when he read those stories. He was not now, nor had he ever been a part of Benson's life. As much as he had wished for a fairytale relationship, he was nothing more than a punching bag or a footnote. He couldn't be sure which.

Travis inherited the condo in Fort Point and a vast sum of money from Benson, but he had no idea what he would do with the money. All he knew for sure was he was never going back into that condo. He sold it along with all the furnishings, the art, the clothes, and the electronics. Stephen and Gabe had gone back to collect his things shortly after Travis was released from the hospital. But Travis could barely even look at those. As soon as he was well enough to leave Stephen and Gabe's apartment, he bought new clothes and threw the old ones out.

His parents called almost every day and came down several times over the summer and fall of that year. He was glad to see them so much, but he wasn't tempted to move back with them, no matter how much he missed them. The world was big, and he was going to be a part of it. It was just going to take him some time to get his feet back underneath him again.

❖

"It wasn't always about the hitting." Travis sat as still as granite, curled up into a ball on the couch. "Don't get me wrong—there was more hitting than I let on."

"I think I knew that," Stephen said.

"It's okay." Travis made a weak smile across the room at his friend. "I did a fairly good job of hiding things. Not just from you, but from myself too."

"I should have seen it though," Stephen said. "Gabe knew there was more going on, but I didn't want to admit it."

Travis waved his hand as if dismissing his friend's words. "Like I said, it wasn't always hitting. Sometimes he'd say really mean things, or sometimes he was silent for days. The silence was the worst, for me…even worse than the physical fights."

"Really? The silences were the worst?" He was sitting on the red leather chair across the room from his friend. Stephen struggled with feelings of helplessness as he was relegated to the sidelines of both Travis's physical and mental healing. He could do little more than change bed sheets, administer vitamin E and antibacterial lotions, and sit and listen.

"Yeah, I know it sounds really strange." Travis picked up the line of conversation dreamily. Stephen had noticed him doing that a lot lately. He still didn't want to have some conversations, but he knew Travis had things he had to say. "He would get angry and he would just, I don't know…he'd go silent. He would sit there and glare at me and not say anything and I wouldn't know what to expect.

I didn't know what was going on—if he was mad, or unhappy, or whatever. I was in this constant state of suspended existence where I felt completely frozen by him."

"How long would they last—the silences?"

"Oh, I don't know. It always depended on how he was feeling." Travis looked at the ceiling of the small apartment, then out through the window, letting his gaze rest blankly on the rooftops of Beacon Hill. "Sometimes it would go on for a day, sometimes up to a week or two."

"Would he ever tell you why?"

"Oh, yeah." Travis managed a half-baked smile. "That's the worst part about it. He said it was for me." A sarcastic laugh and a sigh slipped through Travis's lips. "He said it was like a safety-valve when he got that way."

"A safety-valve?"

"I know what you're thinking—some safety valve, right? I mean look at what happened to me—time and time again."

Stephen said nothing.

"To be fair, the two things didn't ever happen at the same time, though." Travis got up off the couch, his achiness still clearly visible even after the weeks of recuperation, rendering his movements stiff and rigid. Stephen found himself wondering if his friend would ever be as young as his age again. Travis got a glass of water and shuffled back to the couch, curling up where he had been. "I think I hated the silences more than the beatings. I didn't deserve that—I was better than that."

"You are better than that."

"Then why did I put up with it?" Travis stared out the window for a few moments. Stephen could see he was trying not to cry, but it didn't work; eventually he was forced to smudge away a tear forming in the corner of his eye. "I'm just so embarrassed," he said.

Stephen got up and sat next to Travis on the couch. "No, no, no. Travis, you can't think like that. Whatever Benson was doing, it had nothing to do with you."

Travis took a jagged breath, and the tears started to run down his cheeks in full force. "No, it didn't have to, but I let it. I sat there and let him shut me out and make excuses for it. I accepted those excuses, and I hate myself for it. I should have put more value on myself. I should have spoken up and walked out. I should never have said it was okay when he came out of the silences and apologized. Maybe if I had, he wouldn't have thought he could…"

"Beat you?" Stephen finished the sentence.

"I still have so much trouble saying that," Travis said. "But yeah, that's what I wonder."

"Hey, whatever you need to work through to get better, do it." Stephen put his arm around Travis and drew him close. "Whatever conversations you need to have with yourself, have them. But don't let this consume you. He's gone now. Gone for good. And you may not believe this right at this moment, but someday you'll be okay again."

Travis buried his head in Stephen's shoulder. They sat like that on the couch for hours that night, neither one of them saying a word. The sun set outside the window, and the glittering lights of Beacon Hill sparkled at them through the glass, hinting at the bright world waiting for them both once the wounds had healed.

The following spring Travis finally realized he had spent too much time living on Stephen and Gabe's couch. He knew they didn't mind. In fact, they had become something of a family in the months following the accident. And he would never be able to repay the kindness of helping him to find a new normal.

He had decided that he would spend a year traveling. When the fog finally lifted, Travis realized he had inherited a significant fortune. The company he had worked for had held his job, so that spring, he finally telephoned the HR department and told them he would not be returning.

Jenny from Marketing emailed him once after he had officially quit. She wrote that his desk was empty now, and she had read about what happened to Benson. Her email didn't offer any condolences, but the last sentence said, "Now you're free," which had made him smile but not in a happy way.

The lady in HR asked where he would like his personal effects sent, and he told her to throw them all away. When she hesitated and asked if he was sure, he just sighed. He was used to people not being able to understand.

He had felt forgotten until he was in the middle of everything, and then the attention from everyone was too overwhelming. He'd gone from being someone no one expected to speak at a dinner table to someone everyone wanted an answer from. *How are you feeling? Are you doing okay? Where do you want to live? What are you going to do now? Why don't you want the condo?*

All of it was too intense, too much for him. Stephen and Gabe were the only ones who had known—or seemed to know—enough to just be there beside him. They knew they didn't have to say anything. It was enough knowing they were there.

He told them about his travel plans over beers at the Sevens one night. He had planned it all out on his own, and he was set to leave in two weeks. He would spend the spring mostly in Paris, but he would go to the south of France for the month of June. He would head to Norway for July and spend August hiking through the Nordics. Then he would go to Australia and on to China for the balance of the year. He promised to keep them posted on his journey.

Both Stephen and Gabe sat silently staring at him over their beers as they listened to the details of his plans. When he had finally concluded, Gabe spoke first. "If that's what you need to do to clear your head, then I think it's a good plan."

"It's not what I need to do to clear my head," Travis said. "It's what I need to do to find myself again. I'm not sure who I am anymore." He took a gulp of beer. "I don't know if I ever really knew. I spent my whole life trying to impress others, trying to live up to this image of the perfect person I thought everyone expected me to be. I never really took the time to find out what I wanted to do."

"But Travis," Stephen said, "you always went to the beat of your own drum. You were out and proud early, and you were so brave about it."

"Was I really?" Travis looked his friend squarely in the eyes. "I eventually came out, but that only made everything worse. I had to try harder, be better, be louder and funnier and sweeter than anyone else to make up for it. I had to show everyone how wonderful I could be and hope that would make the gay thing okay." He shook his head as if trying to shake off the severity, the seriousness of his words.

"It's okay," Travis went on. "I don't regret that. I don't regret anything, not even what happened with Benson. It was just my journey. But now I get to decide how the rest of my journey is going to go. Who knows? Maybe I'll even join City Year when I get back. All I know is that I want a reset."

Stephen and Gabe looked at each other and then at Travis. Stephen put his hand on Travis's shoulder. "Then you get a reset, Goddamn it."

"Here's to resets," Gabe said softly, raising his beer. Travis and Stephen raised their beers and the three of them toasted to new beginnings.

KNOWING

"Where do you think he'll go after he returns?" Stephen said. "Do you think he was serious about City Year?" He sat across from Gabe at the small table in the kitchen of the Charles Street apartment.

"I don't know," Gabe said, his head buried in a newspaper.

Stephen watched him reading, so silent, so peaceful. Without really knowing why, Stephen reached across the table and traced the scar on Gabe's forehead.

"What is that scar from?"

Gabe didn't answer. He dropped the newspaper and stared at Stephen for a long time before looking down at the table.

"I think I know," Stephen said gently.

Gabe shook his head. "No," he said. "I don't think you do know, and I don't think you really want me to tell you. Do you?"

They sat in silence for a few more minutes.

"Gabe…" Stephen wasn't sure of the right thing to say, so he trailed off before he could finish his sentence and let the unspoken phrases pass between them.

"There's nothing more to say about it." Gabe's eyes began to glisten. "My mother used to say there was no sorrow worse than the tears of the unforgiven."

"Benson would have killed him," Stephen said. His voice had an edge to it. "There was no other way for this to end."

"Why didn't he just leave? I could never understand that."

"I don't know." Stephen brought his hands up to his forehead and ran them through his hair. "Sometimes I felt like we were all just standing on the sidelines watching him, leaving him to die at the hands of that crazy man." He touched Gabe's scar again. "Because that's what would have happened. You know that, don't you, Gabe?"

Gabe sighed and said nothing. He tried to hold back the tears, but it was too late. One streaked down the side of his left cheek.

"Benson would have killed him eventually," Stephen said. "He damn near did that night. I have thought about that every day since it happened. Every single day. And do you know what keeps me up at night?"

"No...What?"

"I wonder how I could have lived with myself if Benson had killed him. We're so lucky—I'm so lucky that he's alive. Because the guilt would have killed me too. I would have always thought of myself as an accomplice, guilty through my own silence, guilty because I sat on the sidelines, guilty because I listened to Travis when he told me not to interfere."

Stephen was near tears, his face red with anger.

"Stephen..." Gabe started to say something but his mouth was dry and he couldn't get the words out.

"So you see, Gabe," Stephen said at last. "You really didn't have a choice, did you?"

"Stephen, I didn't do..."

"I won't ever ask you again. I guess I really don't want to hear you say it. But I want you to know you were the only one who made a decision."

"But what if it was the wrong choice?" Gabe said. "What if I'm having trouble living with that choice? What if the choice wasn't ultimately mine to make? What if I took too much into my own hands?"

Gabe's words hung in the air between them like an abyss, and neither one of them could move. When Stephen spoke again, his voice was tired and he looked suddenly drained. "Travis is alive today because you made the choice you did that night, whatever it was. Maybe it wasn't right, but that choice saved someone we both love, Gabe. And I don't know how that could have been wrong."

Stephen waited for a moment, staring at Gabe. The air in the room around them had grown heavy and dark. Stephen shut his eyes and shook his head briefly, as if he could shake off the coal-grey feeling of the conversation. But they both knew that feeling was there to stay. It might lighten up from time to time, and eventually they would get used to it and things would seem like they were almost normal again. But it would always hover above them, settling down like fine dust on white linen.

Stephen finally opened his eyes again and without bothering to look directly at Gabe, or for that matter at anything in particular in the room, he spoke. His voice was soft and slow and deep, and his words seemed to float out of his mouth. "This time, at least, there was justice."

About the Author

Ralph Josiah was born in a small town outside of Boston and grew up in a Coast Guard family, living in New Orleans, Cape Cod, coastal North Carolina, and Sitka, Alaska. When he isn't writing, you can find him with his nose in a book or running to catch a plane. He loves travel and discovering the way the world works in places that are hard to pronounce. He is inspired by things that are off the beaten path and believes it's good to be different.

Ralph Josiah currently lives in San Francisco and Boston with his husband and partner of more than sixteen years, Dana Short.

Books Available from Bold Strokes Books

A Careful Heart by Ralph Josiah Bardsley. Be careful what you wish for...love changes everything. (978-1-62639-887-0)

Worms of Sin by Lyle Blake Smythers. A haunted mental asylum turned drug treatment facility exposes supernatural detective Finn M'Coul to an outbreak of murderous insanity, a strange parasite, and ghosts that seek sex with the living. (978-1-62639-823-8)

Tartarus by Eric Andrews-Katz. When Echidna, Mother of all Monsters, escapes from Tartarus and into the modern world, only an Olympian has the power to oppose her. (978-1-62639-746-0)

Rank by Richard Compson Sater. Rank means nothing to the heart, but the Air Force isn't as impartial. Every airman learns that rank has its privileges. What about love? (978-1-62639-845-0)

The Grim Reaper's Calling Card by Donald Webb. When Katsuro Tanaka begins investigating the disappearance of a young nurse, he discovers more missing persons, and they all have one thing in common: The Grim Reaper Tarot Card. (978-1-62639-748-4)

Smoldering Desires by C.E. Knipes. Evan McGarrity has found the man of his dreams in Sebastian Tantalos. When an old boyfriend from Sebastian's past enters the picture, Evan must fight for the man he loves. (978-1-62639-714-9)

Tallulah Bankhead Slept Here by Sam Lollar. A coming of age/coming out story, set in El Paso of 1967, that tells of Aaron's adventures with movie stars, cool cars, and topless bars. (978-1-62639-710-1)

Death Came Calling by Donald Webb. When private investigator Katsuro Tanaka is hired to look into the death of a high-profile lawyer, he becomes embroiled in a case of murder and mayhem. (978-1-60282-979-4)

The City of Seven Gods by Andrew J. Peters. In an ancient city of aerie temples, a young priest and a barbarian mercenary struggle to refashion their lives after their worlds are torn apart by betrayal. (978-1-62639-775-0)

Lysistrata Cove by Dena Hankins. Jack and Eve navigate the maelstrom of their darkest desires and find love by transgressing gender, dominance, submission, and the law on the crystal blue Caribbean Sea. (978-1-62639-821-4)

Garden District Gothic by Greg Herren. Scotty Bradley has to solve a notorious thirty-year-old unsolved murder that has terrible repercussions in the present. (978-1-62639-667-8)

The Man on Top of the World by Vanessa Clark. Jonathan Maxwell falling in love with Izzy Rich, the world's hottest glam rock superstar, is not only unpredictable but complicated when a bold teenage fan-girl changes everything. (978-1-62639-699-9)

The Orchard of Flesh by Christian Baines. With two hotheaded men under his roof including his werewolf lover, a vampire tries to solve an increasingly lethal mystery while keeping Sydney's supernatural factions from the brink of war. (978-1-62639-649-4)

Funny Bone by Daniel W. Kelly. Sometimes sex feels so good you just gotta giggle! (978-1-62639-683-8)

The Thassos Confabulation by Sam Sommer. With the inheritance of a great deal of money, David and Chris also inherit a nondescript brown paper parcel and a strange and perplexing letter that sends David on a quest to understand its meaning. (978-1-62639-665-4)

The Photographer's Truth by Ralph Josiah Bardsley. Silicon Valley tech geek Ian Baines gets more than he bargained for on an unexpected journey of self-discovery through the lustrous nightlife of Paris. (978-1-62639-637-1)

Crimson Souls by William Holden. A scorned shadow demon brings a centuries-old vendetta to a bloody end as he assembles the last of the descendants of Harvard's Secret Court. (978-1-62639-628-9)

The Long Season by Michael Vance Gurley. When Brett Bennett enters the professional hockey world of 1926 Chicago, will he meet his match in either handsome goalie Jean-Paul or in the man who may destroy everything? (978-1-62639-655-5)

Triad Blood by 'Nathan Burgoine. Cheating tradition, Luc, Anders, and Curtis—vampire, demon, and wizard—form a bond to gain their freedom, but will surviving those they cheated be beyond their combined power? (978-1-62639-587-9)